# echoes

# echoes

## A.M. CAPLAN

# copyright

This novel is entirely a work of fiction. Names, characters, places and incidents are the work of the author's imagination. Any resemblance to actual persons, living or dead, events or localities is entirely coincidental.

Second edition: May 2020

Cover design by Natasha MacKenzie
Typeset in Palatino by Chapter One Book Production, Knebworth, UK
Printed in the United States

# dedication

For Nathan, who swore he would actually read a book if I wrote one.
Game on.

# 1

The tight, smooth-edged ring the headlights bored into the inky blackness snapped shut behind her car. It was a night that had to be tunneled through, the lane of light the beams carved out so narrow Hannah didn't see the deer until she was almost on top of it, the terrified flash of its eyeball almost level with hers.

She stomped the brake, making the back end of the car kick out on the loose gravel. The last thing she saw before skidding to a halt was a streak of white turned-up tail disappearing into the pine trees.

"Damn it," Hannah let out in a whoosh of breath and eased back onto the road. "Stupid deer." They were everywhere in the late fall, and out of sorts, with hunters disrupting their feeding and running them out of their nighttime cover under the trees. Going anywhere this time of year usually included a close call, and would until hunting season was over. Things would be less hairy after that, calming down just in time for snow and ice to start causing the close calls.

Not that a close call had ever slowed Hannah down for long, whatever the reason. Something about the empty back roads made her foot heavy, and Hannah goosed the gas pedal down a little further, ready to be home and done with this god-awful day.

She looked over at the passenger seat. "Oh, come on. Are you kidding?" The metal canister that had been propped up against her purse was gone. It must have rolled off when she slammed on the brakes. *Please let the lid still be on*, she prayed silently. Just the thought of it open, its contents spilled across the floor mat, made her shudder.

Leaning across the center console, Hannah strained against the seat belt, reaching for the floor. Flicking her eyes back up to the empty road, she nudged the car back into her lane. She slipped the seat belt over her head and leaned a little further, cursing over the music from the radio.

"Gotcha," she said, fingers brushing the smooth metal. It was premature; Hannah felt the canister slide away, briefly catching a glimpse of it as it rolled out of reach.

Holding on to the wheel with her fingertips, stretching as far as she could, she finally got her fingers firmly wrapped around it where it had lodged against the bar that adjusted the front seat. Hannah sat back up victoriously, jerking the wheel to correct from where she'd drifted into the oncoming lane.

It was the correction that did it, the two feet of adjustment that put her right in line with the figure in the road. She didn't see him until a split second before she hit him.

―――――

The quick glimpse before the impact was seared into her mind, a flash of light-colored hair and pale skin, an angular face with a wide-eyed expression, followed by a sickening thud. That brief moment was still burning behind her eyelids like a polaroid picture when the car stalled out and rolled to a halt.

She peeled her face off the steering wheel and shouldered open the door. There was a trickle of blood from somewhere on her forehead making its way down into her eyes, and she smeared it away with the back of her hand so she could see.

"Oh my god. Oh no." Hannah skidded to her knees on the gravel where her car had thrown the man. "Please no."

He was still as a statue; a broken statue, with legs splayed out strangely and one arm pinned awkwardly underneath him. It was horrifying, the broken shape of his body, yet his face was worse. It had been utterly destroyed.

Hannah reached down and put a hand on either side of it, helplessly cupping it in her hands. One of his eyes was deflated like a popped balloon, the eyeball tugged out and lost somewhere in the deep gouge that started in his eyebrow and ran down through his lips, disappearing over his chin. There was slick, pink bone showing between the chewed-up edges of the skin on either side of the gouge, a light-colored streak from his cheek to his jaw.

Everything around that pale length of bone was quickly turning black with blood. There was just so much blood—how could there be so much of it, from one face? —and it ran out from between her fingers in streams while she tried to hold the sides of his face together.

"Help. Help us!" she screamed, hearing the echo of her voice thrown back to her. But screaming was pointless. Out here, she could yell herself hoarse and pray another car would come past, but the chances were next to nothing.

When the sound of her voice died away it was dead silent and completely still, except for the weak movement of the man's heart forcing hot spurts of blood into her hands. It ran between her fingers and trickled over her wrists, cooling as it went, until it puddled, cold and gluey, on the ground.

"Wake up. Come on, mister, wake up." Hannah saw an eyelid flicker open and reveal a silvery sliver of iris. "That's it, open your eyes." She shook him a little, then regretted it, feeling how bonelessly his head moved back and forth. "That's it. Stay with me. Keep your eyes open." *Eye.* Jesus, it was horrifying, that gaping, blood-puddled hole. "Can you hear me?" She had to blink the blood that was trickling from her own forehead out of her eyes. By the time she could see clearly, his remaining eye was firmly shut.

"Help will be here soon. Just hold on." It wasn't true, any of it. It was meaningless garbage, the assurances coming out of her mouth between the choked-off sobs. He didn't look like he was going to be okay, but she couldn't seem to stop the babble any more than she could stop him from bleeding.

Keeping one hand pressed against the side of his flayed face, she looked him over, hoping there was a phone in his pocket that had somehow survived the crash. That was when Hannah registered for the first time that the man was completely naked.

He was a big man, broad and tall, without a stitch of clothing, or even a birthmark or tattoo she could make out. Every inch of him was deathly white except for the dark blood pooling in an unnatural divot in his chest. She looked back to his face when his throat gave a tight, wet gurgle and Hannah felt a shallow breath against her hand. A transparent red bubble formed in the corner of the transected lips and burst. It made a lighter red snail trail that cleared its way through the solid coating of blood down the side of his face.

"Help! Damn it, somebody help!" It was pointless. No one would be coming by, and just sitting here crying wasn't going to help him.

Hannah held his head as gently as she could in one hand while she used the other to pull off her sweater. She wadded it up and tucked it underneath his neck, trying to create a cushion between him and the road. The moment she let go of him, his head flopped over to the side, neck cocked unnaturally.

The front end of her car was accordioned, and she had to stop and steady herself against it. Her head felt strange and her legs kept wobbling unexpectedly, but she dragged herself around to the passenger side. Her hand was slippery, and she lost hold of the door handle twice before she was able to swing it open. When she did, Hannah threw it wide with so much force it rebounded and cracked her across the back and knocked her forward, her head connecting painfully with the frame. She had to pause and waste another moment waiting for the dizziness to pass.

Her bag had been tossed to the floor, the contents all jumbled together under the seat, and the blood on her hands gathered a pair of gloves made of dirt and grit while she groped through the contents until finally she found her phone.

"Please still work. You have to work," Hannah pleaded with the spiderwebbed screen. Mercifully it lit up when she jammed her thumb across the home button and swept aside the red slider.

"911 operator. What is your emergency?"

The dispatcher sounded flatly calm and completely unbothered. How was it the woman sounded so damn complacent when there was potentially a dying person on the other end of the line every time she picked it up? The placid, even voice sounded so wrong next to how desperate Hannah felt.

"911. What is your emergency?" the voice repeated.

"Please, I need help," Hannah said. "I hit a man with my car. He's hurt really bad. He's losing so much blood." She slid on the gravel rushing back to where he was lying. The phone shot out of her hand when she hit the ground, and she missed the tinny words coming from the voice on the line. Hannah crammed the phone back against her ear.

"What? What did you say?"

"Ma'am. It's important that you stay calm. Can you tell me where you're located?"

Hannah faltered, drawing a blank. It was a long, winding stretch of middle-of-nowhere back road. There were almost no landmarks and it was dark as pitch except for what little light her headlights threw.

"Ma'am, can you tell me where you are?"

"I'm headed toward Milltown, on the river road. I'm almost to the railroad bridge—I think. I'm not sure. I'm still on the dirt road. I didn't make it to where it's paved yet."

There was the click of long nails against a keyboard and the muffled murmur of a radio conversation before the dispatcher spoke again. Hannah hoped to god the woman was local, because Hannah couldn't swear to more detail than that with the directions.

"All right, ma'am, I've dispatched EMS and law enforcement to your location," the dispatcher said. "Ma'am, are you still there?"

Hannah was leaning over the man who lay unmoving where she'd left him.

"Ma'am, can you hear me?"

The phone kept sliding out from between Hannah's shoulder and ear, the blood dribbling from her nose and forehead making her skin slippery. Hannah turned the phone to speaker and laid it on the ground next to the suspiciously still man.

"Ma'am," the operator's voice came from next to his head. "Help is on the way. Can you tell me about his condition? Is he conscious?"

Hannah hadn't seen a single movement since the one brief eyelid twitch, other than the sluggish progression of bubbles from the corner of his mouth. Now, a single filmy bubble clung to the corner of his lip. When it popped, she waited, but another one didn't form.

"I don't think he's breathing anymore," Hannah said. She leaned over until her ear was nearly touching his lips, trying to hear a rattle or feel the movement of air coming from his mouth. There was nothing. His face was still a mask of blood, but it looked thicker, growing cool and gelatinous. Where before it had been running in steady rivulets, now it didn't look to be flowing at all. Hannah put her fingers against his neck and tried to feel for a pulse, but she was shaking so badly she wasn't sure if she was feeling his heartbeat or hers.

"What should I do?" Hannah said. "He's not breathing." Should she try to do CPR? Was it even possible, the way his lips were nearly severed? His chest looked like a wet, black swamp.

"Lady, come on. Please, I don't know what to do!" she said. "Damn it! What should I do?"

"Ma'am, calm down. Help is on the way," the dispatcher said, her voice still even and not sounding the least bit rattled. "Until they get there, we're going to do chest compressions."

Hannah eyed the dark puddle of blood in his caved-in chest.

"I'm going to talk you through it. I need you to place the heel of your hand on the center of his chest," the dispatcher said. "Ma'am, are you still there?"

Hannah put her hand down gingerly. Her palm sank into the pool far enough to cover it to the wrist before it came to rest against his skin.

"I don't think I should do this. His chest is all—"

"Ma'am, I have confirmation that a member of the sheriff's department has arrived at your location," the dispatcher broke in. "EMS should be right behind them. Can you see a vehicle?"

Hannah craned her neck to look behind her. Thank god—she could see the flickering pattern of red and blue lights against the top of her car, and a wave of relief rushed through her. Maybe it wasn't as bad as it looked. Help was here, so maybe there was still a chance he'd make it.

Her hand pulled away from the man's chest with a sucking sound, and she rushed toward her car, waving her arms wildly in the direction of the flashing lights, spatter from her hands falling back against her face like rain drops. When she was positive they'd seen her, Hannah ran back to where she'd left the man. She tripped and landed on the ground and sat there, frozen in shock. All she could see was her sweater, lit up in the glow of her cell phone. He was gone.

# 2

The sheriff's department and volunteer firefighters waded through the dark with handheld spotlights and headlamps, searching for him. Their beams did an indifferent job, the light swallowed up by the cover of the trees. They were able to pin back the blackness more completely when tall construction lights began showing up, rolling in from the DOT yard hitched to the backs of pickup trucks.

"Back it in tight to that one, Paul. Then pull the truck around right quick, so we can get the next one in." The sheriff waved the driver of the pickup forward, the buttons of his uniform straining over his stomach when he lifted his arm. The driver jumped out and swiftly uncoupled the light, then squeezed his truck past the next one in line on his way back out.

A few sputtery false starts and the light was pull-started to life, the beam cutting another slice out of the dark. Another set of lights and they'd have a full circle of illumination to crawl through while they looked for the man.

"Sheriff," Hannah said. She hopped down from the back of the ambulance, wobbling a little when her feet hit the ground. "Sheriff Morgan, over here." Stepping in front of him, she lost her grip on the ice pack she'd been holding against the bridge of her nose. He bent over and picked it up for her, dusting off the leaves before handing it back.

He waved the final truck through and gave the driver a thumbs-up before speaking to her. "Yes, Miss Cirric?"

"I'm going to help them look," she said. "I don't know how he even got up, as bad as he was hurt, but he can't have gotten far. He's got to be right around here somewhere." She still couldn't believe the man had been able to move at all, but he must have. Since he'd managed to drag himself off of the road somehow, maybe there was a chance he was still alive.

Sheriff Morgan turned his head and looked down the stretch of road in front of them. Beyond the yellow cordon of plastic tape, lines of people were making a slow study of the ground around the scene. New arrivals to the growing group were being pointed to a place in line to join those already searching. The newest comers weren't police or fire department but volunteers—anyone in the area who had a police scanner or had seen the parade of flashing lights and followed to see what was going on. They were better help than none—the curious rubberneckers—though Hannah thought some of them looked overly excited, so much so that they were struggling to contain themselves and hold their movements to a slow shuffle. They were jostling to be the one to find the victim; the only thing keeping them in check was the more watchful emergency personnel and the possibility of treading too quickly and putting their foot on a dead body.

"If he can't have got far, then we'll find him soon enough. Don't need you; we got it covered. Get yourself back in that ambulance."

Hannah didn't need to be in an ambulance. Her scraped knees and palms had been cleaned and covered. There was a small butterfly bandage over the cut on her forehead, though she'd pulled out the wad of cotton shoved up each of her nostrils.

"I'm fine," Hannah said. She was mostly fine; Hannah blinked away the fireworks display that bloomed in front of her eyes.

"You'll only be in the way, and anyway, the EMTs are gonna give you a ride down to St. Joe's." The sheriff took Hannah's elbow to lead her back to the ambulance, but she jerked it away, almost falling over in the process.

"I told you, I'm fine," she said. "I don't need to go to the hospital. I'm refusing medical attention. I'll sign a waiver or something."

The sheriff planted himself in front of her and crossed his arms.

"You can refuse treatment if you want. Can't stop you. But you're gonna have to go in for a blood alcohol and a drug test."

Hannah's temper flared.

"If they take me to the hospital, is there another ambulance coming?" she said. "For when they find him. Is there another ambulance?"

There wasn't. The sheriff shook his head. "We're lucky even this one wasn't busy or stuck out in the east end of nowhere when your call came in." It was a small town, and this was it. They had to find him any minute anyway. She couldn't believe it had taken this long.

"Fine, then send me in the back of a police car, or even better, draw my blood here," she said. "They can manage that, can't they? Besides, I'm pretty sure you can't demand I give it up anyway, without a good reason to think I'm under the influence." She sure as hell wasn't under the influence of anything other than frustration, and maybe a concussion, but she wasn't going to tell him about that; he'd definitely send her packing then.

To her relief the sheriff shook his head wearily and agreed, mostly so he could get back to the search. Good—that was where he should be; where she should be.

Walking back to the ambulance, Hannah scribbled her signature on a form she didn't read, allowed the EMTs to draw a plastic tube of blood, then resigned herself to sitting helplessly on the back bumper, shivering under the scratchy blanket someone had thrown over her bare shoulders.

———◆◆◆◆———

She was still sitting there when they started to kill the lights. Time had crawled by, and the sun had pushed a pale glowing line over the top edge of the trees. It seemed impossible, but they still hadn't found him. One by one the tall lights winked out. When the last noisy diesel engine died there was an odd silence broken only by murmured conversation.

Hannah looked to where the sheriff was kneeling by her crumpled car. He was deep in conversation with one of his deputies and an officer from the state police. They gave Hannah a sidelong glance before the sheriff heaved himself to his feet, dusting off his hands on his pants.

"Couldn't someone have come and picked him up?" he asked her for the tenth time. The answer was still no.

"There's no way. I left him for less than a minute. I was only gone long enough to flag you down, you watched me. If there was another car I would've seen it," she said. "And the ambulance came from the other direction, straight from town. They said they didn't pass a single car on the way." Hannah rotated her shoulders painfully. She'd grown stiff and sore sitting for hours in the open back of the ambulance.

"And you're sure he was really hurt as bad as all that?" The sheriff looked back at the front end of her car. It had obviously been damaged by something, an object big and solid enough to destroy the grill and crumple the hood.

"Look at the car. There's no way he wasn't hurt that bad. I've told you all this before."

"Couldn't a been a deer, could it? Or maybe a bear? It's around that time of year, when they're getting ready to den up, and the dent, it's about that big. A black bear can look a lot like a man standing up, you know, and it was pretty overcast last night. Hard to really see anything for sure."

"It wasn't a bear, for god's sake. I hit a man. He was lying right there. I didn't just see him, I touched him. I started to give him CPR when you showed up. It was a man, and he's got to be here somewhere."

The sheriff looked her over with an expression she couldn't quite place, then took off his stiff hat and scratched absently at his scalp. "And this man, he didn't just up and walk away without you seeing him?"

Hannah shook her head. He couldn't have. She couldn't believe he'd even moved—he hadn't been breathing, she was sure of it—except he must have, because he was gone. She'd held his shattered face and felt his blood on her hands. Very real, sticky, hot, blood. The memory of her palm sinking into the pool of blood on his chest made her stomach squirm.

"No," she said, "I'm telling you for the last time. I didn't hit a deer or a bear. I hit a man, and he just …"

"He just what?"

"He just … disappeared."

The sheriff flicked a speck off the brim of his hat and placed it squarely back on his head before he looked at Hannah, one eyebrow cocked.

"And he was naked?" he said. Hannah couldn't help but look away when she nodded.

"Well then, if that's the case, what I am now is thoroughly confused. And I'm not the only one. So is that state police investigator over there and anybody else who took a look at the scene."

She narrowed her eyes. *What was there to be confused about?*

"Thing is," he said, "there's a great big dent in your car, that's clear enough. But they didn't find a thing on it, or anywhere around it, except for two little bitty patches of blood on the ground. From what you told me about what happened, I'm gonna guess those came from you." He pointed down at her pants, which had been cut off at the knees by the EMTs, white bandages peeking out underneath the raggedy edge of the denim.

"And for as much blood as you claim this naked man was losing, what with you trying to help him and give him CPR and all that, you don't have a whole lot on you either, except what came from your forehead and nose."

He motioned toward the road. "And then there's that." Just in front of the car was the sweater she'd wadded up under the man's bleeding head. It was lying there like an unseasonable patch of snow in the middle of the road, her now-dead cell phone still lying beside it. It should have been sodden with blood. There wasn't a drop of blood on it.

---

Skepticism—that was the look on the sheriff's face, the one Hannah hadn't quite been able to place earlier. But despite any misgivings, he ordered them to widen the search area and had the volunteers walking an expanded spiral outward from the scene. A pair of hounds on loan from the next county had arrived, but they were nosing fruitlessly around the front of her car, unable to catch a scent. Hannah could hear the low drone of the fire department's rescue boat making passes up and down the nearby river, though only faintly; almost everything was drowned out by the chatter of the Methodist Ladies Auxiliary. As soon as it was properly daylight they'd set up shop and started serving breakfast and hot coffee. One of them consoled the owner of the local newspaper with a donut after Hannah swatted at him and his camera, irritated at him for snapping away in front of her face.

"Thank you, ma'am." The sheriff accepted a donut from a blue-haired lady and took an outsized bite. A spurt of jelly shot out the other side, landing on the ground like a slick red blood clot. He kicked a puff of dirt over it before he walked over to Hannah.

"I'm recalling the ambulance," he said. He waved her down out of it, and when Hannah slid off the bumper, the bored, tired EMTs moved to shut the doors the second she was clear. A spatter of gravel peppered the back of her legs as they tore away.

"I'll give you a ride home," the sheriff said, waving the cloud of dust away from his face. "Even if it'd start, your car's not going anywhere, least not until the crime scene guy the staties called in finally shows up. Taking him damn long enough." He turned around and started to walk away, muttering something under his breath about wasted time and tax dollars. When Hannah didn't make a move to follow, he turned around. The sheriff looked at her for a long moment.

"We're gonna keep looking—for the time being. But you're not gonna be helping, least not now. If it turns out there actually is a man out there like you say, then this is a crime scene, and you of all people can't be roaming around it. Come on now, while the offer of a lift still involves riding in the front."

A short, silent ride later Hannah was sliding down from the front seat of Sheriff Morgan's old green and tan work truck, deposited unceremoniously at the end of her driveway.

"I'll let you know if anything turns up or if I think of any more questions," he said. She watched him nod and pull away, heading back the way they'd come.

When he was out of sight, she took a few steps the way he'd gone, then stopped. Hannah was thinking about walking back to the scene and slipping into the search party. It was only a couple miles away as the crow flies—she could shortcut it through the woods in a couple places and trim off some distance—but she decided against it. She was sure she could make it, lingering wobbliness and all, but the thought of running into the sheriff stopped her. If he had to drag her right back here, it would just waste time he could be using to find the missing man. Hannah turned around and slogged her way down the long driveway and into the house.

Inside, she shot the dead bolt and leaned against the door, the glass pane cold and soothing against the back of her skull. She'd been awake for nearly thirty hours, and between the exhaustion and the collision, her head felt like a loosely tethered balloon. Sleep probably should have been her first order of business, but Hannah couldn't bring herself to go to bed, not without knowing what was going on.

Maybe they'd found him the minute she left the scene. The man could be on the way to the hospital—or the morgue—right now. Hannah took a deep breath and tried to process that possibility. She had almost certainly killed a man; he'd been close to dead after the collision, and every moment that had passed while he'd remained undiscovered made it more and more likely. The thought made burning tears well up in her eyes. But with her phone still lying in the middle of the road, she had no way of knowing for sure, so she put on a pot of coffee and opened up her laptop. The best she could do was to constantly refresh the local news website for information.

Her heart skipped a little when a small blurb about the accident finally popped up, but her hopes deflated quickly: one-car collision, ongoing search for the missing victim, and a picture of the scene, her sitting in the ambulance in the background. That was all, which was exactly no more information than she already had and no consolation whatsoever.

# 3

A flash of light-colored hair and pale skin, an angular face with a wide-eyed expression, followed by a sickening thud. That brief moment was still burned behind her eyelids like a polaroid picture when the car stalled out and rolled to a halt.

She peeled her face off the steering wheel and shouldered open the door. There was a trickle of blood from somewhere on her forehead making its way down into her eyes, and she smeared it away with the back of her hand so she could see.

"Oh my god. Oh no." Hannah skidded to her knees on the gravel where her car had thrown the man. "Please no."

He was still as a statue; a broken statue, with legs splayed out strangely and one arm pinned awkwardly underneath him. It was horrifying, the broken shape of his body, yet his face was worse. It had been utterly destroyed.

Hannah reached down and put a hand on either side of it, helplessly cupping it in her hands. One of his eyes was deflated like a popped balloon, the eyeball tugged out and lost somewhere in the deep gouge that started in his eyebrow and ran down through his lips, disappearing over his chin. There was slick, pink bone showing between the chewed-up edges of the skin on either side of the gouge, a light-colored streak from his cheek to his jaw.

Everything around that pale length of bone was quickly turning black with blood. There was just so much blood—how could there be so much of it, from one face?—and it ran out from between her fingers in streams while she tried to hold the sides of his face together.

"Help. Help us!" she screamed, hearing the echo of her voice thrown back to her. But screaming was pointless. Out here, she could yell herself hoarse and pray another car would come past, but the chances were next to nothing.

When the sound of her voice died away it was dead silent and completely still, except for the weak movement of the man's heart forcing hot spurts of blood into her hands. It ran between her fingers and trickled over her wrists, cooling as it went, until it puddled, cold and gluey, on the ground.

"Wake up. Come on, mister, wake up."

She jerked upright with a start, sending a wave of cold coffee into her lap. Reaching up to touch her forehead, she winced when her hand met her newest injury, a knob growing above her eyebrow next to the butterfly bandage. She'd fallen asleep sitting up, waking when her forehead bounced off the kitchen table.

How she'd dreamed—and so deeply in the brief period before she hit—was a mystery. Even more strange, the accident had replayed with better definition than she remembered with her eyes open. She'd seen the man's face in sharper detail, noticing the slight furrow in his forehead, the faintest shadow of stubble across his jaw, and the shape of his light-colored eyebrows. His eyes were not as eerily pale as she first thought, more slate colored or even a steely blue. Of course, that was before. Her stomach soured when she thought about what came next, his face after, one eye missing, the other not opening—maybe ever again—the torn lips hanging open, the teeth behind them dyed red.

The soundtrack had been more complete in her sleep too; Hannah didn't remember ever dreaming with such clear sound. She would never forget the thud of his body meeting the metal of her car, the screech and crunch of the hood giving and compressing, and the delicate tinkle of the shattered windshield. It was the softer, closing notes of the falling glass that stood out the most, so incongruous and inappropriate, like someone laughing out loud at a funeral.

Rubbing her forehead—the off-center lump felt like she was sprouting a horn—Hannah slid out of her coffee-stained, chopped-off pants and left them on the floor, then dragged herself up the narrow stairs to her bedroom. Giving the bed a wistful look, she pulled on fresh clothes and left the room, shutting the door behind. Sleep could wait a little while longer, especially at the risk of a repeat of that dream.

---

"Come down to the station this afternoon." Hannah jumped when Sheriff Morgan spoke over her shoulder. Hannah had put on her hiking boots and made her way back to the scene, fuzzy-headed but functional. Her tight muscles and aches had worked themselves out on the way, and she felt surprisingly fine physically, except for a lingering trickle of blood from her sinuses that ran down the back of her throat. It had a coppery, spoiled taste—like a rotting tooth—a taste that wouldn't swallow away completely. She kept stopping to do some unladylike spitting as she walked.

At the scene she'd settled for uncomfortably swallowing the blood; Hannah didn't want to draw any more attention than necessary, just to slip in and see if they'd found the man, preferably without the sheriff noticing she was there. Ignoring a couple sidelong glances, she looked around, her heart sinking. The search was still going on. They hadn't found him then. They were still looking for the missing man, though clearly without quite the same level of urgency.

The Methodist Ladies Auxiliary had ceded their territory to the League of Baptist Women, and a fresh gaggle of church ladies were handing out soggy egg salad sandwiches and bottles of water, though they didn't have as many takers as their predecessors. The volunteers had mostly left, and the few that remained were slipping away as soon as they'd eaten.

The sheriff didn't look upset to see her there, or even surprised. She followed his eyes to where he had turned to watch the tow truck trundling in to clear her car from the road. He pulled something out of his jacket and handed it to Hannah; her cell phone and sweater in an evidence bag. He gave her a long look as he did.

"Wait, why do I need to come to the station." Hannah eyed her bright, white sweater through the clear plastic."

"So we can get a statement for the accident report. Not too late now, you hear. If it's after five then the deputy that knows how to use the composite program thing will be gone for the day, and then it'll have to wait till tomorrow. He'll put together a picture of the victim and take your statement for the accident report." He opened his mouth to say something else, then decided against it, clamping his mouth shut like a trout. Turning away, the sheriff tugged his stiff felt hat over his thinning hair and started to walk away, motioning to the driver of the tow truck.

"You're stopping? You can't. He's out here somewhere. He could still be alive."

Turning back to her, the sheriff waved an arm at the now sparsely populated scene.

"I'm calling it. We've been over every inch of ground for a mile in every direction and haven't found so much as a footprint. They've dragged the river from here to the narrows four times and haven't brought up a thing." He pointed at the dogs sitting on their haunches, eyeing the lunch their handler was eating. "Those hounds can pick up a scent that's months' old and follow it a hundred-thirty miles, and they haven't been able to pick up a single thing from your car, human or otherwise."

"What are you saying?"

"You remember anything different? Maybe want to change your story?"

"No. I told you exactly what happened." Hannah's voice had erupted in a shout, and the couple people still milling around turned to stare. The sheriff gave her a hard look, his shoulders raised and tight. He looked ready to shout back, but then let a breath go with a whoosh and took a step closer, bending in and speaking softly.

"I know what the evidence is saying and I know what we've found,

18

which is exactly jack. But I also called and had them replay that 911 call, and I saw you when I rolled up here, so while I'm letting my tired staff that's been in these woods all night go home for a couple hours, I'm also telling you to come into the station this afternoon and put together a sketch."

He leaned back, shook his head tiredly, then turned and walked away. Soon Hannah was left with no one but two old ladies trying to wedge an unwilling plastic folding table into the back of a station wagon.

———◆◆◆◆◆———

Hannah shifted in her seat, leaning closer to the nervous young deputy in the sheriff's department. He fumbled his way through another set of screens in the program that created composite images, and she shook her head.

"No, not like that one. Seriously, nobody has a cleft in their chin like that. And less round." She considered the jaw. "Oh, come on, that's too square. That looks like a robot. Who comes up with these choices?" She thought she heard the deputy sigh, but to his credit, he did a good job hiding it and flipped through some more choices.

She'd gone through one option after another, of face shapes, eyebrows, lips, ears, and noses. As they scrolled by they had been selected or dismissed, then those choices had been tweaked and altered a hundred times. Little by little the image grew closer to the face she remembered.

"Is this him?" the deputy asked wearily.

Closing her eyes, Hannah pictured the man in the second before she struck him, then opened them, satisfied that what was in front of her was a dead ringer for the original. Or a not-dead ringer, she held out a faint hope.

"Yes. That's him."

She saw the relief on the deputy's face. "I'll send this over to the news and to the *Crier* and *Shopper*." He handed her a copy from the sheaf spilling out of the printer and scooted away before she could change her mind.

19

The process had taken hours and now that her attention was off the screen, she could feel the eyes of the people in the room on her, behind her back and over her shoulder. Hannah heard the abrupt halt in background conversation when she walked through to the sheriff's office. Clutching her printout, she waited impatiently outside the glass door while he finished a phone call.

"What else can we do? Can I file a missing persons report? Maybe someone around here knows who he is," Hannah said when she was finally seated in the itchy brown chair in front of his desk.

The sheriff considered her, then shook his head.

"I can't say this is technically a missing person, and we don't have half enough information for that kind of report. We don't have anything more than that sketch." He nodded toward the sheet in her hand. "But I'll see what I can do, and I'll send that out anyway, on the off chance something turns up. Can't hurt anything."

Sheriff Morgan heaved himself up with a little groan and walked past her, stopping to stand in the doorway, clearly meaning for Hannah to leave as well. She followed him reluctantly back through the open room and to the reception desk.

"Could be some kind of practical joke, man running around without his pants in the woods. Maybe it was a dare and somebody picked him up," the petite blonde deputy manning the desk suggested helpfully as Hannah headed for the door.

Sheriff Morgan held open the front door into the dark for her to leave, but he didn't say anything, just shrugged. He looked down briefly at the composite sketch he was still holding in his hand, with a look on his face she could only call resigned. Hannah knew what had happened, but no matter how many times she described it, no matter how certain she was, he was looking less and less convinced the more time that passed.

When the door had closed quietly behind her Hannah took a deep breath and tried to see it from his angle. After all the searching, there was no body, no injured person, and not a drop of blood. He'd spent a long night looking for a nearly dead naked man in the woods on Hannah's word, and when it was all said and done, there was no evidence the man even existed. The sheriff hadn't seen what she'd seen, but when Hannah looked at it his way, she had to admit it sounded crazy.

# 4

The cell phone vibrated in her pocket. Fumbling it out with cold-clumsy hands, Hannah read the number through the cracked screen. The garage—again. Ignoring it for the twentieth time, Hannah slipped the phone back into her coat pocket and kept walking.

She'd gotten a late start. The sun was high enough in the sky when she reached the railroad bridge to draw a blinding white line down the center of the river. Vision spotty from the glare, she took a step and stumbled, catching her foot where the paved road dropped off to gravel. She managed to get caught up in the same spot nearly every time, both coming and going. Hannah had made the hike back to where it happened at least once every day since the accident, so after nearly a month of coming to the scene to look for him, it was a lot of stumbling.

Over the bridge, around the gentle bend in the road that turned with the river, she stopped where a faded piece of yellow plastic tape was wrapped around a tree trunk. Hannah closed her eyes, took a deep breath, and for the thousandth time went over what had happened. She remembered his face, recalled the way it had felt when her car struck him, and the way his blood had felt running through her hands.

Then she shook it all away. She tried to imagine it differently. In her mind she replaced him with a deer, then a black bear standing on its hind legs, front legs outstretched. When that didn't work, she pictured the man lying there injured, but not so badly, only stunned, with a head wound that was smaller than she saw in her memories, one that her panic had made seem worse than it was. Head wounds bled like crazy, didn't they, always looking worse than they were? Hannah swapped out detail after detail, the way she'd examined and dismissed features to create the composite image of the man. But none of the alternate scenarios fit, no matter how hard she tried to convince herself they were possibilities and that she might have misconstrued what had happened. It didn't work. It never worked. Every change to the original memory felt artificial and forced, and she gave up, letting the picture melt back to what she knew.

The blast of a truck horn pulled her back to reality, and she threw herself out of the road, rolling over and sliding to a halt waist deep in the ditch. Hannah popped her head up just in time to see the driver's hand come out of the open window and raise a middle finger.

"Asshole," she said, dusting herself off and climbing back up to the road. The rattle of the truck's muffler died away in time for her to hear another, quieter sound. Shading her eyes from the sun she looked up, trying to find the source. It took a moment of searching and blinking in the brightness, but Hannah saw them.

Above her, over the trees not far away, a trio of vultures circled lazily. As if seeing her watching them, one called again, with the distinct nasal whine that had caught her attention.

Hannah took off. Clearing the ditch with a leap, she pushed her way through the hedgerow. Her sleeve got hung up on a branch but she didn't stop, dragging the branch with her out of the underbrush. She yanked it away while she was moving, ignoring the thorns that tore into her hand, digging her phone from her pocket. She dialed the sheriff while she barreled through the woods.

"Pick up. Pick up. Come on." She tripped and went down on one knee, dropping the phone. It was still ringing, unanswered, when she picked it back up. "Damnit. Don't to go voicemail." It went to voicemail.

"Sheriff Morgan. It's Hannah. I found him. Just past the bridge ..." Hannah trailed off, stopping under a break in the trees to look up. For a moment she thought she'd lost the way, but a dark shape passed overhead, a shadow to match it skipping over her feet.

Another hundred yards and she didn't need to follow the birds any more. She knew she was close because of the smell.

It grew stronger and fouler with each step. The smell of decomposition was thick, and it hung in a miasma near the ground, kicking up in rank puffs when her feet moved. It was so strong she stopped for a moment, covered her face with her sleeve, and steeled herself. After all this time Hannah was about to find what she'd been both desperately hoping for and dreading. She had finally found him, and with the worst possible outcome.

A guttural hiss made her jump. An ugly, bald-headed turkey vulture came winging down through the break in the trees, landing on the ground in front of her. When she took a step back, her foot slid out from under her, sinking with a sickeningly wet crunch into a pocket of what felt like iced-over mud. When she picked her foot back up, part of a ribcage came up with it.

Hannah wheeled backward, landing on her rear, scuttling away and kicking at the bones that clutched at her foot. Vomit rose up in her throat at the putrid smell and the icy sliminess that ran down over the top of her boot and soaked her sock. Hannah scooted across the dirt until her back hit a tree and she couldn't go any farther.

Scattered, disjointed bones were trailed behind her, slick ropes of rotted flesh stretched out between them, the parts of a broken body fallen and flattened into something unrecognizable. The closest pieces were the biggest, the section of ribcage Hannah had shaken from around her ankle, and another spiky knob of bones half buried in leaves.

A spiky, pointed knob of bones. Hannah deflated. Bone, pointed in a way that would have made a brag-worthy trophy on someone's wall. A pair of sizable horns, still firmly attached to the head of the deer whose carcass Hannah had fallen into.

———◆◆◆◆———

"Have a seat. I'll let him know you're here."

Hannah nodded, embarrassed, as the deputy Sheriff Morgan had dispatched in response to her frantic call ducked out of the waiting room, relieved to be rid of her.

"Hey Hannah," Laurel behind the reception desk said, looking up briefly. Her nose crinkled when the smell reached her. Covering her nose with her sleeve, Laurel picked up the buzzing phone. Quickly hanging it up again, she motioned Hannah back.

It was unusual for her to be seen so quickly. Hannah had been haunting the sheriff's department as often as she had the scene, stopping by daily in the month since the accident and badgering anyone who would listen for information. The short wait today might have had something to do with her arriving in a squad car. Or maybe it was because of the smell. Either way, this wasn't going to be one of those days where it slowly grew dark while she read and reread the same old magazines and waited for the sheriff to finish whatever he was working on that took precedence over Hannah—which was pretty much everything.

Walking around the edge of the desk, Hannah turned the corner and stood for a moment, staring at the scattered work stations where every person was looking remarkably busy, their attention turned to anything but her. No one looked up or made eye contact as she walked to the back of the room where the sheriff was visible through the glass door of his office. He waved her in.

The rolling office chair gave out a groan as Sheriff Morgan dropped himself into it. He sniffed, just once, then looked straight at her. On his usually cluttered desk was a single sheet of white paper. Hannah's heart leapt momentarily.

"I told Denny he could've dropped you home. This would a kept till tomorrow."

"You said you wanted me to come by. You have some information for me?"

"First, why don't you tell me what happened out there," he said.

"I was out in the woods looking and I saw vultures. I was sure I found him."

"Deer?"

She nodded.

"Do you know why?" He didn't waste any breath waiting for her to answer. "In all the looking, all you've ever found out there is a deer, because that was all there ever was to find."

He paused for a moment and sat back, then continued less gruffly.

"Miss Cirric," he said. "Hannah." The sheriff pulled his hat off and set it on its little wooden stand by the desk, running a hand through his wispy, carroty hair. "You didn't find him because there's nothing to find. I've been sure of that for a while now, but I've given you the benefit of the doubt, since you were so sure, and since it wasn't hurting anything for you to keep after it. I realize now that was a mistake."

"Sheriff, wait. What are you—"

He put up a hand to silence her. "I blame myself. I let this go on longer than it should have, and it turns out that wasn't the right thing to do. But it ends now."

Hannah sat back with an empty chest, like the air had been punched out of her. This was not at all what she'd thought she'd come by to hear.

"I won't waste another breath on this. It's time to stop coming by here and wasting my staff's time. Same with calling the state bunker every day. All inquiries into this matter have been officially suspended."

He pushed the piece of paper in front of him across the desk to her. "I don't know what you hit, or what happened to make you see what you believe you saw, but there was no man in the road. You didn't hit anybody. You didn't kill anybody. That's a good thing. You should be happy about that."

"Happy? I should be happy? So, you're saying I made this up?"

"Well ... I'm not saying exactly that." He leaned back and thought for a moment. "All I'm saying is that something happened, but it wasn't what you believe it was, and the reason you saw what you think you did needs figuring out. That's why I wanted you to come down here. I had this ready for you before you called, but that just made it even more clear it was time."

She crossed her arms and blinked back frustrated tears, holding in angry shaking with her arms. "Time for what?" she spat out.

Sheriff Morgan nodded at the sheet of paper. She reached out and flipped it over. There were only a few thin lines of blocky handwriting at the top. Hannah read the name, number, and address for the mental health practice down the street.

"I think it'd be best if you spoke to another kind of professional about this, Hannah. Since I'm pretty sure you aren't going to just forget about it, I think you better get some help straightening things out." Sheriff Morgan sounded gruff, but it was a put on. There was pity in his eyes when she looked up at him. A dressing down she could have taken; the pity, she couldn't.

Zombie-like, Hannah got up and made her way back out past the averted eyes, catching her boot on an unraveled seam in the ugly orange carpet and stumbling, batting away a hand that reached out to steady her. Finally reaching the front door, she pushed her way out onto the sidewalk and sank onto a bench, letting out a big, pent-up breath in a cloud of white air.

To her left and right most of the small town was visible, its main street lined with businesses and houses shoulder to shoulder. Past these were gaps and spaces and empty lots, until the decaying buildings petered out into emptiness and long dirt roads. There were few people outside, and the ones that were took no notice of Hannah, hustling into the restaurant or the bar next door. Everyone and everything else had moved forward and moved on.

Not Hannah. He was out there somewhere, a man likely dead because of her. The sheriff didn't believe her; no one believed her, but he was out there. Hannah just couldn't find him.

She crumpled up the piece of paper and jammed it in her pocket. The sheriff could think what he wanted. He could tell himself she'd overreacted or had some kind of emotional breakdown. He could decide to think she'd flat-out lied or was on something. Why wouldn't he? Why wouldn't anyone? There was no body, no blood, no evidence. That meant there was no missing man, nothing to lose sleep over, nothing to worry about.

*Nope,* she thought. *I know what happened. I know what I saw.* She took a deep breath, peeled herself off the bench, and headed home, boots crunching on the scattering of salt on the sidewalk. Hannah made the long trek home in the dark to her silent house.

Once she was inside, she crawled into bed and tried to shut out the world, but one part—the worst part—wouldn't go away. Like every other time Hannah had closed her eyes since the accident, starting with the very first time sitting at her kitchen table, she dreamed of him, replaying the accident over and over again.

Tonight the sheriff had shut her out and stopped the investigation, but it didn't stop the nightmares. It hadn't seemed possible, but it made them worse. When she finally fell asleep, what had been a realistic replay of the event morphed into something more sinister. The phantom bloody trickle that had never completely left the back of her throat grew into a hot, choking torrent in her sleep. The coppery flood filled her mouth and nostrils, drowning her in her bed. She jerked awake sputtering and breathless.

Going downstairs, Hannah poured herself a coffee mug full of wine from the box in the refrigerator and drained it without stopping. When it was empty, she held it out in front of her and stared at it, at the drop of red clinging to the rim. Suddenly furious—at herself, at everything—she hurled the mug across the room. It bounced off the pantry door and broke, hitting the linoleum in two pieces.

The cork board on the pantry door was covered with layers upon layers of papers and newspaper clippings, the sketch of the man tacked on top of them all in pride of place. Hannah considered the face staring back at her. It hadn't been so blank and placid a moment ago in her dreams. Instead she'd seen it streaked with gore, filled with rage. A hissing, slurred voice had hurled accusations at her through flapping, severed lips, the chest that was heaving with the effort now fully caved in, rotting and decaying. He looked like a demon as he cursed her, damning Hannah for killing him, for walking away and leaving him to rot.

# 5

Pulling the door shut behind her, Hannah eyed the bulbous white shape in her front yard. She'd ignored the calls from the garage for so long they had eventually given up and deposited her good-as-new car at a pissed-off looking angle on the lawn. It had gathered an uneven coating of snow since, and some toothy looking stalactites of ice that dripped from the side mirrors. She gave them a swipe when she walked by and sent them crashing to the ground. It was as close to driving it as she'd get this morning, or any morning. Hannah couldn't bring herself to get behind the wheel since the accident. It conjured up all kinds of bad memories, and she had enough of those as it was.

As usual, on foot it was. It was frigid out, but Hannah was thoroughly warm by the time she made it up to the end of the long driveway. At the top where the dirt met the pavement, she turned right—strictly by force of habit—then stopped and looked down the long stretch of empty road.

That was the way she usually went; Hannah probably could have walked to where it happened with her eyes closed. She'd returned to the scene every day since the accident, to comb the woods and walk the banks of the river. If there were anything out there, chances were she would have found it, after all this time. She knew that; she just didn't know what else to do with herself.

This morning, Hannah turned around and started walking toward town, feet crunching noisily through the skim of dirty ice. She hadn't come this way much since she'd stopped making the trip to haunt the sheriff's department, hardly ever since the day he shoved the piece of paper at her with the number for the local shrink. At the time she'd had no intention of taking his advice, but now, if she didn't get a move on, she was going to be late for her appointment.

———◦•◦◦•◦———

There were plastic clings in the shapes of angels and Christmas lights in the window of the therapist's office. Their edges were curling under untidily in a way Hannah found instantly irritating, though if she was being honest with herself, she was determined to find fault even before she walked in the door. Nothing she'd seen so far had given her much incentive to change her mind, starting with the sticky smile the receptionist plastered on her face the minute Hannah opened the door. The look was clearly meant to convey concern and welcome, but all the lipstick was just a thin veneer that did nothing to cover up the smugness underneath.

Making the appointment in the first place was enough, wasn't it? It might be better to reschedule and give herself a little more time to get used to the idea. *If only that were an option,* she thought. If Hannah cancelled it was at the risk of ending up in jail or committed.

"Good afternoon," the woman chirped. "Can I help you?"

"Hannah Cirric. I have an appointment at eleven."

The woman leaned forward and whispered conspiratorially to Hannah. "This must be your first visit. We only use first names and last initials here, for your privacy."

She actually winked, closing one mascara-encrusted eye in a ridiculously exaggerated fashion. Hannah looked around at the otherwise empty waiting room.

It was even more comical, considering this town was so small everyone knew exactly who everyone else was and what they were up to all the time. It didn't help that the office was a glass fishbowl of windows in the middle of Main Street. Hannah sincerely doubted there was any privacy left for her first name and initial to protect.

Shaking her head in disbelief, Hannah sat down to wait. *Was there a holiday or something today I missed?* she thought after a few minutes.

It felt like half the population of the town paraded by while she sat in the uncomfortably warm waiting room flipping through a ratty *Better Homes & Gardens*. Almost to a person they paused ever so slightly to peek through the unshaded window before moving on. While she was enduring a bundled-up child with his nose pressed up against the glass like a pig snout, the door behind the receptionist opened and a woman emerged, red-eyed and clutching a wad of crumpled tissues. Once the woman had walked out the door, the receptionist announced Hannah C. in a ridiculously loud whisper to the still-empty waiting room. Hannah rolled her eyes.

Inside the therapist's office, the dislike was instantaneous, and, swallowed up in the faux leather armchair across from the man, Hannah had to force herself to take a deep breath and at least try to be civil.

"So what brings you here today, Hannah?"

*Lack of a better option,* she said to herself. "I was required to make an appointment as a condition of my release from the hospital," she said. "A couple days ago I got … confused and was, uh …" It was tough to say out loud, so she didn't. "I was involved in an accident." That was one way of putting it.

What had really happened is that Hannah had seen him. She'd seen him, the man she'd hit—would have sworn she'd killed—with her car.

It wasn't the first time. In her nightmares Hannah saw him every night. But after the sheriff had given her the brush-off, Hannah started catching sight of him while she was awake. He was never close, always just too far away for her to make out clearly, and she could never seem to get nearer than that. She'd get a quick glimpse of golden-blond hair in a passing car or a flash of big shoulders on a man crossing the street and would take off after him, but he always seemed to slip away like magic, leaving her standing confused in an empty street, or following a shadow around a corner to find no one in a dead-end alleyway. Every time she missed catching him was like a jolt, and a thud, and it all came back, just as bad as when it'd happened. And it left her even more bewildered. Hannah had been looking for a body, certain he was so badly injured he couldn't have survived. Now she was seeing what she was sure was him, but alive. Was it even possible? What did it mean?

Then, two days ago, she'd spotted him—closer than any time before—and she wasn't going to let him get away. He was behind the wheel of a sleek black car, and when it passed by she'd caught a glimpse of his hair, the shape of his jaw, and his size, the top of his head brushing the ceiling inside. It had to be him.

He nearly slipped away again, but the traffic light had turned at just the right moment, and his car had been trapped there in the intersection. Heart pounding, Hannah ran toward it, willing the light to stay red for just a moment longer until she could reach him. He was sitting there in profile, facing forward. He hadn't seen her. She was only a few steps away.

Then the minivan hit her.

It only clipped her, thank god, the side mirror spinning her around and tossing her backward into traffic. The car behind it shrieked to a halt just in time, so close they had to back up to get the hood of her sweatshirt out from under the tire to move her.

It was a freak accident, a whoops with an all's well that ends well at the end, maybe a little road rash and a couple nasty bruises. Or it would have been, if she hadn't opened her mouth and told them what she'd seen when the sheriff's department got to the scene. And if they hadn't done a blood alcohol at the hospital where they'd insisted on taking Hannah to check her out. And if she hadn't been over the legal limit at ten in the morning on a Tuesday. Whoops was right.

"So, this accident, it happened because of the man you thought you saw in the car," the therapist said. "Who is he, this man you were trying to get to? Tell me about him. Where do you know him from?"

Hannah raised an eyebrow. Maybe it was a therapist thing, where he wasn't supposed to act like he knew just as much about this story as everyone else in town. She was sure he knew exactly who Hannah was. She'd recognized him immediately. He'd been part of the human chain walking through the woods after the accident, poring over the ground looking for the very man he was asking about; his extremely white sneakers and gray community college sweatshirt were hard to forget.

Taking a deep breath, Hannah shut her eyes for a moment and compelled herself to cooperate. It was not going to kill her to sit here and talk about it, especially if it was the only way around any more threats of involuntary commitment from the sheriff. She wasn't sure he could do that, but at the very least he could press the issue about the public intoxication and the jaywalking. An hour in therapy was the easiest solution. And a teeny-weeny little part of her admitted that maybe it would actually be good to talk about it. Hannah let out the breath she'd been holding, opened her eyes, and started talking.

It felt like she was listening to someone else speak as she told the therapist the story he already knew. He nodded and mmmh hmmm'd as she spoke.

"It's the same man. I know it was him," she said.

"But all these times you've seen him—starting with the accident and leading up to the most recent time when you were struck by the van—has there been any evidence he's actually there?" the therapist said.

"I know what I remember. I know what happened. They didn't find any evidence, but why would I make something like that up? My mind can't just have created a person. And something destroyed my car. I know the rest doesn't add up, but it doesn't prove anything the other way either. And two days ago, I saw him. He was in that car, I know he was." Hannah was getting a little hot under the collar, and when the therapist sat back and smiled down on her with a look he probably thought appeared genuine, she had to suck in a breath between her teeth to keep her temper in check.

"And you were intoxicated when you were struck by the vehicle. Is alcohol consumption something you struggled with prior to the initial accident, or is this a new development, since all this happened?"

She crossed her arms and stared at him.

"I see." The therapist nodded sympathetically and scrawled something on the yellow legal pad on its cheap plastic clipboard, making it wobble where it lay propped on his crossed knee.

33

"Are there any other substance issues at present? Are you using any illicit drugs? What about prescription medications?" He raised an eyebrow, and she wondered if it meant he thought she was on drugs, or that she needed some.

He finishing writing, uncrossed his legs, and set the clipboard squarely on his knees, leaning forward. "I think we need to look at the root of this man's appearance in your life. It might be helpful to look farther back, at things that might have happened before the event. Were there any big changes in your life before all this transpired? What about since then—how has this affected your relationship with your family?"

Maybe he genuinely didn't know, or maybe it was all part of the oblivious act; Hannah couldn't tell, but she told him the truth because there was no reason not to. It hadn't changed her relationship with her family one single iota because Hannah didn't have anyone, no family. Hannah was alone. There had only ever been her uncle—she'd been raised by him her entire life until a little over a year ago. Now he was gone.

The thought of him was like a punch in the chest, unexpected enough to take her breath away. Hannah missed him in a way that physically hurt, and the house was an empty rattling shell with just her inside it.

He must have thought he was on to something, because the therapist handed her a tissue she didn't need. Hannah crushed it in her palm. This would have been completely different if her uncle were alive now, every part of it. He would have known how to handle it, and he would have believed her. He would have somehow made this situation tenable, because that was the way he'd been. Uncle Joel had taught her to be strong and resolute, and he always operated with complete and total confidence in what should be done, no matter what the situation was. Now, left to her own devices, the determination and absolute belief in herself he'd taught her had backfired. She believed in herself alright. Problem was, no one else believed her.

She crammed the flowery-smelling tissue down in the crack of the seat and stared at the man who had gone back to scribbling. It was difficult to explain how she felt to a figure that instinctively made her bristle, but she made an attempt despite herself. Hannah didn't think for a minute it had anything to do with the accident, but losing her uncle had been crippling, and maybe she did need help in that department.

Swallowing the lump in her throat, Hannah described how close she'd been to her uncle, and how different her future looked now.

"I mean, my life was good. I finished college, I got a job I really liked. And it's not like I was a child. When he died I was perfectly capable of taking care of myself. It was just so unexpected. He'd been there my entire life and then he wasn't." Hannah swallowed back a lump in her throat. "I never got to say goodbye. All of a sudden he was just gone. For the longest time I kept expecting him to walk back in the door. I had just stopped listening for his footsteps on the porch when this happened."

Hannah eyed the nodding therapist, wondering what he was thinking.

"My uncle was my best friend, more than that," she went on. "I didn't realize it until it was too late. He was my best friend, and my father, and my mother, and a big brother all rolled into one. I know he was only one man, but he was all those people for me. It's like I lost my whole family in one day."

It actually felt good to put it in words, she had to admit, even when she wasn't sold on the man in front of her as the best outlet for her feelings.

"Your relationship with your uncle, it sounds like you were extremely close, more than most nieces and uncles would normally be." The therapist lowered his voice, leaning toward her slightly. "Was it ever too close?"

"I'm sorry, I don't really think I understand what you're asking," Hannah said. Actually, she was afraid she did. She just hoped to god she was wrong.

"You say your uncle was your whole family. With the lack of

other adult figures in your life and the number of roles he filled beyond uncle, were there any other parts he might have played, ones that crossed into territory that might have been hurtful to you as a person or damaging to the psyche maybe? That kind of relationship and the loss of it might drive you to create a male figure ..." The therapist was staring directly at her, expectantly, almost as though hoping there was a salacious part, something grimy and titillating for him to uncover.

"What in the actual fuck does that mean?" Hannah got up slowly and deliberately. "What kind of screwed-up bullshit are you into that would make you think something like that you—"

She couldn't even finish. Let them drag her into an institution or jail, she didn't care. Hannah swiftly raised two middle fingers in front of his face, then slammed her way out of his office, enraged. The suggestion appalled her and she had to resist the urge to smash a boot through the receptionist's desk. She settled for swiping the stack of magazines onto the floor in a cascade of pages and subscription card inserts, sending all the slick, artificial cheerfulness face down on the carpet. When she left, she slammed the front door as hard as she could, putting all her anger into it. It was a substantial amount of anger, and Hannah heard the crash of glass behind her. She didn't look back.

———————◦•◦•◦———————

After the rage had subsided from that first unpleasant experience with therapy, Hannah made an appointment with the only other therapist in the area. She'd spent another week not sleeping and rambling the woods, with the new addition of sitting on the bridge and staring blankly down into the river for increasingly long periods of time. But that really wasn't why she made the appointment. It was because Sheriff Morgan had called repeatedly, and after being ignored, had finally stopped by to let her know that once again she didn't have a choice. He was a persuasive man, what with the possibility of charges for property damage added to his previous list of threats.

This appointment was in the next closest town, which wasn't

actually that close, but was near enough that Hannah could at least make it there under her own steam. She still couldn't bring herself to get behind the wheel, and her other option was asking someone for help. Hannah would have rather risked the car.

She hauled her bicycle out of the shed and climbed on, then climbed off to root out the pump and inflate the tires. *Maybe the bike wasn't the best idea after all*, she thought as she huffed, pedaling it doggedly down the logging road that cut through the woods, the shortest way to the two-lane on the other side of Route 14.

By the time Hannah dragged her bike through the brush between the forest and the paved road she was baking in the layers she had piled on against the cold. By the time she managed to pedal to the top of the hill above Newton, sweat was trickling down to her waist. Unzipping her coat to let the breeze blow through her, she coasted down the last stretch of road onto Newton Street.

Hannah didn't walk into the psychiatrist's office expecting any ridiculous insinuations. There wasn't any way there could be another mental health professional in the world as inept as the last one, let alone in such close proximity. Still, she was on edge, not knowing what to expect.

She needn't have worried. From the moment she sat down, Hannah could see this was going to be a different kind of appointment.

"Now tell me, Hannah, what brings you here today?"

The therapist didn't interrupt or make fake sympathetic noises, just sat back and listened while Hannah waded yet again through her story. Aside from a tendency to pat her tightly pulled-back hair for stray strands, the woman seemed perfectly normal. She didn't take notes and appeared to be listening intently, only breaking in once or twice to ask appropriate questions.

"Now tell me about the man you remember hitting. Who do you think he might be?"

Hannah opened her mouth but was interrupted by a soft ding; time flies when you're having fun.

"I'd like to see you next week, Hannah," the psychiatrist said. "I believe this situation really bears some looking into. I also think the problems with sleeping and rumination are something that can be helped." She scribbled on a few pages of pastel-pink prescription pad and tore them off, handing them to Hannah. "And these"—she added a handful of pamphlets on grief and depression to the pile— "you might find some things that ring true."

Hannah wordlessly accepted the stack and an appointment card for the next week, the thought of which made her legs hurt.

"I want you to really think about the man from the accident. Really think about who he is, who he might be. We'll talk more about him next week."

Hannah pushed everything into her pocket and stepped blinking into the bright, biting cold. As she pedaled back through town, she considered the question about who the man might be. Who was he? What kind of man was he, or more likely, what kind of man had he been? Did he have a family who was looking for him, or was he a bad person running from something? Was that why all the searching had turned up nothing? Was there something more beyond the random man who had the misfortune of meeting the front end of her car?

Then it hit her. The psychiatrist hadn't really meant that. Hannah realized that while this appointment might have seemed different, the outcome was the same. The psychiatrist was looking for who the man might have been inspired by. She wanted to know why Hannah had invented this particular man. Though the woman had listened quietly and not questioned his existence outright like everyone else had, she too thought he was a specter Hannah had cobbled together from the damaged bits of her psyche. In the end, everyone believed the same thing: that he was all inside her head.

As soon as she got home, legs like jelly, Hannah poured herself an oversized glass of cheap boxed wine. Bad habit, yes, but her biggest problem right now? Not hardly.

What if they were right? She set the full glass down on top of the prescriptions and watched a dull red ring soak into the little squares of paper. She'd hit a man with her car and watched him die, but no one else had seen him. There was no evidence he'd ever existed. But Hannah, she was still seeing him. She was seeing him even more frequently, and alive now, but still it was just her. Everyone believed her mind was broken. It was starting to feel like it was. What if it was?

Picking up her wine, she downed half of it then sat back and stared at the canister in the center of her kitchen table.

Small—about the size of a soda can but shorter and fatter—and a uniform matte silver, the canister contained all that was left of the man who raised her. The day of the accident had marked exactly one year since he died so unexpectedly, and she'd spent the entire day on Barclay Mountain, picking her way upward through the overgrown trails to the knob. It was a hell of a climb, but it was a place that meant something. Hannah couldn't begin to count the days the two of them had spent up there, camping when the weather was good, hiking until winter set in with determination.

At the very top of the narrow trail with its obstacle course of glacial erratics and old, nearly nude pines, part of the mountain had crumbled off into a sheer cliff, leaving a view that was worth the miles of hiking. Far below, small clearings were scattered here and there with cabins like dollhouses set neatly inside them, invisible from anywhere but this high above. The Susquehanna snaked around the town to where it swallowed Pine Creek, and on clear days the mountain ranges went on forever, disappearing into the distance like endless smoky blue waves.

Hannah had intended to spread Joel's ashes from the edge of the mountain that day, to let him go and say goodbye. She'd opened the can and looked at the gray coarse sand and bits of bone that were all that was left of the only family she had, but standing there, she couldn't bring herself to do it. It was the pieces of bone, the dirty, chunky reality of them that stopped her. A human being reduced to the contents of a can, not in a smooth, final way, but in a crumbly, uneven mess. Instead of a graceful cloud of ash drifting away on the breeze over the mountaintop, there would be bits and pieces tumbling down the endless cliff to be part of the dirt at the bottom. Hannah had screwed the cap back on and made her way down the mountain, heading back home in the fading light.

A tap of the brakes, a clunk of metal, and seconds later her life had changed so much she didn't recognize herself.

# 6

"**O**kay then, I'll just leave it on the porch again," the voice called through the door. "The bill's on it."

Hannah held still until she heard the crunch of retreating footsteps and the delivery truck backing up and pulling away. Only then did she get up from the kitchen table and open the door to the front porch. She wouldn't have bothered, but if she let the box of merlot sit outside in these temperatures too long it would freeze, and it was crappy enough wine to begin with.

Her bill was rolled up and jammed into the cardboard hole that was the handle; today there was a bright pink flyer stapled to it. *Get Ready to Spring into Savings!* it said, a childish clipart tulip between the heading and delivery price list. Huh.

Spring then. Time had drifted by unnoticed, and somehow in the haze of days she'd managed to entirely miss her birthday, the new year, and a few odd months on top of that.

There may have been some text messages and voicemails to mark the occasions, but Hannah didn't recall. Everything had chittered by like stones skipped across water. A couple of cards in bright envelopes stood out like flags, shoved between the unopened bills and junk mail in the pile that threatened to spill off the counter and onto the kitchen floor, but she hadn't opened any of them, just jammed them into the stack. It was only standing because it had grown large enough to touch the underside of the top cabinet.

Stuffing the wine in the fridge she slid back into her seat, still in

41

a groggy haze from the medications that were supposed to help her sleep and keep the nightmares away. Were supposed to, but didn't. Maybe she'd just stop taking them, with what little good they did. There had to be a notice somewhere in the stack of envelopes that her health insurance had lapsed—the prescriptions had started ringing up full price—so she probably wouldn't be able to afford them much longer anyway.

The insurance bill was just one of many being crushed to death in the mountain of mail. She hadn't worked since the accident, and at some point, the publisher she edited for stopped sending her jobs. The lights were still on, so her bank account hadn't dried up completely, but that was probably because she'd stopped paying almost everything but the bill for the Beer Barn.

Pushing aside a pile of old newspapers, Hannah stared at her laptop. When she wasn't walking the woods, she was huddled at the table in the unkempt kitchen scrolling through websites, looking for the face that consistently haunted her dreams. She looked over at the police sketch that still hung on the cork board. There was a cleft in his chin from the mug she had thrown at it. She found the look quite dashing.

Obituaries and crime reports, faces in crowds at accidents and rallies, until her eyes were sandy. When the actual news sites were thoroughly exhausted, she poked a finger into less reliable sources, delving into seedier stuff that gave her the urge to look over her shoulder, like she was about to be caught watching porn.

None of it was actually risqué—or at least the majority of it wasn't. Some of it came disturbingly close to what she was looking for. Disappearing bodies and people who should be dead mysteriously walking around weren't unheard of—if you were a conspiracy theorist or super-duper religious. But those sites were as near to familiar ground as she'd ever gotten, and something kept her from going too deep into that world. Maybe because there was an underlying fanaticism that hit a little too close to home. Some of these people sounded completely off the rails. What did that say about her?

Once, just once, she thought she'd really found him. In a grainy scan of a photo from a crime scene she caught a glimpse of a head far above the others, someone in the background of a crowd of spectators. Hannah had squinted, sure it was him, for a moment unable to breathe, turning blue while she dialed the phone.

"Sheriff Morgan, it's Hannah. You're not going to believe this but ..." She'd let the phone slide out of her hand and back to the table with a clunk. She'd read the caption under the photo.

It had been taken outside the home of a serial killer from the 1960s. Maybe it was a relative? It had to be, he looked so similar. She examined it from every possible angle, made every adjustment she could to the low-resolution image. Hannah even tried to contact the newspaper, which turned out to be long-since defunct—big surprise there—and the photographer had died in 1978. In the end she'd ignored the phone when the sheriff called back and had tacked the image up on the board with the rest of the dead ends.

Shaking her head to clear it, coming back to the present, Hannah repeated a familiar mantra in her head. *He doesn't exist. If he were real you would have found him, dead or alive. That man you think you see but can't ever catch—it's because he isn't there. No one else believes because there's nothing to believe. You made him up.*

And a tiny, even less welcome voice chimed in after it.

*You're sick. Sick in the head. That's the explanation that makes the most sense. Accept it and it will all be over. You'll stop seeing him when you admit he was never there.*

Some days one of the voices resonated, sometimes both. Some days it was nothing at all. Today was one of those days.

Hannah just couldn't let go of it, couldn't accept that her mind might be so badly damaged it had created such a detailed false reality. How could she have created an event and a person so real that even though none of what happened made sense, she couldn't accept that it hadn't been real.

She let out a sigh, exhaling a plume of white. Spring might be coming, but it wasn't here yet, not by a long shot. It was still miserably cold, the way the end of February here always was, making you question whether warm weather would really ever come. The sun that managed to fight its way through her window was murky gray and carried no warmth with it, and she shivered.

"Wine would have been frozen inside today." She heaved herself out of her chair and went into the living room. The little plastic toggle that operated the thermostat moved when she nudged it with her index finger, but there was no familiar click and rumble of the furnace trundling itself to life. Hannah went down into the ancient stacked stone cellar where the boiler sat wreathed in cobwebs, and brushed the film of dust off the gauge on the tank. Seeing it buried below empty didn't surprise her. Having it filled hadn't been a priority.

Back up the stairs, she paused at the top and watched her breath puff out white in front of her, then yanked the string hanging from the bare bulb in irritation, swearing when it broke off in her hand. Shrugging on a coat, she sat back down at the table, pulling the worn collar up around her ears. It still smelled like her uncle, retaining ghostly scents of old leather and coffee. She wished he were here.

*What would you make of all this, Uncle Joel?* she wondered. *Would you be sitting here, freezing to death because you hit someone with your car and they disappeared? Even if you were sure it wasn't a tree or an animal, could you convince yourself that somehow you blocked it out, replaced it with something else inside your head? What would you have done? At what point would you have just accepted it and moved on?*

She didn't know. She wouldn't ever know what he thought again.

*I wouldn't have sat there and frozen to death,* a small voice that sounded like his whispered inside her head. *Hannah Cirric, get the hell up,* the voice said a little more loudly. Now that sounded more like him.

"What's the point? What's the point of any of it?" she said out loud. It sounded strange in her tomb of a house where there was only ever silence. Great, now she was answering the voices in her head.

*Get the hell up.*

"Don't tell me what to do."

But she got up.

She only paused in the mudroom for a knit hat and work gloves before she braced herself and stepped out into the yard.

The woodpile was buried under a crust of iced-over snow. Hannah scraped off the large, round section of tree she used for a chopping block, stood up a short section of log, and hitched the heavy axe, praying that everything wasn't so frozen she'd bounce the blade through one of her legs. God she was out of shape; it felt like she was lifting a cinder block.

She took a breath, hitched the axe up again, then brought it around, the sharpened head whistling as it cut through the air. The section split neatly in half and she tipped one of the halves up and split it again, quartering it down to size so it would fit in the stove. She propped up another, then another. Sweat trickled down between her shoulder blades and she shed the coat, flinging it aside onto the snow where it landed splayed like a sad brown snow angel. When she was gasping for breath, she buried the axe in the block with a crack that echoed around the snowy yard. Scooping up as much split wood as she could carry, she wheezed her way to the door.

The kitchen wood stove was an ornery black dinosaur that had been in the house longer than she had been alive. It protested its age by being next to impossible to light, especially when fed unopened mail and pieces of empty wine box. The cold, uncured firewood that should have been split and stacked months ago didn't help, but after blowing and pleading, the flames finally took. She left the grate open and plopped down on the slate in front of the stove, hands outstretched toward the warmth.

The fire cracked and popped while she sat, and little by little it grew, until the frigid air around it was steaming. It was snapping and roaring by the time she was finally warm enough to move. Hannah used the wire coil of the door handle to carefully close it and groaned her way to her feet.

When she spun around to warm her back, the coffee maker on the counter stared at her and she swallowed. She couldn't remember how long it had been since she used it, and for once the thought of a warm drink didn't instantly give her the phantom taste of rot and blood in her mouth that soured her stomach and killed her appetite. Instead, she could almost feel the coffee warming her from the inside out, and taste the hot bitterness, cut with just a little bit of milk to tame the acidity.

Rummaging through the cupboards, she pushed aside boxes and canning jars until she found the sadly crumbled remains of a bag of grounds; there was maybe enough for two stingy cups. She gagged and almost changed her mind when she saw the mold farm growing on the old grounds in the top of the machine. Dumping them into the sink for lack of room in the overflowing garbage can, she rinsed them down, then scrubbed out the filter and pot tolerably well.

It smelled glorious. While the pitiful pot brewed, she opened the refrigerator. No milk, no cream, pretty much no anything, except some ketchup in an interesting shade of brown and a box of wine trailing a sticky stream of red from the spigot to the bottom of the refrigerator. A search of the mostly barren pantry produced a single dusty can of evaporated milk. It would do, probably.

Suddenly she laughed out loud. It was a bizarre sound here, where there hadn't been anything like it in so long. It had just come out when she'd looked at the date on the can.

*Expiration dates are only a suggestion. That's exactly what you would have said if you were here, Joel.* She could almost hear his voice saying it.

He would have been right; the canned milk wasn't going to kill her, though by normal standards it was probably an awful cup of coffee. To her, it tasted amazing. She poured the last drop into her cup and added another slop of the milk, then wrapped her hands around the ceramic mug.

Hannah sipped thoughtfully, staring at the steady drip from the kitchen faucet. Suddenly, out of nowhere, her stomach tightened and growled audibly. It took her a moment to place the sensation; she didn't remember the last time she'd actually felt hunger.

Little by little, on those rare occasions when she both remembered to eat and could get past the terrible taste in her mouth, she had picked her way through the carefully labeled glass mason jars of spiced peaches, pie filling, apple rings, and the dill and bread and butter pickles.

After that she had made her way through the odd jars of things like sauerkraut, bean salad, and relish, the back-of-the-cupboard, old-lady concoctions put up to avoid wasting what grew in the garden. Waste not, want not—she'd heard it a million times growing up, but she had made the preserves without ever actually planning to eat chow-chow or pickled watermelon rind.

She was never going to be hungry enough to eat the pickled watermelon rind, but miracle of miracles, there was a quart jar of applesauce hiding behind a crumpled box of pasta. Hannah pried off the lid with the edge of a spoon, releasing the vacuum with a pop. Nearly half the jar was gone before she came up for air, sticky sweetness dripping down her chin. Sighing, she let the spoon fall into the jar with a clunk and set it down on the table.

For a few minutes she stared at the bulletin board, at the black and white sketch. Her mind began to slide back into its usual rut: see his face, remember the accident, try to convince herself to accept something else, give up, repeat.

Today, though, she didn't quite slide. Maybe it was the coffee or the activity, but something had changed. Nothing was tangibly different, but somehow there was the tiniest sliver, a thin icicle down her spine that poked at her and made her move. With a great effort, she pushed herself back in her chair and stood up.

Sliding her feet into her boots, Hannah sucked in a deep breath and threw open the door. It was still and crisp outside. The sun had managed to cut its way through the clouds and was blindingly bright against the layer of clean, white snow. Closing her eyes and resisting the urge to turn around and go back inside, she let the cold air wash her lungs clear of the funk of indoors and woodsmoke. Then she started walking.

———•◦••◦•———

Hannah was sweaty and out of breath by the time she topped the last small rise before Main Street. Coat unzipped and flapping open in the breeze, she covered the last couple of blocks into town more slowly, walking carefully down the uneven sidewalk that passed the smattering of buildings.

First, she passed a faded flower shop that had never been open in the time she'd lived in the area, its for-sale sign swinging at an angle on a single rusty length of chain. Next, a duplex house, one side well kept with neatly swept front steps, the other side with a child's blanket hung askew in the window as a curtain. After that came the gas station with its dirty windows and rusty, cock-eyed sign.

She trudged on for a few more blocks, past the nicer houses and the hardware store. Passing the mental health office she kept her middle fingers tucked in her pockets and frowned at the glass door. Maybe they should put her name on it, since she'd paid for it. She finally crossed the two empty lanes and walked through the small parking lot of the Shur Shop just shy of the center of town.

"Welcome to Shur Shop," a tired-sounding greeter called out. Hannah ducked past him, head down. Inside the store it seemed overly warm and unnecessarily bright. There were only six or seven aisles in the store, compared to the much larger, more popular Giant Foods on the other side of town, and she registered with discomfort how busy the store was despite being the worst place in town to shop. A glance at her phone confirmed her suspicion that it was Saturday.

Slinging a red plastic shopping basket over her arm, she dodged a woman with a car seat balanced on the handle of her cart and a sugared-up toddler jumping up and down beside it. Hannah skirted the old ladies blocking the way while they squeezed wan, off-season tomatoes, and made her way quickly down the next aisle. Tossing coffee, a bag of pretzels, some pasta, and whatever else crossed her path on top of each other, the basket got heavy quickly and she headed for the checkout with her sad haul. She was near the limit of what she could carry home, small, nutritionally void selection that it was.

"Hannah, is that you?"

She jumped at the voice, losing her grip on one of the plastic handles, the box of rigatoni hitting the floor before she could right the basket. Sheriff Morgan picked up the box and balanced it back in her basket. He was looking at her with an expression she couldn't read in the second before she looked down at the linoleum.

"Haven't seen hide nor hair of you in some time. You doing okay?"

She mumbled something with embarrassment and started to walk away, the memory of her walk of shame out of the station rushing back, reddening her cheeks.

His big meaty hand caught her shoulder. He wasn't in uniform for the first time in her experience, the sweatshirt over the crisply ironed jeans making the whole situation seem more surreal.

"You take care, girl. Good to see you out and about. I mean it."

Hannah couldn't meet his eyes or stand the pity in his voice. She shrugged out from under his hand and toward the checkout.

All the foot tapping in the world didn't make the line she was in move any more quickly. Hannah looked over at the other open check-out, which had a line twice as long. Sweet, white-haired, arthritic Betty was behind the counter, which explained the backup. Betty was the soul of kindness but not the speediest operator, so Hannah kept her place. She jiggled impatiently through a price check on condoms for a red-faced teenager, finally getting her basket to the conveyor and unloading it.

"Why, Hannah Cirric, is that you? I barely recognized you. Haven't seen you in ages. Have you been sick?"

Hannah should have waited it out in Betty's lane.

Sheila had been working the Shur Shop checkout for as long as Hannah had lived in town. She was the town busybody, something Hannah had at first found more amusing than annoying. The woman had at one point harbored a serious crush on Joel, and after he died told anybody who would listen about the affair they'd been carrying on in secret. Hannah knew it wasn't true, because she was pretty sure she would have known if her uncle was seeing someone. Also because Sheila was a blowsy, overdone chain-smoker who always had a little too much cleavage on display and a heavy-handed spackling of makeup. She couldn't know for sure what Joel's type had been, but Hannah imagined Sheila was the total opposite. Joel wouldn't have given her the time of day beyond common politeness, let alone carry on some type of clandestine affair. The thought made her laugh.

Hannah had told Sheila as much in an uncharacteristic snit right after he died, something Sheila clearly remembered. Hannah was sorry she had ever stooped to the woman's level and opened her mouth, especially today, when it seemed like every bit of temper and source of shame she'd ever had was coming back to bite her in the ass.

"That'll be eighteen seventy-eight." Looking up to place a crumpled twenty into the outstretched hand with its lacquered claws, Hannah's vision was drawn in by the reflection of herself in the mirrored glass window of the manager's office behind Sheila's head.

Maybe the self-righteous tone from the checkout was justified. No wonder the Sheriff hadn't immediately recognized her. She didn't recognize herself.

Her unzipped jacket was hanging open, displaying the grimy, stained sweatshirt underneath. The hair escaping from under her snagged knit cap was a matted wad, greasy and lank and in a dark ball of tangles. Under the cuff of the hat was a gaunt, pathetic stranger with hollow eyes shadowed by purple rings like fading bruises. How many times in her life had she walked by a person in a comparable state and looked on them with pity or, even worse, derision. Her disgust with herself rose in a hot tide up through her face, burning the tips of her ears.

Hannah grabbed her groceries and forced them roughly into her shoulder bag.

"Your change!" Hannah ignored Sheila's voice with its thinly veiled laughter and dashed for the door, determined to get as far away as she could from the sad reality of the level she had let herself reach.

A swirly dizziness washed over her and she sank onto a concrete parking barrier. Look at what she had become. Her obsession over proving herself right, finding someone the facts told her didn't exist, was destroying her life. She hadn't been able to get past what she was sure she'd experienced and accept the reality of what must have really happened. Now she was as broken and degraded on the outside as she felt on the inside.

Her pulse pounded in her ears and she choked on heaving sobs, growing even angrier at herself for the tears. Carts rattled by, pausing, then passing by without stopping. A car door opened and closed, and someone spoke to her but didn't linger when they got no response.

It was ultimately the shivering that pulled her back to reality. Hannah stood up shakily and leaned back against the cart return behind her, taking a few less frantic breaths to steady herself, feeling as wrung out and limp as a wet rag.

Somehow she still needed to walk home, make her way back into bed, and find some oblivion. Mostly she needed to get away from herself.

Maybe she should go back inside and have the sheriff haul her off to an institution; she felt ready for one. Maybe that was what she needed. But the thought of walking back past Sheila was a more painful prospect than being committed, so after one more deep inhalation Hannah stepped over the concrete divider and into the snowy parking lot.

He was standing there, just across the parking lot, under a sadly naked winter tree. Light hair, fair skin, tall and broad, just like she remembered. Like she always remembered. Hannah put her hands to her face, grinding her fists into her eye sockets. When she looked up, there was no one there.

This was never going to end. One cruel pause so that time could show her how far she'd fallen, convince her maybe there was a way back up, then back into the blender. Hannah had seen him everywhere for months, glimpses that kept mocking her, jerking her mind back and forth, asking her whether he was her invention or not, never letting the memory of his face fade. It never would; she had really and truly lost it.

Hannah let her bag slide to the ground with a thud, and began to run.

# 7

**B**y the time Main Street was behind her she'd lost her hat, and her matted hair hung down her back in a heavy knot that thumped her between the shoulder blades with each step. She hadn't slowed the entire trip back, and when she finally reached her driveway, she was exhausted and tripping over her own feet, dragging her coat by one sleeve. At the turn she finally lost the coat altogether, then tripped over it and skidded, falling face first toward the ice. When her hands went out to catch her, Hannah didn't feel the crusted surface cutting into the skin of her hands. She didn't feel the pain or the cold. She didn't feel anything at all.

At the front door she reached automatically to her side for her keys—keys that were in her bag; the bag that was lying somewhere on the ground outside the supermarket. Hannah made a fist and punched out one of the glass panes in the door and reached through, raking her wrist over the jagged edge in the process. She barely noticed the red bracelet it drew across the pale underside of her arm, or the blood that ran down from the ragged cut, except that it made her fingers slip and slide on the lock. When she finally managed to fumble it open, she pushed her way inside and slammed the door shut behind her.

The stairs looked like a mountain, and she climbed them like one, dragging herself up the narrow flight on her hands and knees, desperate to put the world behind her, anything to get the hell away from this nightmare that wouldn't stop.

*And it won't stop, will it? I'll close my eyes, and he'll be there. I'll open them, and he might be gone for a little while—just long enough for me to scrape myself back together and drag myself out the door—and then, he'll be there too.*

In the bedroom she crawled into bed, still in her boots, arm bleeding, and burrowed like a mole under the mountain of covers into the familiar mustiness of unwashed sheets. Even in the rank, warm dark, it didn't disappear, the image of him standing under the naked tree, staring at her with strange, pale eyes. He was so real, so detailed and defined she couldn't comprehend where in her mind she'd gotten him from.

*Leave me alone. Leave me alone. I'll admit it, I'm messed up. How's that—I'm fessing up. I'm crazy and none of it is real. I made it all up. I made it all up. I made you up, now leave me alone. Leave me alone, you're killing me.*

Unburying one arm, Hannah groped for the bottle on the nightstand. She knocked it off, sending the contents skittering away across the bedroom floor. She felt around blindly until she managed to close her hand around some pills and crammed them into her mouth, not caring what they were, or how many, only about making it all stop. Chewing them and forcing them down dry, Hannah prayed they would take effect quickly and give her a moment's peace. She'd do anything just to make it go away.

Hannah lay rigid as a statue, every muscle clenched, seeing him under the tree, seeing him before she hit him, seeing him after when he was torn up and bleeding, seeing him in the car at the stop light before the car hit her. He was there again and again, mocking her, disappearing and reappearing until finally the drugs began to take effect. Blessedly he began to blur, and fuzz, and grow indistinct, until finally he melted away into nothingness.

———

*Uncle Joel's home, thank god.* She heard him coming in through the front door, jiggling the finicky old lock until it opened. Maybe he'd make the coffee, since she wasn't ready to get up. He couldn't cook, but he made coffee just fine. "Don't make me get up. I want to sleep in," she mumbled to herself under the blankets. "I've been having such a terrible dream." A terrible double dream, a dream within a dream. But he was coming up the stairs; she heard the squeak of the second step. He was going to make her get up. Were they supposed to be somewhere today? She didn't remember. Were they going hiking, up Barclay Mountain?

It was the squeak that made what she'd thought was a dream step sideways into reality; suddenly she was fully awake. It was a house of clicks and rattles, filled with the sounds of loose glass panes in shrunken wooden frames and wind under shingles, the constant death clacking of its old bones knocking together. But the squeak of the second step from the bottom, it was unique, the way it protested when someone stepped on it. She'd know the sound anywhere, and it sliced cleanly into her foggy oblivion, poking a finger into her stoned sleep. Hannah was wide awake, and there was someone in the house.

She opened her eyes in the dark, listening to the shuffling sound of someone moving up the stairs. Dropping her arm down the side of the bed, Hannah felt around silently for the shotgun she'd kept there since her uncle died, quietly picking it up from under its cover of dust bunnies. Sitting bolt upright in total stillness, she tried to listen around the sound of her own racing heartbeat, trying to focus on what was coming. There was another sound, a thud this time, heavy, somewhere higher and nearer to her than it had been before. It was the sound of someone setting both feet down on the landing at the top of the stairs, just in front of her bedroom door.

She considered calling out, but the jiggle of the bedroom doorknob made her throat constrict. Her words stuck, but a squeak forced itself out when her sliced forearm protested against the weight of the shotgun when she raised it and trained it on the door. Hannah was shaking, and it made the gun quiver up and down, the moonlight reflecting in thin, wobbling lines on the top of the barrels.

"Who's there?" she tried again to call out, though it came out as a hoarse croak. Focusing, taking a deep, silent breath, she stilled the gun at the door and forced the lines of light steady and unmoving like a laser sight. No one answered. The doorknob stopped moving.

"I'll shoot …"

Suddenly the door swung inward, the opening fully blacked out. A large shape moved through it, toward Hannah. She pulled the trigger.

The gun bucked against her shoulder, pushing her backward and slamming her head against the headboard with a painful crack she felt but didn't hear, deafened by the blast of the shotgun. She lost her grip on the gun and it dropped off the side of the bed. Hannah barely heard the second barrel discharge when it hit the ground, just saw a flash of fire, then it was dark again.

The spent gunpowder burned her nostrils and stung her eyes. Shaking, Hannah reached over to turn on the bedside lamp. When it threw a ring of smoky light across the room, she wished she hadn't.

A man was crumpled against her doorframe, still moving, sliding sideways slowly against the wall. Finally, he came to rest with a thud, slumping on the floor. His chest was a scatter of bloody dots that were quickly growing toward each other, turning the white shirt red. He was staring straight at her, eyes wide open. She recognized those eyes. It was him, all over again. Cramming her fists into her eyes, she ground them to tears then opened them back up.

He was still there.

She got up and stood over him, watching the red spread over his chest. He was motionless and bleeding, but Hannah was afraid of him, this man who had climbed so fully into her mind. The only explanation was that this was some kind of full-blown psychotic break and none of it was really happening. But if that was the case, it was pretty damn convincing.

It occurred to her that maybe this was some kind of screwed-up cosmic test. If this was a do-over of her failed attempt to save him the first time, this could be her chance to make it right. She needed to do something either way, whether this was as real as it felt or a breakdown-induced fantasy. She'd hesitated before and failed to save him. She wasn't going to this time, delusion or not.

Reaching out, she put her hand on his neck, feeling for a pulse; there was a beat, but it was faint. She pulled her hand away from the almost feverishly warm skin and groped through his pockets—this time he had pockets, thankfully—searching for a phone. He felt real enough to Hannah, and her hands came away sticky with blood, though empty. No wallet, no phone. No way to call for help. She didn't have a landline and the nearest neighbor was a mile away, and that was as the crow flies, through the snow and in the dark. She was on her own.

"Oh no. Don't you dare die. Not this time." She'd hoped he'd give her some sign of life, but there was nothing. Hannah reached over to the bullet-ridden dresser, pulling out a clean T-Shirt. She ripped apart his shirt—now entirely red—the scattered holes making it shred like paper, and covered the worst looking places the best she could, putting pressure on them to try to stem the bleeding.

"Come on, don't do this again. Either you need to wake up or I need to leave you and find help. Don't you dare do this to me again."

As if to respond, his head suddenly tipped sideways, and a trail of blood ran from the corner of his mouth.

"No, no. Don't you dare." She felt for a pulse again. This time she didn't feel even the smallest movement. Making sure his airway was clear, Hannah tipped his head back up, put her lips on his, and forced his chest to rise. She did it again, watching it lift and then fall back into place. Blood sputtered out of one of the wounds, air escaping from where the buckshot had punctured his lung. She grabbed another shirt and covered the wound, pushing down, hoping it was the right thing to do.

Was she just making it worse? "Damn it," she cursed, "why is this happening?" She didn't know what to do, other than to keep trying. Interlocking her fingers, Hannah put them on his chest.

"Stayin' alive, stayin' alive," she mumbled under her breath while she did chest compressions. When she reached thirty, she returned to his face, forcing air into his lungs again. His lips and face felt colder now than before. Again, she laced her fingers and pressed against the wet, red chest.

"Come on now, don't you die. You're going to survive and you're going to tell me what the hell is going on. I don't care if you're real or not. You need to wake the hell up and let me off the hook."

Nothing. She needed to get help, but she was afraid to leave and stop trying to force blood through his body and air into his lungs. And she was afraid if she looked away for even a moment, he would be gone.

She breathed into his mouth again. His skin was colder and clammy and she thought it looked paler. There was still no pulse she could feel. Hannah sat back on her heels, stunned. He was dead, again. Why was this happening?

Suddenly frustration and fear overwhelmed her and she screamed out loud. "You can't die!" Hannah slammed her fists down onto his unmoving chest.

His eyes shot open, rolling crazily back in his head and he jerked forward, sitting straight up. One of his giant arms swung wildly and struck Hannah, throwing her backward into the bed's footboard. When her head connected with the wood the world went gray, and she saw him sliding back to the ground before it faded away completely.

---

It was so cold her limbs didn't want to move at first, and she just lay there blinking away the weak sunlight coming through the bedroom curtain. Watching dust motes drift through the light, Hannah tried to remember how she had gotten there, lying on her bedroom floor. She reached a hand up and felt the lump that was throbbing on the back of her head, and it all came back.

It felt like a dream, but it hadn't been, at least some of it. There was a scattering of buckshot like a negative constellation in black on her white wall. But that was all there was. There was no one there. He was gone. No body, and no blood. None on the pale floor boards, none on the wall where he'd left a red arc when he first slid to the ground. None on her. She looked at her hands in disbelief, completely clean except for the crusty bracelet of dried blood around her wrist. None of it was his, though she'd been covered with it.

Why was this happening? Was this really her life now, the same insane nightmare repeating over and over again? How had she become so far detached from reality? Hannah felt like the toy gyroscope she'd had as a child, which started in a stable spin, over time its grip on the axis deteriorating into wobbling chaos, more and more off center in ever-widening circles. She had gone too far off center and now spun wildly, beyond recovery, about to skid to a lopsided halt.

Pulling herself to her feet, Hannah walked past the splintered remains of her dresser and out of the bedroom, pausing only to trace the dots in the doorframe with her fingers, feeling the rough edges of the irregularly spaced holes.

One methodical step at a time, she made her way into the hallway and down the stairs. She retraced a trail of frozen blood drops—her own—out through the front door, leaving it open behind her as she stepped onto the porch. In the bitter cold she walked across the yard and up the driveway.

Hannah floated, the bite of the air rolling off her, oblivious to the speckles of snow that stuck to her hair and freckled her face. She didn't move to brush them away as she walked toward the place where she had first seen the man's face and turned it into a pulp of blood and mangled flesh. Tripping in the slush, she continued to place her numb feet one in front of the other. Her head felt broken.

She heard the whoosh of the rushing water and followed it to the center of the metal railroad bridge. Hannah stopped there, dislodging clots of snow with her boots, watching the frozen snow tumble haphazardly downward. The wind was blowing harder here, buffeting her body, the cold cutting through her thin sweatshirt like a knife. She climbed over the rail to stare at the river below, like she had done so many times before.

A small splash. That would be what she left behind. An ungraceful ripple in rushing water, a barely perceptible disturbance, swallowed whole and whisked away. Without a doubt, she was afraid of dying, but at this moment, under the weight of all these moments, she was sagging under the burden of living.

With a whoosh, a gust of icy wind pushed off by a passing car gave her a nudge of encouragement. Even the air wanted to tip the scales, bullying her toward the edge of the rusty girder. Chips of paint whirled away on the wind like crusty brown snowflakes.

It would probably hurt for a moment, being chewed up by the freezing river with its jagged border of ice like ugly broken teeth. But hurt, she had learned, was cumulative. What was one more little hurt on top of so many other hurts?

Leaning forward, one freezing hand wrapped around the railing, she held the other hand out as far as it would reach. Palm flat and facing up, she weighed the resistance of the frigid air against the nothingness of empty space. When she closed her eyes the weights balanced, and she floated. It was simpler here in the middle of the bridge, above everything, where there was only the most basic of truths. You can hold on, or you can let go.

"Hannah. No."

The voice, so close, startled her. She lost her grip.

She thought she heard her name again as she fell.

# 8

The hurt was everywhere. She could feel it deep in the center of every bone and poking its way out from the inside of her skull. It needled its way up and down her spine and over every square inch of bare skin. The hurt and the cold. She was so cold she couldn't manage to shiver, her entire body locked in ice and clenched as tightly as a fist. The very air inside her body felt solid, like a congealed, viscous fluid too thick for her lungs to push out.

And if that wasn't enough, suddenly the pain, this incredible pain beyond anything she'd ever experienced, somehow managed to get worse. Hannah was dropped into a pool of fire. She tried to scream but nothing came out of her raw throat.

The burning crept slowly inward, chewing into her skin, eating away at her flesh. She couldn't move, couldn't thrash against the heat on the outside that fought an inch-by-inch battle against the razor-sharp frozenness inside her.

She hadn't expected it to be like this, not remotely. Didn't anyone know this was what came after? Was this what dying had earned her? What the hell was wrong with her? It would have been better to suffer through life completely out of her mind than this. What a goddamn coward she was, to waste even a single day—no matter how miserable, no matter how painful—when this was what there was to look forward to. Was this it, an eternity of fire and ice fighting to see which could cause the most pain? This was her punishment for wasting so much perfectly good time not appreciating being alive.

The fire sloshed around her wetly and Hannah grew aware of solid bounds against her body. Strange how insanely hot it felt, considering the distinct crack as she clove open the ice on the river with her body. Maybe she was in hell. She'd been pretty sure there wasn't really hell; the joke was on her. Hannah had done some things she wasn't especially proud of, but if she was in hell, the bar for admission must be pretty low.

It had to be that she was still dying. Maybe the impact hadn't killed her instantly. She remembered reading, somewhere far away, in another lifetime, that after the intense coldness the late stages of hypothermia felt like gentle warmth, followed by peaceful drifting off to sleep. But this was anything but peaceful; this was more like being inside a volcano.

It hurt so badly, still hurt in the most unimaginable way, but suddenly a little part of her could take it. The pain abated enough for her to take a full breath, and she wasn't so locked in ice. Here it was then; this must be the dying part, the growing warm and drifting off. She was so very scared. In the place beyond the hurt, through the burning and freezing, she was coherent enough to be terrified at knowing she was going to die.

But she didn't fade away. The pain did, just a little more. It was still excruciating, but less so. With the abatement of the hurt, the world outside started to come back into focus. She could hear the slop of water and the sound of soft, even breathing.

"Hannah, can you hear me?" a gravelly voice said, rumbly and deep like a big jungle cat. "Wake up, Hannah." She struggled to open her eyes, able to force one to oblige just a crack; the other didn't want to cooperate. Through the sliver all she could see was haze and a blurry figure. She let her eye fall shut again.

"Hannah, you need to wake up. Open your eyes."

The words were more urgent, and there was a faint pressure against her face that felt like a hundred bees stinging her cheek. She forced her eye open again. Above her was the white, curved ceiling of her small bathroom. The solidness against her back was the old enamel of her ancient claw-foot tub, filled to overflowing with water. This was not what she had expected.

She couldn't get her head to move so she could look around. All the parts of her body were refusing to work together the way they were supposed to. Closing her eye again, she decided it was easier to sit here petrified.

"Are you awake, Hannah?"

The voice was close enough now for her to feel the movement of breath against her ear. With another squinting look—out of the corner of her eye at an angle that made her already painful head scream—she saw the owner of the low voice.

There he was again, still following her, close enough for her to see in misty detail. His eyes were staring at her intently, a strange shade that reminded her of something—a star sapphire, or the silvery blue butterflies that drifted across her lawn in the summer.

She had seen him enough times, though for the first time she could hear him, even feel the warmth from where his hand had touched her face, and she wondered what that meant. Hannah let her eye close again and sat in the blackness behind her lids, not knowing if when she opened them next everything would have changed yet again. It probably would, so she kept her eye closed, because she wasn't prepared for that to happen again quite yet.

There was silence for a moment, the only sound breathing and the soft slosh of water. The pain abated some more as well, and with that came a great sense of relief. Where before she hadn't been so sure, Hannah was right now certain she was still alive, and she was extremely grateful for it.

"Hannah, I know you can hear me. You need to open your eyes."

She was most certainly alive, but was she in her right mind? That was still in question, but it had been for so long it wasn't really her prime concern at the moment. The pain was more urgent. Though marginally better, she still hurt absolutely everywhere, in a sickeningly throbbing way that turned her stomach.

"Open your eyes, Hannah." He sounded different; the words had an edge to them. She obliged, one eye mostly cooperating, the other glued shut. It hurt too much and suddenly she heaved from the pain, vomiting water and bile. Unable to move, her throat filled and she began to choke. Warm hands tipped her forward and her airway cleared.

There was a pop and a sucking sound and the water began to drain from the tub. Her skin began to be exposed an inch at a time, but it felt like someone else's skin, numb from the cold. She must have finally been thawed out enough to shiver, because she was quaking by the time the water level dropped to her backside. A blanket dropped over her and she felt herself being lifted up in a big, damp bundle, aching where his arms were under her.

A moment later Hannah was buried under a mountain of blankets, the familiar feeling of flannel sheets beneath her. She had done something so incredibly stupid, yet somehow she was alive. Tears leaked in a steady stream down her face. Something wiped them away.

"I think you will be okay," the low voice said. "You will be fine. Rest, Hannah. You can rest. You are going to be okay."

"Are you real?" Her voice came out in a raspy whisper. She wanted to reach out a hand and feel that he was actually there, but her arm didn't want to move.

"Yes, Hannah, I am real. Go to sleep."

"Will you still be here when I wake up?"

"Yes, Hannah."

———◦•◦•◦———

She forced her good eye open and kept it that way this time. He was still there, directly in front of her face, even larger and more solid than in her memories. He filled up the space in her small bedroom, and the mug in his hand looked like a child's teacup. When he set it on the nightstand and sat carefully next to her on the edge of the bed, his weight dipped her mattress, tilting her toward him. She groaned at the movement.

He must have thought she looked panicked because he put his hands up slowly, palms forward, leaning away from her.

"No need to be frightened."

She didn't feel afraid, every other sensation overshadowed by overwhelming thirst. He must have seen her eye flick toward the mug and he reached over to pick it up. She tried to take it, but her arm wouldn't quite close the gap, making it halfway then dropping back to her side. He put a hand behind her head and brought the mug to her lips.

The lukewarm liquid felt like fire in her throat, and she sputtered and choked. He wiped her chin with his shirt sleeve.

"More," she croaked before he could take the cup away. She drank greedily, though it burned, until the cup was empty and she gasped to catch her breath.

He let go of her head and it sank back into the pillows. His eyes probed hers, his forehead furrowed.

"Hannah, how do you feel?" he asked very quietly, returning the mug to the nightstand. "None of your injuries appear to be serious, but there is no way for me to know that for certain. Do you think you need to go to a hospital?"

Her eye widened. "No. No, please don't take me to a hospital. I think I'm okay."

He surveyed her face, lifting an eyebrow. "If you are sure?"

She leaned back and closed her one working eye.

"Going to the hospital would mean a lot of questions, and I'm in enough trouble already. Last time I was there ... well anyway, when they find out what happened they're going to think I jumped. I'd end up in an institution for sure this time, no doubt about it." She turned her head a little toward her shoulder, the motion making her draw a painful breath. His expression tightened a little around the eyes but he nodded.

However it may have looked to anybody else, Hannah was happy to be alive. The man she had driven herself nearly mad trying to locate and thought she had killed, *twice*, was not only alive but sitting on the side of her bed looking uncomfortable. Everything told her he was real, from the way she could feel his hip against her leg through the blankets to the outdoorsy smell she remembered from some dreamlike place.

"You're alive?" It was both a question and a statement.

"Yes. It appears we both are. Are you sure you are not seriously hurt?"

Hannah took a moment to analyze herself, top to bottom. She was sore, more sore than she could believe was possible, but her toes moved when she wanted them to and her fingers flexed. She rotated her arms with a groan and took in the mottled bruises that covered her skin.

"You are very scraped up, all over that side. From the ice. It was jagged when you broke through and you had to come back up over it on the way out."

It felt like she had been dragged over a cheese grater, now that he mentioned it. She noticed the backs of his own hands, raw skin peeking out over the cuff of the plaid shirt.

"You pulled me out?"

He looked grim and nodded.

"Thank you."

"Thank you?" He spoke in a whisper. "I am fairly certain that I am the reason you went in."

Before she could speak again there was a knock on the door.

"Miss Cirric. Are you in there? Hannah, it's Sheriff Morgan," a voice called from far away, outside the front door. There was a brief pause, then the brisk double knock came again.

Her mysterious man got up from the bed swiftly and crossed to the bedroom door. He was far less lumbering than his size would have had her believe, and he moved noiselessly. The voice called out again.

"Hannah. It's Sheriff Morgan. I came to check on you and make sure you're okay. Holler if you're in there."

She rasped a reply, not able to make her scratchy voice loud enough to be heard. When she tried to roll over and get up, the movement sent a jolt of pain through her body.

"You should answer the door." He had her robe over his arm. Hannah nodded, because that was all she could manage. He picked her up as gently as he could and opened the bedroom door.

"Can't you answer it?" she asked him. She wasn't sure she could stand up.

He shook his head firmly. "Send him away."

The sheriff called out again. "Hannah, I'm gonna come in now, for your own safety. If you can hear me, I'm coming in the house to perform a welfare check." She could hear the door rattle, and she hoped it was locked.

"Tell him you are coming," he hissed into her ear, carrying her down the stairs. He had to duck to miss the low ceiling above the last step.

"I'm coming, Sheriff." It was a weak attempt, but the rattling stopped for a second. "Just a minute," she said, a little more loudly. She reeled dizzily when the man set her down and threw her robe around her.

"Tell him no one else is here." He looked at her, his eyes begging for acquiescence.

"I don't think I can. I'm going to fall over." She wobbled a little, and not for effect. Her legs felt like Jell-O.

"Send him away, and do not tell him what has happened."

"What if he—"

"If you send him away, I will stay and explain everything. If not …"

She nodded. He'd disappear again, she knew, if she didn't do this the way he asked. Hannah took a deep breath and steadied herself as he slipped silently into the dining room as the door swung open.

"Oh, Hannah, there you are." The sheriff stopped short and took his hand off his holster. He ducked inside, shutting the door behind him against the cold and removed his stiff felt hat. "I just stopped by to check in on you." He really looked at her for the first time and his brows dropped. She must look as rough as she felt. He paused for a moment then continued. "I was relieved to see you at the supermarket, out and about for a change. Then I ran into Dan from the Beer Barn down at the diner. He mentioned he'd tried to deliver you a couple boxes like he usually does." Sheriff Morgan looked down at her like a disapproving father. "He said you had a broken front window that hadn't been that way before and thought maybe it looked like there was some blood on it. He knocked and yelled in and didn't get any answer."

He was looking at her suspiciously. She only nodded slightly, clutching the sides of her robe closed at her neck. Holding her arm up felt like trying to lift a cinder block.

"Dan's a fool," the sheriff went on, "and didn't think to call me right then. Instead he waited to tell me about it till he ran into me today. Course everybody knows Dan's his own best customer so no surprise there. I tried calling but your number goes right to voicemail, says the box is full."

It probably was. God knows where her phone even was at this point.

"Anyway, I thought I'd stop on by to check in on you." He made to leave but stopped, turning back. "I don't wanna pry, but it's my job. What the hell happened to you?"

She smiled, hoping it looked more convincing than it felt. "I fell coming home. I haven't been doing so well after … well, you know. I was finally feeling a little more like myself and decided to walk to town for some groceries and overdid it. I got overwhelmed, I guess, and kind of freaked out. Then I made the mistake of going through Sheila's line in the checkout, and she can be a little … um …"

Sheriff Morgan rolled his eyes. "Yeah, I know what you mean."

"I was cutting back through by the logging crossover since it's quicker and ended up going ass over teacup down the bank. I'm a little out of balance these days, apparently." She tried to look sheepish, but it probably leaned closer to creepy, as twisted up and swollen as her face was feeling. "When I finally made it home I realized I forgot my bag with my keys and phone. I had to break a pane in the door to get in and managed to cut myself. On top of all that I think I'm coming down with a cold or something. It's been a rough couple of days."

"Want me to run you over to St. Joe's to get looked over?" Sheriff Morgan asked, looking down at the white bandage around her wrist she hadn't noticed until then. He was putting his hat on, thank god.

"No, I'm fine. Only thing really injured is my pride," she said. Maybe slightly more than her pride. Her legs were done and were quavering from the effort of standing.

He laughed, zipping up his coat and straightening the radio at his shoulder. She felt a twinge of guilt for lying to him. For all the threatening he did, it was all meant to help her, and in his defense, he'd put up with a lot from her. It wasn't his fault she'd dogged him about finding the man based on some admittedly sketchy evidence, a man who was probably in the other room listening to every word they said. That, or was running away as fast as he could.

For a moment she considered telling him, but just as quickly dismissed it. If the man had meant her harm he wouldn't have pulled her out of the river. Now that he'd appeared, Hannah desperately wanted answers. The possibility of getting them outweighed the lie, at least that was what she told herself. The rest could be cleared up later.

"Sorry to give you grief, Sheriff. I appreciate you looking out for me. I'm fine, really."

He had the door cracked open, letting the cold in, and she could see where the broken window had been neatly patched with a square of plywood, the jagged pieces gone. He nodded and slipped out the door but still didn't close it. Hannah had a death grip on the back of the couch to keep herself upright.

"Make sure you lock this up tight behind me. And I'd avoid taking that logging crossover, if you haven't learned your lesson this time. Been some people I don't recognize around here. Never hurts to be cautious." He gave her one last appraising look, shaking his head a little, but finally he pulled the door closed.

She reached forward to shoot the deadbolt but lurched dizzily, the floor currently in the midst of some kind of localized earthquake. She was caught before she hit the ground and set carefully on the beat-up couch. Hannah peeked through her tightly shut eyes to make sure he was still really there, then shut them against the spinning. He sat down in the dainty chair beside the couch. When it creaked in protest he quickly moved to sit down beside her.

"I know you have a number of questions. I will answer those that I can. But first, are you hungry?"

*How could anybody be thinking about food right now?* she thought. The last thing on her mind was eating. But her stomach thought otherwise and answered for her. She was pretty certain they both heard it growl.

# 9

It was the strangest day she'd ever had, and she'd had some strange ones. It had begun with falling off a bridge and ended with sitting across the table from a dead man, eating dinner in the most bizarrely normal way. That anything edible had been thrown together from the contents of her kitchen was almost as miraculous as the company.

She was still challenging what she was seeing, testing the reality of it. He was still there, no matter how many times she screwed shut her one working eye and opened it again.

"Is there something wrong with your eyesight? Is your vision blurring? I fear you may have a concussion."

"It's possible, between the fall and you launching me across the room."

"I what?" His eyebrows furrowed, and he leaned forward.

"Nothing. Anyway, I'm fine." She shook her head, which made her vision swim a little. Maybe she did have a head injury. Hannah closed her eye until she could open it and see just one of him, then leaned back in her chair at the kitchen table and let out a little groan. Only part of it was from the ache; the rest was her uncomfortably full stomach.

"I don't know how you managed to put this together from what was here, but thank you." She was painfully aware of the strange state of things, and also of a sudden shyness, sitting across from this man she had never met but had seen and thought about more than anyone else these last months. "Where did you find pasta? I'm pretty sure there were about three pieces of penne in a box in the pantry."

He took his empty plate to the sink and washed it thoroughly, then set it precisely upright in the dish rack to dry. He set his silverware up rigidly next to it and turned back to her.

"When you saw me at the grocery store you dropped your bag and took off. I picked it up and followed you home. Along the way I also ended up with your hat, a jacket, and one glove. I fear the other may not be recoverable." He smiled a small smile, showing white, even teeth. "Your pasta made it home. The pretzels were a total loss."

He turned to look out the kitchen window over the sink and she stole the moment to evaluate him. There was a shadow of red-blond stubble across his chin and up the line of his jaw now, but otherwise he was very close to how she remembered him. Her eyes flicked with embarrassment to the drawing of him along with all the other random bits of information tacked to her bulletin board.

It was a close match, except in real life his face was a little bit softer around the edges. His skin was light, but not as fair as she had thought, and incredibly smooth and even—unusually so. The hair had been cut since she first saw him, not long enough now for the wave she recalled falling over his forehead, and darker than she remembered, not white blond but closer to the color of honey. He was very tall but not awkwardly so, just larger than normal in scale, the kind of person you would think was a professional athlete of some kind, a football player maybe, if you passed him on the street.

She took one last bite of the now-cold pasta and pushed the plate aside, turning to face him. "Will you tell me what's going on now?" Hannah took a shot at getting up against the protests of her stiff body, but he picked up her plate and she gratefully sank back down.

He set it in the sink with a faint clink and turned back toward her, nodding.

"But on the couch," she said. "I don't think this chair and I can be friends right now. Tell me your name." She'd been mentally running up a sizable list of questions while they had eaten in silence, and it seemed like a good place to start.

"My name is Asher."

It fit him. It was old fashioned but not too out of the ordinary here, where families handed down the same names generation after generation. It wasn't strange to hear someone on the street calling for an Ezekiel or Job or even a Malachi.

"No last name?"

He smiled, but at what she wasn't quite sure.

"Smith." Sure it was.

"I hit you with my car. Six months and ..." Her eyes flicked to the calendar. Apparently she had lost a couple days somewhere. Months was more like it, looking at the calendar page that hadn't been turned, twice. She did the math.

"Six months and three days ago. I hit you and you were lying on the ground bleeding, and you died." She took a deep breath and it all spilled out in a rushed jumble. "And then I saw you in a car on the street, and then you were in my house—or at least I hallucinated you were—and then I shot you. But if you're here now then you were real the first time, so you must have been real those other times too, right?"

So much for the neat mental list. This was question vomit.

He leaned back against the sofa and crossed his arms across his chest.

"I was only stunned by the collision. I got up and walked away and an acquaintance picked me up. As you can see, I am very much alive. No worse for wear. You must have dreamed I was here before now." His tone was a little too flippant, and his eyes dared her to question the truth of his words.

"You're admitting that I hit you, then where are the scars? Your face was cut down to the bone from top to bottom. One of your eyes was gone." Hannah tried not to sound accusatory, but there was definitely acid creeping into her tone. She made an effort to calm down. After all, wasn't this what she had been wanting so badly, to know he was real? The added bonus of finding out she hadn't killed someone wasn't a bad thing either. Getting an honest explanation was what she wanted, and she was at risk of blowing it with her temper.

"It was just a scratch. It must have looked worse than it was; it was very dark out if you recall. Everything healed up without a mark." His arms were still crossed against his chest and his foot jiggled just the smallest bit.

"I don't believe you."

He raised an eyebrow. If this had been a poker game, that jiggle would definitely be his tell. Funny, while the story was exactly what she wanted to hear, it wasn't the truth and she knew it.

"Who picked you up then?" she said. "There wasn't another car on the road, I would have seen it. You didn't have a cell phone on you to call anyone with, and I got up for less than a minute. You just disappeared, and you didn't even leave a drop of blood behind. They looked for you with bloodhounds and search parties. There wasn't a trace of you or anyone else."

She was exhausted and in pain, she'd almost died, and she was starting to lose the war against holding her temper. While he'd just saved her life—which she was grateful for—he was the reason for all of this in the first place, and now he was definitely lying to her. He'd better have a good reason.

"Fine," he said. "No one picked me up. I was alone. I was poaching and was afraid of being caught. So, after you hit me, I got up and walked away to avoid any trouble."

"You were hunting naked?" He didn't have an immediate answer for that question. "And how did you end up with my bag and my groceries?" she said.

His arms were still crossed defensively, and his expression had grown stony. "I saw you at the grocery store and you took off running. I gathered up your things and followed you here and left them on the porch. I was never in your house. Maybe you imagined I was."

"Why were you there when I was on the bridge?"

"I just happened to be passing by on my way home and saw you about to jump. You have answers to your questions, and no reason to further upset your life with worries about my well-being."

"Okay, let's pretend for a minute that any of what you just said is true. That still doesn't explain where all the blood went. What about the bullet holes in my room? I shot you. I tried to give you CPR, but you died, *again,* and then you just vanished."

*Cool it, Hannah.* She took a slow breath and thought for a moment before she continued. "I don't believe you. Thanks for saving me and making sure I'm in one piece, but I don't buy it. I know what I saw. Everyone, including me, has tried to convince me I made it all up or that there's some other explanation. But since you're sitting here right now, I believe myself. I know it happened, all of it."

A sharp pain was settling in the middle of her forehead. She squeezed her eye shut until it subsided slightly, then changed tack.

"Listen, I hit you and I thought I killed you. I was sure you were dead, and I have been paying for it every day and night since then," she said. "I did everything I could to find you, and when I couldn't and everyone believed I was making it up, I tried to come to terms with having lost my mind. I failed. Miserably." Hannah opened her eye. "Then it happened again. I shot you, though what you were doing in my house is a whole other question. Anyway, I'm at fault for hurting you, so you don't owe me anything, but you could at least tell me the truth."

He opened his mouth to speak but closed it again, staring at her intently for a moment. Then he stood up abruptly, looking out the front door and across the yard.

"After all this," she said, "after everything that has happened, you aren't even going to tell me what's going on. Do you know what my life has been like, trying to find you?"

Finally, he came and sat back down, beside her where she couldn't see the expression on his face.

"Does it make a difference?" he said. "You believed you killed me. I am clearly alive. Is that not enough? You can pick yourself up, get back to your life knowing you were right and there is nothing wrong with your mind. Do you need to possess every detail?"

They sat in loaded silence for a moment, the only sound the tick of the ugly Swiss clock between the doorframe and the window.

"Yes!" It came out angry, and she stopped, made herself control her temper. "And no," she said more softly. "I'm alive right now, and despite how it may have looked to you, I'm happy about that. It's apparent now you aren't dead, and you actually exist, so that's supremely helpful with the crippling guilt and the overall sense of insanity I've been living with. On the other hand," she said, "if I hit you and I didn't kill you, and you just walked away and disappeared, then why are you here? Why did you come in here in the middle of the night like an intruder? Why did you follow me off a bridge yesterday?"

Hannah swallowed and hoped he would turn to face her. He was eerily still, like a giant stone man. Suddenly he got up again and walked toward the kitchen. Her head turned to follow him to where he stopped in the doorway and put his hands on either side of the frame, leaning forward wearily.

"I am sorry my explanation does not satisfy you," he said. "I hope you will be okay after this point. I am clearly alive; there is no need to continue to suffer for my sake. I did not intend to drive you to where you ended up, but I hope now I was able to keep the situation from becoming fatal. It would be best if you accepted what I have told you and moved on." He walked through the kitchen, opened the back door, and left, closing it behind him with a click of finality.

Hannah sat there, shocked. Her head drifted forward until she was staring straight ahead at the front door, at the neat wooden square that covered the broken pane. Eventually she swallowed and stiffly hauled herself up from the couch and to her feet. She went to the kitchen and looked at the messy room with its overflowing waste basket and rolls of dust in the corners. The only clean thing was his plate and cutlery, standing rigidly at attention in the drainer. With a sigh she turned off the light and dragged her protesting body up the stairs.

# 10

Her body and mind were both beyond exhausted, but even burrowed warmly under the layers of blankets, shotgun napping on the other side of the bed, Hannah struggled to fall asleep. She tossed and turned, rerunning the jumbled, unbelievable bits of the day over and over in her mind. Finally, through sheer inability to keep her beat-up body awake, she drifted into a fitful, dream-filled sleep.

Hannah found herself falling from the bridge again, but in a world that had been upended, so the sparkling river was like a waterfall, and she was sliding headfirst, down across its surface, edges of white ice reaching together on either side of her. She could see her shadow, arms stretched wide like wings, the water shimmering and wavering like old green glass just in front of her, close enough that she could have reached down and trailed her fingers over the surface as she fell.

Each time she tried, she was pulled back by an unseen hand. Finally, she saw the black pool at the river's end, but there was no fear in the landing, like there had been none in the falling. She broke through the surface like a diver, but instead of being sharp and icy, it was like falling into new snow that was strangely warm and soft as cotton batting. No water rushed into her sinuses, just the smell of wood smoke on the air. Instead of the weight of the dark pool, Hannah could feel the sun against her skin. Under the water it was calm. Perfect meaninglessness calm.

It was wonderfully peaceful because it was the first night since the accident she hadn't seen him when she closed her eyes. Hannah was pulled gently from the dream by the morning sun cutting directly through the sheer curtains and warming a line across her face. She stretched under the blankets, her body protesting, though not as violently as yesterday. It felt more like a day after too much exercise, like she had run a marathon. Or had run a marathon, finished first, and been trampled by every other person in the race.

Both eyes opened today, and flipping back the covers, Hannah could see the side of her left leg was covered in an unattractive camouflage of red scratches and purple and black bruises. The mottling continued up her thigh and under the hem of the T-Shirt she'd slept in, popping back out from the armhole. The other side had fared a little better, not visibly marked up, but as sore as she expected when she raised her arm.

She quickly put the arm back down. She stank. Like pond water and old sweat.

In the bathroom she turned on the shower and waited for the water to heat up. When she took off her shirt it peeled away audibly, and she winced as the fabric separated from where it was glued to the scraped skin on her back. Hannah dropped it to the floor with disgust and toed it in the direction of the trash can.

The hot water was a revelation. She sat in the bottom of the tub watching it circle the drain in a dingy swirl and disappear. After wrapping her hair in a towel, she swiped a hand across the mirror to clear the steam.

The dark bags under her eyes and the hollow cheeks she had seen in the mirror at the grocery store were now accompanied by a swollen and split black eye. Purple and red ran down her cheek and over her chin in one continuous bruise that traveled downward to her shoulder. She let the condensation build back up and her reflection fade away to a blurry, indistinct outline of someone more recognizable.

After several minutes and no small amount of swearing, she'd managed to work most of the knots out of her matted hair, and it finally fell straight and dark, clinging in damp hanks to the middle of her back. Hannah shivered, cooling down quickly out from under the warm spray, and threw on a pair of sweatpants and a fleece shirt.

Looking around at the accumulated piles of dirty clothes on the floor and draped over every available surface, she sighed then stuffed the hamper full and lugged it to the top of the stairs with her less sore arm.

Thunk. Thunk. She jumped. There was a thump against the side of the house, then another. She paused. It came again, making the loose windowpanes rattle.

Abandoning the hamper, Hannah tiptoed quietly down the stairs. By the front door she pulled the curtain aside, jerking backward when a quartered piece of wood hit the siding and fell onto a stack under the window. Hannah opened the door to see a retreating figure in plaid flannel making its way back to the woodpile. She wasn't sure if Asher heard her open the door or not, but he didn't turn.

Deftly, he placed a section of log on the block and split it cleanly in two, again and again until the last of the pile was split. He leaned the axe against the block and gathered up a giant load of wood, balancing all of it carefully in one big arm.

Asher didn't look at her when he stepped onto the porch and tossed the last pieces on the pile. The crib was full of split wood, and what wouldn't fit was stacked neatly down the length of the porch.

"You should lock your door at night." He brushed the wood chips off his arms and turned back toward the woodpile.

That was the second bossy man to tell her that in as many days. Truthfully, living where she did, locking or not locking the door at night was about a fifty-fifty occurrence. She figured if a person really wanted to get in, a locked door wasn't going to keep them out for long, and Asher was the only shady character she'd ever seen in the area. The town was so small they didn't have a resident peeping Tom or even a lecherous old guy to worry about. Dan from the Beer Barn stared at her ass sometimes, but that was about the extent of the local creepiness.

Anyway, she hadn't been raised helpless. She knew how to handle the shotgun in her room—as he well knew—and in her mind that leveled out some of her lack of diligence in use of the deadbolt.

She closed the door against the cold but didn't lock it, mostly out of petulance, and went into the kitchen.

The situation hadn't improved overnight. She turned the radio on, pushed up her shirt sleeves above her elbows, and dug in.

By the time her ambition started to lose ground against her aches and pains, the room was shining and smelled like soap and pine cleaner. It was nearly back to normal except for the mountain of bagged trash that needed to go out, and the mail pile she was ignoring. The dish rack was loaded with clean dishes and the cork board was empty of clippings and the drawing of Asher, the blank grocery list pad and the calendar turned to the correct page the only things on it.

She almost didn't hear the tap on the glass of the back door over the music. Looking out, Hannah opened the door for Asher. She didn't hesitate, telling herself again that if he meant her harm, he'd had plenty of opportunity and she'd be buried in the woods somewhere by now.

His hands were filled with the pile of faded envelopes and flyers that had been crammed in her mailbox, and she winced at the red past-due stamps that had somehow managed to avoid fading with the paper. He didn't come inside, just stood, filling up the doorway.

"Just put it with the rest." She nodded toward the counter.

Adding it to the now-neater pile, Asher still had to cram it up under the bottom of the cabinet to keep the pile from avalanching onto the floor. He turned to go.

"Hungry?" She spoke to his retreating back. The pot of oatmeal simmering on the stove gave a glurp as if on command. He turned back and nodded.

Her kitchen table had never seemed tiny before he sat at it. Asher just took up more space than most people. Hannah was relieved to find out the oatmeal tasted better than she'd expected, since the main ingredient was imagination. She'd dumped in the rest of the jar of applesauce from the other day and a healthy amount of cinnamon, nutmeg, and anything else from the spice drawer that seemed appealing. After drizzling the oatmeal with homemade maple syrup, she handed him a heavy bowl. She sat down across from him with her own and they ate in silence.

"Thank you." He set the spoon down in the empty bowl.

"Would you like some more?" She filled his bowl a second time without waiting for an answer. She imagined it must take a lot of calories to run a person his size. She poured them each a cup of the coffee that had been brewing while they ate, then Hannah sat back down across from him, feeling oddly out of place in her own kitchen.

"There is a delivery for you on the front porch. Appears to be from the beverage store." His voice didn't necessarily carry any judgment, but she winced. Her recurring delivery of a sad quantity of the Beer Barn's cheapest wine. She had almost no food, but boxes of crappy merlot showed up on her doorstep like clockwork. There were probably three or four slushy boxes out there at this point.

Hannah would have poured a glass now if she was alone, and just the thought made her flush with embarrassment. The downhill track that had been her life recently had turned her into a person she wasn't proud of.

Asher finished his second helping in silence, then rose to wash his bowl while she stirred her oatmeal into a congealed clump. He balanced the clean bowl carefully on the precarious pile, then drying his hands on the dishtowel, he folded it precisely in half and hung it over the edge of the apron sink.

For months Hannah had felt like she was stumbling through a dense fog. Today was different, a little less hazy at least, even if still undeniably strange. The efforts of the morning had brought her up some, but stopping reminded her how sore and battered she felt inside and out. She wasn't surprised. Things were better, but they weren't just magically perfect, all the problems blown away on the breeze. The thought made her sigh. There were just so many unanswered questions. She put her head down in her hands.

"What is it?" Asher turned from peering out the window.

Through her hands she mumbled, "I still don't understand. I don't understand any of it."

"Why do you have to?" he said. "What made you dwell on it for so long? Accidents happen every day, people die. You could have come to terms with any explanation, whether you had every detail or not. Why did you spend all this time searching the woods for me and staring at the river as though I would be there? Anyone else would have just moved on. You still should."

His tone was even but not irritated, like the words themselves made her think it should be. It was speculative, even, and it made her wonder. If she kept her temper in check this time, maybe he would let his guard down and some of the truth would slip out on its own. She picked her head up and took a breath. Getting carried away didn't used to be her at all, and it certainly wasn't going to get her the answers she needed.

"You're right," she said. "There's obviously something I'm hung up on. I believed what I saw and I wasn't able to accept anything else, because I'm stubborn. And yes, people die every day, but not because of me. All I could picture was you rotting in the woods somewhere while your family wondered why you never came home." Hannah stood up and took her bowl to the sink. "But you're right. I need to get past it. Coming as close to dying as I did makes that clear."

She shuddered at the memory of the crack, the feeling of ice caving beneath her before it all went black. "But I'd like to be able to do it with all the facts, then I can walk away from it, end of story. If not, I guess I'll figure something out. Thanks again for pulling me out of the water. I'm glad you did, and you can leave here with a clean conscience and my eternal gratitude."

He looked at her levelly, smoothed out the already smooth dish-towel, and walked toward the back door. She reached for the knob, disappointed, and started to open the door for him. Then she closed it before he could leave.

"How did you know I've been searching the woods and staring at the river?"

She took a step sideways and leaned against the closed door, glaring at him, though feeling silly. As if she could stop him if he decided to go. Asher was the size of a bus. He stared past her, out the window over her shoulder.

"Asher, how do you know what I've been doing? Why were you at the grocery store? And you were here when I fired the gun. I know it. Don't deny it. Have you been following me?"

He didn't answer her, instead reaching out toward where her hand rested on the doorknob. She froze, holding her ground, waiting for him to push her aside.

"It can wait. Right now we need to step calmly away from this door." Asher turned the lock above the knob with a click. "There is someone watching us from the tree line."

# 11

She turned her head slowly toward the edge of the woods, but from so far away all Hannah was able to pick out were the shadowy spaces between the thick firs.

"I don't see anything," she murmured. He motioned for her to get back, and she slid behind him.

"They may know that I saw them, but there is no way to be certain," Asher said, whispering over his shoulder. "They slipped back into the trees. Where is the shotgun?"

It was still upstairs. He didn't wait for her answer.

"Go get it. Stay clear of the windows. Does the room at the end of the hall lock?"

"It locks, kind of," she said to his back.

"Now, go quickly. Get the gun and lock yourself in. Do not open the door until I come get you. Do not open it for anyone but me. The gun, do you know how to use it?"

Hannah didn't bother to respond to that one.

"Where are you going?" she said. He backed away from the door, shuffling her behind him.

"I will leave by the front and see if I can discover who is out there. It may simply be the sheriff again, or a neighbor."

Hannah didn't have any neighbors close enough to be casually walking by, but it wasn't unheard of for someone to cut across the back of the property from time to time, taking a shortcut to the logging road.

"Who else would it be? Why would the—"

"Go now." It came out of his mouth as a hiss. The ferocity silenced her and she slipped out of the room, away from the glass panes of the kitchen door. As quietly as possible Hannah went up the stairs and retrieved the shotgun.

The boards creaked twice as loudly as they usually did, it seemed, as she made her way through the hallway downstairs. Pausing at the linen closet, she dug out a box of shells by touch on the little shelf between two studs. Pocketing them, she crept the rest of the way down the hallway, pausing by the narrow window to look through the space between the curtain and the frame.

Hannah jumped back, whipping the gun to her shoulder by force of habit as a figure passed by the window. She dropped the barrel and stepped back from the window when she saw it was Asher, crouched low and padding stealthily by. Not hesitating any longer, she scooted past the window and went into the downstairs bedroom, dropping the old-fashioned thumb latch in place and slipping the little pin into the slot above it. Technically it was locked, just not in a way that would do a whole lot of good if someone really wanted to get in.

Trying to be quiet, Hannah set the shotgun down and tipped up the bench that sat at the foot of the bed, turning it sideways and jamming it between the heavy footboard and the door. With the reassuring weight of the shotgun back in her hands, she dropped open the barrels and checked the load. The smell of spent gunpowder drifted upward when she ejected the empty casings and she remembered the last time she'd fired it. After pushing a fresh shell into each chamber, she closed the breech with a soft click.

She slid down into the space between the nightstand and the far wall, out of sight of the window. A crow called just outside and made her jump, and she jerked the barrel up. Probably a good time to put the safety on—firing a gun at her own doorway twice in one week was a little much, even for her.

Settling back down, gun across her knees, Hannah looked around the room. She hadn't been in it more than a handful of times since her uncle passed away. It hadn't changed since then. Aside from a thin layer of dust, it was the same as he'd always kept it, much the same as he'd kept his room in all the homes they'd lived in over the years. The bed was made with military precision and the nightstand was bare except for a book he'd never gotten to finish, a piece of paper sticking out halfway through to mark the page. There were hundreds more books on the shelves, each one lined up exactly with its neighbor, organized by size and color in an attempt to impose order on the crazy variety of titles. Each one Hannah had read at some point; Pyle's *Robin Hood* and *The Prince.* Two fat volumes of Norse mythology, *The Libertine*, and Steinbeck's *The Grapes of Wrath. Dracula* and *The Transit of Venus.* Countless others, the most eclectic of collections, with classics touching books still on the best-seller list. Fiction, history, autobiography, true crime, and horror, together taking up a full wall of the room.

There weren't many other personal items, besides a few drawings she'd made him as a child and cringe-worthy graduation pictures, Hannah looking awkward and uncomfortable in a polyester gown and mortarboard. The only other picture was of her mother and her aunt, identical and lovely, with dark eyes and black hair. They beamed happily, arms wrapped around each other in their matching dresses. That was everything in the room, except another door, the one to his closet, still filled with his evenly hung clothing, the row of clean shoes lined up underneath. Hannah wished her uncle was here now.

There was a shuffling in the hallway and Hannah pulled the gun off her lap, pointing it at the door. She heard it again and pushed down the little lever that controlled the safety, a little shake in her finger.

"You can come out now." There was a quiet tap on the door. She lost hold of the gun for a second, catching it before it fell. It took her a moment to un-wedge the bench from beneath the doorknob.

"There is no one out there now," Asher said, "but someone definitely has been. I found footprints, several sets of them, running all along the trees and back into the forest. Some are fresh, the others I cannot tell."

It sounded so ominous coming out of his mouth. It could very well have been a hiker or an out-of-season hunter looking to fill their freezer. But all this tiptoeing around and his obvious concern made her uneasy.

"Who would it be, unless it's a hunter or something? Unless this is about you." She took a step backward. "Is this about you? Did someone follow you here. Are you in danger?" Her eyes widened. "Wait, am I in danger?"

Asher eyed the gun as it crept upward while she was talking. She dropped the barrel slightly but didn't drop the subject. Hannah didn't really know anything about him, other than he wasn't currently as dead as she'd previously thought and was the size of a small truck.

"Asher … who do you think is out there?"

"It may not be anything," he said. "There may be an entirely innocent explanation. But it is also possible I may have brought danger to you. The figure in the woods, they were too far away for me to see clearly, so at present I am not certain."

She thought about waving him out the door with the double barrels. Hannah knew almost nothing about him, and very little of what she did know made sense. For all she knew he was in some sort of trouble and someone dangerous had followed him to her home. Maybe it was time for him to go. Or for her to go to the authorities. As badly as she wanted answers, getting them wasn't going to be worth much if she was dead.

With a small step, she moved toward the door, wondering if he would move aside. The way he filled the entire doorframe, there was no way past him.

He put up a hand, stopping her. "I know what you are thinking. If I was certain you would be safe, I would leave right now. But as I have gone to some lengths to make sure you are alive, I intend to stay for now and see that you remain that way. I think it is safer for you to stay inside the house right now."

The way he was staring down at her was intense, and his hand had reached out to completely encircle her forearm, but for some reason Hannah didn't fear him, as stupid as that probably was. There might be something to fear, but somehow she knew it wasn't in the room.

On the other hand, she wasn't a total idiot.

"Why should I trust you? I don't believe any of what you've told me so far is true. You can stay, for now, but we're going to lock up this house, and then we're going to sit down and you're going to enlighten me as to what the hell is going on. Then maybe we can find out who the people creeping around my backyard might be." She tried to look bold and defiant. "And I'm not letting go of this gun."

Hannah might have been able to sell it if she hadn't wobbled a little bit trying to hold the shotgun up with one arm. If he thought of commenting, he had the sense to hold his tongue and simply nodded. She dropped her twitching arm with relief. "Okay then," she said. "And make some coffee. I think we're going to need it."

———— ◈ ————

Maybe it was overkill, but they erred on the side of caution. The house was now as secure as it was capable of being, which was to say it would keep a mildly motivated intruder out a little bit longer than someone who had a real mind to get in. It was an old, cobbled-together farm-house, but they did the best they could, shooting the deadbolts and locking the windows, covering them against prying eyes. While the coffee brewed, Hannah propped empty cans with a handful of change in them on top of the windows. It was a little much, but it wouldn't take a genius to jimmy one of the old-fashioned locks, and it would give them some notice if anyone tried to slip inside. Finally, Asher wedged chairs under the knobs of the front and back doors.

Avoiding the kitchen with all its windows and glass-paned door, they sat with their coffee in the tiny, never-used dining room. It was a late addition to the house, a tacked-on rectangle of a room with only one small, high window. Hannah had intended to turn it into an office but never got around to it, preferring to work at the kitchen table in its sunny little nook.

Hannah sipped the strong and scalding coffee appreciatively. She was running on fumes, her energy fading fast, but she was unwilling to concede defeat until she got a little more information. Besides, she was a jittery jangle of nerves, so as badly as she needed it, sleep was probably a pipe dream.

When Asher didn't speak immediately, she settled for examining him from across the dining table where he was sitting straight and upright, staring off into space, still as a statue. He seemed to do that a lot.

In the low light his eyes looked darker, almost completely gray, the blue lost in the dimness. His nose, she decided upon seeing it in profile, was rather attractive and perfectly straight. The hands enveloping the coffee mug were sprinkled with pale, fine hairs up to where they disappeared into the frayed cuffs of the shirt.

He looked, catching her staring. Hannah put down her coffee and stretched, trying to look nonchalant, her shoulders creaking with the effort.

"You're still here," she said. "Explain."

Asher twisted the heavy stoneware mug around and around, studying the organic swirl in the glaze as it turned.

"Please understand." He stopped and set the mug down, turning to face her. His gaze was unnerving, but she made an effort to not look away. As the short staring match went on, she wondered what he saw, or what he was trying to decide.

"Fine," he said. It was a defeated *fine*. "I woke up lying on a road. I opened my eyes and stood up, and the first thing I saw was headlights. I do not remember being struck, but I remember hearing your voice. I felt your hands against my face, and the blood running down my neck. Then it became incredibly cold, and everything went black."

Yes, well, she was there for that part.

"Okay, so you just woke up there, and then I ran you over with my car?" Hannah raised an eyebrow. "But how did you get there? And where did you go after? You were really hurt, so how did you even move? Oh, and where the hell were your clothes?"

He blew out a breath and ran a hand through his hair, standing the front of it up.

"I was ... are you familiar with the gas station at the four-way intersection to the east of town?" She nodded. There were only two stations in the area, and the one he was talking about was the bigger of the two, a truck stop for semis off the highway.

"I was by the gas station and my car was hit by a very large truck. I really only remember seeing the bulldog emblem on the front, and I woke up next in the road where I had my second unfortunate meeting of the day with a motor vehicle."

"Now wait …" She started to speak but he raised a hand. She raised an eyebrow but conceded, nodding for him to continue.

"After you hit me, I found myself waking up rather uncomfortably in a small creek I believe is not far from here."

Hannah laid the shotgun across her lap and closed her eyes. She rubbed her temples, wincing at the pressure against the one that was still swollen and painful, willing herself to hear out the story.

"So, you got in two horrible accidents in one day, and you just woke up somewhere else, not knowing how you got there, even though after at least one of those accidents, you should have been dead?" She opened one eye to look at him.

"Yes, that is what happened. You asked for the truth, and now you have it." He sat back, arms crossed. "You can choose not to believe it, if you wish."

"I'm beginning to think I may have hit my head harder than I thought. You were hit by a Mack truck. Then you woke up in the road, and I hit you with my car. Six months later you show up breaking and entering and I shoot you."

Hannah took a deep breath and crossed her eyes, the pain shoving her thoughts into alignment a little more cleanly.

"I know how bad you were hurt when I hit you with the car. I didn't just see it, I touched you. I remember how much blood you lost. Then you were gone, not just you, but the blood too. You were nearly dead and you just disappeared without a trace."

"I was completely dead."

She laughed out loud, then choked it off at the look on his face. "I'm sorry, obviously it's not funny. But really, you died and then just vanished, and then you woke up in a creek. How about when I shot you upstairs?"

"I died then as well. Sadly, I have a rather long-running habit of doing so."

His face was deadly serious, and she would have sworn he believed every word he was saying. Everything about this was absolutely crazy. But what about how he'd actually disappeared right in front of her without a trace? And even worse, what about the fact that this was the first explanation she'd heard that in any way matched what she had experienced?

"You know what?" she said, standing up. "My brain hurts. I need some time to digest things. Thank you for your ah, story. Now, Mr. Shotgun and I, we're going to try to get some sleep." She got up and started toward the door, then turned back to him. "You can sleep on the couch, so if whoever you say you saw in the woods comes through the door, they're going to have to go through you. Good night."

She walked out the door to the stairs.

"Hannah."

She paused without turning.

"Please stay away from the windows. Lock your door."

She nodded.

"And do not try to sneak out. I do not know who might be out there. If you try, I will stop you, for your own safety."

Crap. She'd been absolutely considering sneaking out.

# 12

How was it possible to be so exhausted and yet so entirely unable to sleep? Hannah tossed and turned crankily, flipping the pillow and attempting to punch it into submission. The house was quiet, save for its familiar shifts and moans. Usually they were something she found companionable, the aches and complaints she knew so intimately. Tonight, each tick and snap sounded like the crunch of snow underfoot or the groan of a hinge.

Finally, she gave up altogether and got out of bed. Pulling back the curtain, Hannah looked out over the silver-white backyard toward the line of trees that was black in the thin slice of moon. There was no movement, not even the shapes of the group of deer that usually fed there, where the snow was never too deep. Dropping the curtain back into place, she shivered at the thought of someone out there looking back at her. Rubbing the gooseflesh from her arm, Hannah pulled on her robe against a chill that wasn't entirely from the cold and locked herself in the bathroom.

The bathtub gave off billows of steam and she let out an involuntary squeak of pleasure as she lowered herself into the water. The heat melted away the knots in her back and legs, and she felt weightless and light, the tightness in her head loosening up, her thoughts slowing and untangling. Hannah did her best thinking in the tub.

Uncle Joel; she missed him so much. None of this would have gotten to the state it was in if he was still here. He'd been the most resolute, determined person she knew, and he'd raised her to be resilient and sensible. At least she'd thought she was until recently. He also would have been the one person she could have asked about this.

"You have to look at things from more than one angle, Hannah." She could almost hear his voice. "Believe what you can see." That one rattled around in her head.

Letting a tear slide the short slope into the bath water, she tried to shove away the great lump of guilt that rose in her throat. Hannah hadn't been raised to fall apart like she had, to crumple and give up. Joel certainly would never have imagined she'd fold altogether and think about walking away from life. And what about now? Things had turned on their axis again, but where did it leave her? *What would you say to this one, Joel?*

Sinking until only her face broke the surface of the water, reveling in the silence, Hannah stared upward, counting the thin white strips of lathe in the funny curved ceiling above her head. Like the dining room, the upstairs bathroom had been tacked on to the original saltbox farmhouse. It sat directly on top of the flat roof of the kitchen, and when they'd climbed on top of it one day to fix a leak in the roof, they found that the long and narrow room had been topped off, in true waste-not want-not fashion, with the curved top from an old cattle trailer, tar papered and shingled over.

The problem of creating a ceiling for such an odd curve was solved by the small strips of wood, tightly fitted against each other above her head. One by one she counted the thin lengths of white and the hair-widths of black between them. In her mind she drew labels on them, scribbling out the facts, the feelings, the disbelief, and the belief as well. Truth, falsehood, possible, impossible. Did reasonable always mean right? Where did the parameters of the things she could believe and the things she couldn't even come from?

Mentally she pulled them down and rearranged them, trading them like pieces of a puzzle, parsing them like words in a sentence.

Finally, Hannah sank under the surface of the water, expelling a stream of bubbles on the way down, watching the white lines and black spaces blur together through the ripple of water.

When she couldn't hold her breath any longer, she popped up and stepped out of the tub, drying off before the chill could seep back into her skin. Not wasting more than a second looking at her bruised face, she ripped a comb through her hair and coiled it into a heavy, wet bun at the nape of her neck. With her robe tied tightly against the cold, she opened the door.

"Damn it! You scared me!" She walked out to a broad back sitting in the near dark on the top step, silhouetted in the light from the kitchen downstairs.

Asher didn't turn. "I was concerned. I heard you get up, but there was no sound for a very long time." She was touched by his concern, she guessed. Maybe he thought she'd drowned. At least it would have been warmer if he'd had to pull her out of the water again.

She stood behind him in silence until he got up and went back downstairs.

"I made some tea," he said to the air.

It was some minutes before she decided to come down, then several more by the time she pulled on a pair of leggings and her favorite sweater, old and holey but soft as a kitten. She went back for a pair of thick wooly socks after stepping on the cold wood of the floor. When she finally made it down the stairs, she could smell chamomile and lemon.

Asher sat at the kitchen table, holding a mug. When she appeared, he rose and took the kettle off the burner and filled her mug on the table across from him. Hannah sat down and savored the smell that rose up and the burning heat cradled between her palms.

"There has not been any movement outside." Asher spoke quietly, his oddly colored eyes fixed on her. His way of staring so intently was growing on her, and she stared right back.

Hannah nodded. "I feel like someone is out there, watching. I don't know if it's because you put the idea in my head, but the darkness out there seems"—she searched for the right word—"loaded. And there're no deer. There are always deer in the backyard, especially this time of year. They come by every night, you could set your watch to it." Even the birds had grown silent. She hadn't heard the call of an owl all night.

He nodded, finally looking away toward the kitchen window where a towel was draped to block out the light.

"So." She took a sip of tea and burned her tongue. "How long?"

His eyes looked back to hers.

"You said you've gotten in terrible accidents or something and"—she hesitated to even say it out loud— "and ... died, then woken back up in another random place, and it's been going on for a while. So how long?"

He was trying to make a decision, she could see it in his eyes, but he didn't speak for a moment.

"Does this mean you have decided to consider what I am telling you with some seriousness?" he finally asked.

She thought for a moment before answering.

"All I know is what you told me is the first thing I've heard from anyone that remotely makes sense with what I know happened. I've been feeling like part of my brain has been missing for half a year, so if this is what I have to entertain, I'll entertain it. Better to feel like I'm in my right mind."

He laughed aloud, which startled her. And irritated her, until she realized it wasn't directed at her.

"Strange, is it not? The most unbelievable thing you can imagine is the only thing that makes you feel like you are not losing your mind."

"Does all of that have something to do with whoever might be out there?"

The tea was finally cool enough to not burn her mouth, and drinking it gave her something to do. She finished it too quickly, then rose to turn the kettle back on. When he still hadn't answered, she pretended not to be bothered and gathered up a stack of mail, pulling over the trash can. The pieces began to fall one at a time into their appropriate places. Trash, bill, trash, bill.

"They may be related," he finally said, "myself and whoever is out there, though right now I cannot say for certain. I will tell you the rest, if you want to hear it."

She nodded without looking up. Trash, bill, trash, bill.

"You heard a small part of this earlier, or yesterday actually. Before the first time I ended up here I was at my home, sitting outside watching the sun set. The next moment I awoke in the middle of a field full of very surprised cows, not too far from here, as it turns out. I was able to get hold of a vehicle and intended to make my way back home. When I pulled out of the station after filling the tank, my car was hit by a large truck, as I told you. The next part you were there for."

The kettle whistled, making them both jump. He turned it off and filled their mugs again.

"So, you've died three times now in six months, and you've ended up here?" she said.

Asher nodded. "Four. I died that night, sitting on my porch. But yes. Though even three times is well above my average. I make a habit of avoiding death as much as possible. I have passed on and come back more times recently than has ever happened in such a short span. It has never happened with such frequency before, and I have been around for a very long time."

"How long is a long time?" Hannah was down to a small stack of envelopes that couldn't be thrown out or ignored. She paused in her sorting for his answer. He looked around the room but didn't speak. Hannah decided to humor him.

"Who was the president?" she asked.

"It was pre president."

"Pre automobile?" She raised an eyebrow.

"Pre plumbing," he offered.

"Pre horse?"

"I do not think anyone was pre horse." He smiled.

Silence. She couldn't even believe she was trying to think of things with hard dates between plumbing and horse.

"Gives new meaning to the phrase older than dirt," she said.

"Dirt was around. Newer than dirt."

"You know what, I'm going to leave that alone for a minute." She was laughing now, trying to do it quietly, but it was building in a big way, down in her belly, tears beginning to leak from the corners from her eyes.

94

It took a full minute for her to calm down, and longer before she could completely stop. When she finally wiped her eyes and looked at him he was leaning back, unsmiling.

She probably shouldn't laugh at a potentially crazy person. Except herself.

"Okay. No. Sorry. Please go on."

He was still looking at her, stone-faced. At least he didn't look mad, just serious. She studied his expression. There was a time when Hannah had been pretty sure she could spot a liar. If that was still true, he was either really good, or he believed what he was saying.

"I mean it. Please keep going. How long ago?"

He leaned back for a moment and thought.

"Births were not recorded the way they are now, so I do not know the year with any certainty. I know now, from what I remember of the time and what I have been able to discover, that it was sometime around the Battle of Hastings. I recall my father's stories of it when I was a child."

She was staring at him open-mouthed.

"Battle of Hastings? As in William the Conqueror, the Norman Invasion and all that? Come on." She shook her head. At least it was a good story. He was still selling it, no jiggle or anything.

"I am surprised you are familiar with it."

"I read a lot. That was hundreds of years ago." She couldn't believe she was even encouraging this conversation.

"It grows closer to a thousand," he said.

She didn't laugh at him. If he was making it up, he was going all in.

"Okay, go on." She might as well hear it out. "So, you've been returning to life every time you die ever since then? For almost a thousand years?" It sounded way worse coming out of her mouth.

He nodded. "That I am actually telling you this, something I have not told anyone in a great many years, should give you some indication of the seriousness of the situation. If it would make you understand the potential danger, I would take the shotgun you so unwisely left upstairs and prove it to you."

"Prove it? What are you going to do, shoot yourself?"

He got up and rinsed out his mug, moving the window covering aside a slit to peer out.

"That is not a route I ever choose to take, if there is any other option, and now is certainly not the time. It is still dark and there is no telling who might be nearby. If I were to go right now, it would leave you vulnerable."

She was about to protest the need for him or anyone else to protect her, but something stopped her. She had always thought she was more than capable of protecting herself, but sitting here, not knowing what she needed protection from, Hannah was afraid.

# 13

Hannah rolled over and nearly hit the floor. Somehow she was on her squashy living room couch, covered in the crocheted throw that was usually draped across the back, daylight leaking in weakly around the edges of the windows. The floor creaked behind her.

"It has been some time since I have seen someone fall asleep while sitting straight up," Asher said. "It was a bit disturbing. One moment you looked like you were about to speak, the next you were falling over. I thought you were ill until you started snoring."

"I don't snore." She sat up groggily to accept the mug of coffee. His hair was wet, dark toffee colored instead of honey blond. He was also shirtless and wrapped in a towel. Coffee slopped down the front of her sweater.

"Sorry, still half asleep." Hardly. The dryer buzzed and stopped thumping, and Hannah blotted her wet front with her sleeve while he walked toward the kitchen. He was tall and broad, that much had been obvious from the beginning, but without the heavy shirt he'd been wearing, she could see he was more finely built than she'd guessed. Big but not burly, and very muscular, tapering to a trim waist. She was pretty sure she was blushing to no one, and concentrated on her coffee.

He came back into the room, buttoning up the freshly laundered shirt.

"I am glad you slept." She felt the dip as he sat at the other end of the couch, and she scooted her feet away. "You must have been entirely exhausted to fall asleep like that. One moment you were there, the next, headed face first into your tea."

"Must be," she said. She *had* been exhausted, but it wasn't just that. Hannah was pretty sure she had also reached total mental overload, trying to process his crazy story. And she'd been frightened, felt trapped in her house, hemmed in by the dark and not knowing what might be out there. Her brain had just decided enough was enough. "I don't even remember getting up."

He must have carried her to the couch. That was kind, and she was sorry she'd missed it. Was she usually this kind of a disaster? Hannah was getting red in the face over a man who was undeniably very easy on the eyes, but who was one hundred percent crazy. Unless he was telling the truth, which was two hundred percent crazy.

"I think we should venture out today, during daylight, while it is safer, if you are willing." His voice seemed loud, booming after so much whispering in the dark.

She nodded. Maybe they should. Her mind was wrapped around things as well as it could be, but a little distance and a little reality outside of the house would be good for perspective.

"Good. You are in dire need of supplies, and I think I should take a better look around. Assess things a little more broadly. Can you be prepared to leave in an hour?"

She set down her empty mug and folded the blanket.

"I'll be ready to go in thirty."

It was closer to fifteen; high maintenance, Hannah was not. Since the clothes she had fallen asleep in were mostly clean, she quickly changed her coffee-stained sweater and washed her face, half of which was the color of a ripe eggplant. She looked briefly at her concealer and decided that she needed about a half gallon more than was there, so she skipped it. A minute after yanking a brush through her hair she clomped down the stairs in her boots.

Asher was waiting at the bottom, holding her heaviest coat and a winter hat he must have dug out of her coat closet. She grabbed her bag, the one he'd rescued from outside the grocery store, and slung it across her chest.

She almost went down on the ice, two steps out the door. He grabbed her by the elbow and righted her, then went ahead of her.

"Do you think it will start?" She dug around in her purse for the car keys but didn't hear the expected jingle. He pulled them from his pocket and clicked a button, the locks popping up on command.

"I unearthed it and checked it this morning before you woke up, in case we should need it. It appears to be working just fine." He went to the passenger door and opened it for her. She didn't protest. Last time Hannah drove the car she'd hit him with it, so she figured that entitled him to be behind the wheel. Maybe not to rummaging around her place for the keys, but she'd apply that against shooting him.

"What is it?" she asked, her eyes scanning the tree line where he was staring, frozen.

"Nothing," he said while they got in, but he was intent on the rearview mirror as they started up the driveway.

———————

Instead of making the left into town they had turned right, toward Newton, taking the long route around by the highway. The grocery store there was larger but more expensive, the kind where you had to pay for the luxury of having too many choices and a florist, nail salon, and bank branch.

"Do you drink milk in your coffee or cream?"

He didn't answer.

"Asher. Earth to Asher."

"I beg your pardon?" He was staring through the front window of the store and out into the parking lot. "Cream." He didn't look at Hannah when he spoke but started scanning the faces around them. She wondered if it was all due to the current situation, or if part of it was that at his size you were just more prone to be on guard, knowing you were more noticeable than the average person wherever you went.

Hannah didn't really stand out in a crowd and was accustomed to—and perfectly fine with—blending in.

"What is it?" she asked, looking over the list she'd made in the car.

"Nothing. I saw a face I thought familiar."

It was familiar to Hannah. They rounded the corner, and when she reached up for a box above her head she almost ran into a bleached blonde in a tight coat, lips painted bright red. The same obnoxiously bright shade of red Hannah had last seen at the Shur Shop.

"Oh, Hannah! How are you? I was just thinking I should give you a call and see how you were doing. I'm so glad I ran into you."

Hannah was seriously confused. Last time she'd run into Sheila the woman could barely contain her amusement at Hannah's misfortune. Now she sounded like her long-lost best friend. Then she realized Sheila had gotten an eyeful of Asher.

"Well now, who's your friend? Aren't you gonna introduce me?" Sheila asked, her voice syrupy.

Hannah looked at him with a grimace, scraping for an explanation.

"Oh, um, Sheila, this is …"

Asher nodded at her from behind the cart, forcing a sliver of a smile on his face.

"Tony. Tony Barilla. I knew Hannah's uncle. We were friends from the …" His eyes flicked to Hannah.

"From the air force," she added, knowing how completely unconvincing it sounded. Sheila wasn't the least bit bothered though, and she beamed, wiggling past Hannah to get closer to Asher, holding out a manicured hand for him to shake.

"Well, I am pleased to meet you, Tony. I'm Sheila. Sheila Gates."

If Sheila mentioned anything about knowing her uncle intimately, Hannah was going to punch the smile off the woman's face and go on the run.

"Are you just visiting?" Sheila said. Asher nodded, dropping her hand and trying to move away, but Sheila took another step toward him. He looked a little uncomfortable as she tapped a long red nail on the handle of the cart. "You gonna be stayin' long?"

He looked squirmy enough for Hannah to have to fight the urge to laugh as she edged her way closer to the turn of the aisle in an effort to escape.

"At present, I have no immediate plans to leave."

This was news to Hannah, and it made Sheila smile. God, the woman was a freaking shark, an apex predator.

"No, you're not from around here, are you? But my, you do look familiar? Have you ever been in the Shur Shop in Milltown? I work there, though I admit to cheating on them to shop here. Better selection, you know." She winked at him. "Our little secret." Sheila was looking at Asher closely, head tilted to one side. "Now where have I seen you?"

All of a sudden, Asher threw her a dazzling smile and leaned forward over the cart handle.

"You must have an amazing memory, Sheila. I believe I *was* in that store. It is incredible you would remember me after only ringing up my groceries one time."

Hannah thought Sheila's face was going to break, the quizzical look replaced with a grin that made her lipstick crack in the center. Asher turned to Hannah, engaging smile still pasted onto his face.

"Do you have everything you need, Hannah? It looks like it might snow and I would like to get back in case the roads get icy." She didn't have everything on her list, but she'd do without toilet paper and bread to get out of there as soon as humanly possible.

"A pleasure to meet you, Sheila." Asher pushed the cart forward, bumping Hannah with the front to get her out of the way, not waiting for a response from Sheila.

They blew through the self checkout and loaded the car without looking back.

"Way to turn on the charm there. Might have been a bit much though; Sheila might decide to follow you home," Hannah said. "Still, nice job, Tony Barilla. Would have been a little less obvious if we weren't in the pasta section." Apparently, he didn't think it was as funny as she did. "It went slightly better than my last trip to the grocery store, anyway." Still nothing, just her voice and the click of the blinker.

Finally he spoke. "I did not mean for you to see me. I wish that you had not."

"What do you mean, you didn't mean for me to see you?"

He didn't answer right away, silent as they drove out of town. He finally spoke after they had turned onto the highway.

"I did not intend for us to actually meet," he said. "I was aware of who you were, after you hit me. I kept an eye on you because I was attempting to figure out why I kept running into you and waking up in the same town again and again. That is the strangest part. Never in all my years have I found myself in the same place after dying more than once, certainly not repeatedly."

She didn't think that was remotely the strangest part.

"I was here for some unknown reason, and then you continued looking for me, and there were descriptions and pictures of me all over. I stayed nearby longer than I intended to, to see how far you would dig and at what point you would leave it alone and the interest in finding me would die down. I was concerned it was because you knew what I was, though I could not imagine how. I discounted the idea after a time, seeing that you were just stubbornly looking for a normal missing man."

"So you *were* here, watching me."

"In the beginning. Not that it was a difficult task. You only left the house to look for me. It was worrying; you looked like death, growing paler and thinner by the week."

She snorted. "Yeah, well, you could have done something about that." Hannah said it light-heartedly, but inside, it angered her, that she had gone through everything she had trying to find him.

"I know this, and I had every intention to. I had decided to walk to your door, knock, and give you some made-up explanation, anything, to make you stop looking. Then I could leave town confident my face would cease showing up on posters and online. And I still thought maybe my happening to reappear here in the same vicinity was a fluke, some random occurrence."

"Then why didn't you?" Her words were clipped. He could have saved her so much pain. If he had showed up, even if he hadn't told her the whole truth, at least she would have known he was real and she hadn't killed him. It wouldn't have answered all her questions, but at least she would have known she wasn't completely crazy.

"I was going to, Hannah. I swear to you I was on my way to do just that when you were struck by the car trying to reach me. Oblivious me, I did not even know you had seen me until they were pulling you out from under that vehicle."

He was staring straight ahead, intent on the road, and she saw his expression harden, his jaw tighten. "You would have had me then, you know. It would have been better if you had, I think now, but I fled, knowing the questions it would raise when the authorities arrived and found a man they did not believe existed."

Asher shook his head. "I should have risked it, if I had known what would happen the next time you caught sight of me. Or maybe I should have just left the area for good, because the next time I saw you was when I passed you on the road walking. Instead of leaving I followed you to the grocery store. It was a mistake. I should have driven away right then. I should not have gone there and waited for you to come out, because if you had not seen me then, you would have been okay. Now that I have met you, I know you would have been. But I stayed, and you saw me."

He was gripping the steering wheel, knuckles whitening.

"And then I managed to make it infinitely worse. I picked up your things, thinking I would return them to the porch, make sure you were okay. When I got there, I saw the broken window and the blood. I was about to go in, but a man pulled up to make a delivery. I was thankful, since I imagined he would see what I saw and call for help."

The steering wheel gave off a strange grinding noise, and Asher let go, color returning to his knuckles. There were now sizable finger-shaped divots crushed into the wheel.

"Geez, take it easy on the car. It's the only one I have." She was slightly less angry now, partly because the look on his face was so agonizingly sad.

"Hannah, I was certain whoever it was would do the right thing, or I never would have left. I know now that they did, just not immediately. When I returned, I could not believe the snow in the driveway was undisturbed. There were no lights on, no smoke from the chimney, and the window was still broken. I will not deny I thought you were dead. I came into your freezing, wide-open house expecting to find your corpse. Needless to say, I was surprised."

He actually smiled then, a small, wry smile.

"It happened again, and I woke up outside in the snow. It took me some time to put myself back together, find clothes, car keys, and come back to confirm you were safe, especially now that you had watched me die a second time only to have my body disappear once again."

They drove in silence for a moment, a thin line of slate sky visible above them between the walls of frost-tipped green. The heavy clouds of a coming storm loomed overhead.

"I was almost too late, did you know that?" His eyes were staring fixedly at the road, his face in profile appearing cut from stone. "When I put myself together and came back you were not in the house. The front door was hanging open. I could see your tracks, but at the road there was no way to know which way you went. I went back to where it happened, when you hit me, and then I drove to the only other place I could think of. I never imagined for all of the time you spent sitting, looking at the water, that you would go in. I saw you leaning over, reaching out over the river, like you were flying. I yelled your name, and you let go. This is my fault. All of this happened, is still happening, because of me."

They were waiting at the crossroads close to her house, stopped at the intersection of the pavement and the dirt, and he paused, putting his head down on the steering wheel.

"I heard you call my name." She laid a hand on the crook of his arm, tentatively. "I heard you call out and I lost my grip. I didn't let go, I slipped and when I went in, you came in after me. Asher, I'm glad to be alive. I couldn't make the world make sense, and it became my entire life, and that was wrong. How I handled things was a mistake

I almost didn't live to see the error of. Blame yourself all you want. Whatever happened, whoever you are, whatever you are, when it's all said and done, you risked your life to save mine, and I'm grateful for it."

Hannah had been angry, but what she had just told him was true, and remembering how close she'd come to dying had snuffed out a great deal of her rage. She paused for a moment, then laughed out loud.

Asher picked his head up to look at her.

"Well, I guess you didn't actually risk your life. According to you, you probably would have just woken up on my couch or something. But still, the end result was the same, and I appreciate the effort." She punched him on the arm playfully, and he shook his head, which she told herself was in amusement.

"Come on. It's going to start snowing any minute. We better get home before it gets bad, or Sheila comes looking for you."

# 14

Hannah's phone started ringing the moment she set foot on the front porch. Juggling both shopping bags into one hand, she rummaged around in her bag until she found her house key. Ignoring the ringing, she unlocked the door and held it open behind her with her foot for Asher, who was bringing up the rear with the rest. By the time they were inside, the phone had rung itself out.

"What is it?" She balanced the bags on the counter in the kitchen, still dark with the towel over the window. Asher looked on alert, as he had been the entire time he hustled her out of the car and quickly to the door. She couldn't imagine what he was anticipating, but he looked like an animal sniffing the air for danger.

"Maybe nothing. Just a feeling."

Her phone began to ring again and she sighed with annoyance, pulling it out of her bag. "Shoot. It's the sheriff." Two missed calls from him, the third still ringing. Great.

"Answer it."

She shot Asher a glare in response, but he was right. She would prefer not to answer it, but if she avoided the sheriff's calls there was a chance he would just stop by. If her suspicion about why he was calling was correct, he would definitely be stopping by.

"I guess I'd better." She made a face and hit answer. Sheriff Morgan didn't waste time on pleasantries.

"I'm on my way to your house. I'll be there in five minutes, and your friend better be around when I get there."

Funny how she'd previously been dreaming about this very moment. Being able to convince Sheriff Morgan the man she'd hit was real, and with the added bonus of him still being alive. Knowing one hundred percent she hadn't completely lost her mind and proving it. Everything she'd hoped for neatly tied up in a bow. But now that it was happening, it was going to be little more complicated.

"Well, Mr. Barilla, any idea how we should handle this one? I mean other than telling the truth, which I don't think is going to fly. We could, but he's threatened to have me committed before, and this won't convince him that was a wrong move. Maybe we can share a rubber room."

Asher wasn't smiling. He was looking at her in a way that made her think he did have an idea, and that she wasn't going to like it.

---

"Hey, Sheriff Morgan." Hannah opened the door and let him in, trying to look sheepish. He actually had his hand resting on his gun, and the strap across the top was undone.

"Hannah. I just got a phone call from Sheila Gates, you know her, works over to the Shur Shop. She swore to everything holy that she just saw you in the grocery store in Newton with the man whose face has been plastered on every phone pole and board in this town for going on half a year."

Hannah took a deep breath.

"He's in the kitchen."

The sheriff stopped short, like he'd expected her to deny it, despite believing Sheila enough to be standing on Hannah's doormat.

Asher—Tony for the moment—was sitting in one of the kitchen chairs. He looked a little less giant and threatening sitting down, at least that was what they were hoping. The sheriff was glowering down at him from the kitchen doorway, hand still uncomfortably close to his gun.

"Hannah, I really hope you have a good explanation. I see a real live missing person sitting at your kitchen table." Oh sure, now he believed there had been a missing person. He took his hand off his gun and crossed his arms, which was a small improvement. His tall, stiff hat was still on, which wasn't.

"Coffee, Sheriff Morgan?" Hannah asked, sidling her way toward the sink.

"No, Hannah, I don't want coffee. I want an explanation."

She set the coffee pot back down and turned around. This was where they hadn't agreed. Hannah wanted to tell the sheriff everything had really happened the way she'd been saying it had since the beginning, but that Asher—Tony—had walked away and been in a coma until now or something. The problem was that explanation would have raised some questions they couldn't answer, like why there wasn't a mark on him, where his blood had gone, and where he'd been the whole time since then. They'd needed a story that would encourage the least amount of follow-up, so they'd settled on a different version of the events.

Hannah took a deep breath and did her best to sell the sheriff a big fat lie.

"So, the day of the accident, you remember I was coming from up on Barclay Mountain, where I went to spread Joel's ashes?" The sheriff nodded. "I wasn't in too great shape that day. I was pretty broken up about Joel, and I wore myself out climbing up and back. On my way out I guess I must've hit something, like a tree or phone pole or one of those big boulders in the parking lot there, you know the ones I'm talking about."

The sheriff was still looking at her, both eyebrows raised now, his forehead crinkled like a hound dog's.

"So anyway, on the way home I guess things just really caught up with me and something just … well. Anyway, I really thought I hit a person and killed him. I swear I did."

"Keep talking," Sheriff Morgan said. "That still doesn't explain the man sitting over there."

Hannah put down the mug she'd been fiddling with.

"Yeah, about him. So right after you stopped to see me this last time, there was a knock on the door, and would you believe, the same man I'd been looking for all this time was standing on my front porch.

It kind of all came rushing back then, who he was. I actually did know him, kind of. Tony is—was—a friend of Joel's. They were in the air force together, and I met him years ago, when I was a lot younger, when we were living in Alaska, I think."

She looked over at Asher who was sitting just a little too woodenly. "It was in Alaska, wasn't it? Were you stationed there?"

He nodded but unhelpfully didn't offer up any supporting falsehoods.

"I don't know why my brain put him in the road. Maybe I had a little schoolgirl crush on him at the time"—she was going to hit Asher with a frying pan later for that part—"or why he happened to be um, nude, but anyway, there he was."

The sheriff's arms were at least uncrossed and he was leaning one shoulder against the doorframe. The man looked exhausted now that she looked at him properly. She poured a cup of coffee and sugared it heavily, recalling the way he took it from her time haunting his office. She handed it over, and thankfully he accepted it with a nod.

"Tony." She'd almost said Asher, and took a shallow breath and reminded herself to stick to the story. "Tony hasn't been in the country and, when he finally heard about Joel passing away, he came to pay his respects. I know I should've come and told you right after, but I was embarrassed. I've been putting off telling you." She couldn't summon up any tears so she settled on a look she hoped came across as remorseful.

The sheriff didn't look convinced, but he didn't look ready to put them in cuffs either, so she held her breath.

"Is that true? Tony, is it?"

Asher nodded and finally spoke.

"I knew Joel when we were both in the service. I was saddened to hear of his passing and that I missed his memorial service, so I decided to call on Hannah. I remembered her from back then and was surprised to see the state she was in when I showed up. When I finally got her to tell me the whole story, I decided to stick around a little bit, get things around here put back together, make sure she gets any help she needs."

Sheriff Morgan eyed Asher.

"You look a little young to have known Hannah too many years ago."

Asher smiled. "I was just a new recruit when I met Joel. He took me under his wing, looked out for me."

The sheriff considered Asher for another moment, then nodded and looked back to Hannah, then back and forth once again.

"You were right, you know," Hannah said to the sheriff. "You were right when you sent me to see someone, as much as it kills me to say it. I was so messed up with losing Joel and everything. I just …" Hannah trailed off. Remembering that therapist was going to ruin her ability to look contrite, so she ducked her head in fake remorse.

Sheriff Morgan took his hat off and scratched his head through the thin layer of hair. Hannah let out a secret sigh of relief. She'd spent enough time in his presence to know that when the hat came off, nobody was going to get more than an ear chewing.

"Well, Hannah, lucky for you going a little distracted isn't an actual crime, what with losing your only family and all," the sheriff said. "And everything in the accident report was technically true when you get right down to it, since you really did think you saw what you said you did; it wasn't the same as thinking it up and lying on purpose." He set down his coffee cup and crossed his arms. "But on the other hand, a lot of man hours and money were wasted looking for the man sitting over there. We had the state police and EMS and a hundred volunteers out there. That's a pretty serious matter, especially seeing as it was all for nothing."

She hung her head. "Sheriff, I understand if you have to pass some of that cost on. I'll figure something out. If I have to sell this place …" Hannah managed to squeak out a crocodile tear at that one.

"Now come on, I'm not going to send you a bill, I just want you to understand the gravity of the matter."

Hannah did understand the gravity. That part was absolutely true.

"Well, at least I can button this up. I admit, the whole thing was a head-scratcher. And I'm glad nobody's really missing. There's enough people missing for real, don't need any more." He looked at Asher and shook his head. "Darn good likeness now that I see you in person."

At the front door, the sheriff fiddled his hat back on and stepped out, then paused. "I almost forgot." He looked back past her to where Asher was standing, blocking out the kitchen doorway. "You don't happen to drive a big white SUV, matte paint job, weird silvery window tint?"

Asher shook his head no.

"Where's your car?"

They hadn't considered that in the frantic minutes of cobbling together a story, but Asher didn't miss a beat.

"I came in a rental. Hannah followed me to Newton and we returned it today. Stopped to get some groceries after."

The sheriff nodded and looked at Hannah. "I was out past Davidson's, you know that place with all the junk cars on the dirt road, the one that comes around the edge of your property on the side towards the lake."

She knew it well, eyesore that it was.

"The car I was asking about was parked in the pull-off there. Blended in so well with the snow I wouldn't a seen it 'cept for the tires being black. Anyway, no plates, nobody in it that I could see, and locked up tight as a drum. I went down past the hedgerow to see if I could find the owner. Thought maybe they were lost, or hunting out of season or something, but I didn't come across anybody, or tracks even. By the time I came back out of the woods it was gone. You see anybody strange around there lately?"

Hannah cocked an eyebrow at Asher, and he just looked levelly back at her. Nope, nobody strange around here.

"No, I haven't seen anybody. We didn't take the dirt road today. Looked like it might snow so we came the long way around."

Sheriff Morgan nodded. "Good call. It's already started. Wouldn't be February if we didn't get another doozie of a storm or two before the month's out. Anyway, keep your doors locked and all that, and if you see anything out of the ordinary, give me a call."

"Will do, Sheriff. Thanks."

He slipped out and Hannah made a point of shooting the bolt as loudly as possible behind him, watching through the curtain until his truck cleared the drifted turn of the driveway and disappeared from sight.

Dropping the curtain, Hannah turned around to an empty room. She found Asher in the kitchen, unpacking the last of the grocery bags, his back to her.

Maybe it was time for him to leave. She wondered once again if there was any danger except what had come from him being there. If he left, would he take it with him?

The problem was, after all the time she'd spent trying to locate him, it was like finally being able to draw a full breath after holding it for too long. Asher had slipped from being a ghost to a real person, one who was trying to protect her. But what was he protecting her from? Saving her from herself had been one thing. Protecting her from an unknown quantity he might have brought into her life was another. She didn't believe he would harm her, but that didn't mean harm wouldn't come to her. Maybe he should go. Right now.

The closing of the pantry door snapped her back to reality. Hannah opened the cutlery drawer and pulled out a sharp kitchen knife, eyeing the wicked edge on the blade. She held it thoughtfully for a moment. When Asher turned around he looked at it, raising an eyebrow. Then he looked up at her.

Maybe it was a terrible mistake, but she put the knife down on the scarred cutting board and slid it closer.

"Hungry?"

# 15

Hannah waved aside Asher's half-hearted offer of help with dinner, after which he quickly made himself scarce, slipping out the back door to take a look around. After going upstairs and retrieving the shotgun, she leaned it carefully against the end of the counter while she cooked. The act of cooking was familiar and comforting, and for a moment she felt like life had skipped backward, to a time before her life had taken such a drastic downhill turn. The rattle of the lock brought her back to reality.

"That smells very good."

She nodded to Asher when he stepped back in and shook the snow out of his hair. He locked the door behind him and wedged the chair back under the handle.

"There are new footprints out there, mostly the sheriff's, I would guess. They will be covered over soon enough. The older sets are gone already, though it makes no difference. I was not able to follow them far when they were fresh, so where their maker went, I cannot be sure."

Avoiding the spatter of grease from the skillet, she set it on the trivet in the middle of the table. "Who do you think was in the car?" Hannah said. "I'm guessing not poachers, not in that nice a vehicle. Other than that I don't get a lot of people just wandering around out there, especially in the winter. And they probably wouldn't be on foot. Everybody around here has an ATV or a snowmobile."

They ate in silence, him steadily, her picking thoughtfully. Midway she got up and poured herself a glass of wine from the box in the fridge.

It occurred to her that it was the first drink she'd had since he'd pulled her out of the river. The urge had stopped with the nightmares and the rotten bloody taste she'd had in her mouth since the accident. Both had disappeared when Asher arrived.

"Wine?"

He shook his head, and she sat and took a sip while her chicken grew cold. It was pretty terrible wine, now that she really tasted it, and she set it aside unfinished. Maybe it was time to level up from the cardboardeaux.

He cleaned his plate in silence before looking up.

"I think we should consider going to stay somewhere else for a time."

She frowned. Not that *she* should, or *he* should, but *they*.

"Do you think that's necessary?" she said. He didn't answer immediately, eyeing the skillet of chicken in the middle of the table. She spooned the rest of it onto his plate and pushed the salad bowl in his direction.

"If this is about you, and you're concerned about putting me in danger, you think us both going somewhere is the best thing to do?" It sounded harsher than she intended, but it was true. She wasn't ungrateful for his help, and she'd decided not to ask him to go just yet, but leaving her house to go somewhere with him, a strange man she'd just met, sounded like a generally bad life choice.

He paused, fork in midair, to speak. "There is a chance there is nothing going on beyond mundane trespassing. If I were certain that was the case I would have left when I knew you were on the mend and no longer in danger. However, if the person out there is someone else, my leaving might do you no good."

"You've said as much, so enlighten me then. If it isn't out-of-season hunting, then who is it? Who's the monster in the woods who might be after you, and why should that mean anything to me? You seem pretty concerned, and it'd be nice to know what I'm supposed to be afraid of."

He chewed slowly and swallowed his last bite before looking up.

Asher was looking at her that way again, straight at her, but she'd be damned if she was going to look away. Hannah was getting better at their stare downs, not as thrown off by his strangely colored eyes and his habit of not blinking.

"Beyond my better judgment I told you about myself. I did it because you refused to accept any other explanation, and that turned out to be hazardous to your health. Why could you not accept an alternative? Any one of them would have been far more believable," he said.

Answering a question with a question. But she bit.

"Because none of those other explanations cut it. So far, what you've told me is the only thing that actually matched up with what I know happened. It seems unbelievable, but in all this time it's the only chain of events that works, even if it doesn't make sense, at least not in the normal way." She paused to collect her thoughts. "Last night I kept asking myself why it was so hard to believe what you told me. My answer was because it's impossible, but the more I thought about it, the more I wondered why that mattered. It happened, I know it happened, so that means it *is* possible. And why not? I've watched movies and read books where unbelievable things happen, and never blinked because I've decided it's okay because it's fiction. I'm choosing to apply that to reality. I'm broadening my horizons of possibility, for the present at least."

She put her clean dish in the drainer with a little more force than was necessary, as if physically putting an explanation point after her words. Strangely, saying it out loud had served to make it more true for her. She turned and leaned against the sink, facing him.

"At least until I wake up and find out I've really been in a coma hallucinating this whole time, or that I'm really heavily medicated in a rubber room somewhere. Then I'll be forced to reevaluate."

He considered her for a moment, then nodded, the corners of his mouth tugging up into a smile.

"So now that you have decided you are willing to believe me, at least at present, consider this: would it be too much more of a stretch to believe I am not entirely unique in my condition?"

Her mouth opened into a little o. She pulled out a chair and flopped down into it. "It's not just you?"

"Sorry, but as it turns out I am not terribly unique. There are others like me out there, scattered through the world ..."

She sat back, trying to wrap her head around it.

"Knowing there are more of us," he said, "and seeing as you know what I am, can you imagine then that you are the only person who is aware of our existence? Beings like myself are of great interest to a number of people and groups, and for a variety of reasons, some good, some rather nefarious."

"Okay, I get that," Hannah said, "and I get that you don't know which one might be creeping around outside. But no offense, none of them has anything to do with me. I mean, if you're worried about my safety, maybe you should just make your own little trail in the snow and let them follow it the hell away from me."

He shook his head. Hannah wasn't sure, but he looked a little hurt. She looked down, suddenly sorry.

"I hope it has nothing at all to do with you. If I were sure who it was, and that they would not harm you strictly because of association, or try to use you as leverage, I would leave today," he said. "But there is no way for me to be sure just yet. So I think it best if you remain with me for the immediate future."

"But you have an idea who it might be."

He nodded. "Rather a fear. I can't be certain, but there is the party who concerns me most."

"Who?"

He didn't answer immediately, looking down at his hands.

"My sister."

Just when she thought things were as weird as they were going to get today.

Asher stood suddenly and went to the sink. He pulled aside the towel covering the window and looked blankly out across the yard.

"Well?" she asked.

He turned to her. "Well what?"

She shook her head in disbelief. "Oh, come on. You can't really throw that out there and then stop."

He turned to look out into the waning light one last time before letting the towel fall back across the window and sitting down.

"My sister—Amara is her name—she is like me," he said. "I imagine you gathered as much since I am concerned about the possibility of her presence. One would think having a sibling in the same circumstances would be a good thing. Maybe it would have been, if things had gone differently. Unfortunately, our relationship is rather … strained."

Asher looked suddenly older, like his face was carved from stone. "Hannah, in my very first life, all those centuries ago, I did something I will always regret, and because of it my sister died—for what we could only have imagined was the only time—hating me. She hates me still. And because of it, Amara has made sure, even after all these years, that I never forget what I did. As if I needed her to remind me. But she persists, and she has made it into a twisted, never-ending game between us." He had been talking to his folded hands, but now he looked up at Hannah. "Whenever she finds me, which she always eventually does, she tortures and kills whomever might cause me anguish, and then she kills me. She kills me and resets the game so she can play it over."

Hannah sat back, silent for a moment.

"So you think if it's your sister out there, she might kill me because it would hurt you? That's stupid. It's not like we're dating. I accidentally killed you with my car."

He shook his head. "It does not matter what the reality is. That I have shown an interest in your well-being will be enough. She has killed people for far less."

"What did you do to her?" Her voice was timid.

He shook his head.

"Hannah, please listen to me. I have lived many years and done many things I do not care to look back on, but given enough time, nearly every wrong fades and lifts away. Except one. There is one burden that cannot be lifted, no matter how many years pass. The weight of human life is heavy and it is permanent. Since I cannot escape it, I can at least try not to accumulate the weight of any more deaths on my conscience." He stood up suddenly and walked to the door. "As soon as I can find out for sure who has been skulking around out there, I will be on my way and you will return to your life. That is my hope. Unless it is my sister. If it is my sister, I do not know if it is possible for you to be made safe. My sister Amara is …" He stepped outside into the snow without finishing.

Locking the door behind him, sitting back down, and laying the shotgun across her lap, Hannah thought about what he had said. It was dire, and it was frightening, but it made sense. She'd wondered why he was still here, what possible interest a being that has been around as long as Asher could have in her welfare. This at least she could understand.

Because she thought she understood his regret. The heaviness that had weighed her down all those long months when she thought she'd killed him had been crippling. Imagine carrying that for a hundred lifetimes, putting more and more on top of it year after year. What would it take to keep going under something like that? She wouldn't want to add to that burden either.

Hannah gathered up what was left on the table and set it in the sink, pouring the remainder of her wine down the drain, watching it swirl away in a twist of crimson.

---

The sun had begun to redden, and she got up to turn on the kitchen light. Before she sat back down, she heard a rattle at the door. Hannah grabbed the shotgun and took it with her the few steps to peek around the towel while Asher came back in.

"The storm is growing worse. The snow is coming down more quickly." Asher stomped it from his boots and relocked the door behind him. "You have been productive." He nodded toward the neat stack of envelopes, stamped and ready to go in the mailbox. It seemed silly that she'd bothered to do it at all, knowing there was a chance someone dangerous was lurking outside. It could end up being utterly pointless, opening bills, writing checks, and sealing envelopes.

She frowned. She'd done it because the monotony and normalcy of it had been relaxing, but it had ended up being a painful experience as well. A notice from the bank Hannah had expected to be an overdraft was confirmation that her uncle's affairs had been settled and the contents of his accounts had been transferred into hers. She'd propped the notice up against his urn where it now sat on the windowsill. Hannah missed him so much, and it appeared he was still caring for her. Without the funds she would never have been able to settle the pile of bills in front of her.

"Have you given any thought to my suggestion, that we go somewhere more secure for a time?"

Looking away from the container of ashes, Hannah considered Asher. She hadn't really thought about it; there were a couple more pressing things on her mind. She couldn't deny she was considering it now. The prickle of discomfort in the back of her mind that something was dangerously off here had grown.

The thick woods behind the house, with their girdle of shadows, used to be welcome, a natural fence around her little house. With the thought of the shadowy figure prowling behind the house and the possibility of being penned in by the weather, it now made her uneasy, like she was trapped inside a snow globe.

"Seems reasonable enough, I guess. Where were you thinking?"

He dropped his voice, speaking so quietly she struggled to hear. "I have a place in mind. It is not too far from here." She nodded but didn't ask more. The feeling of being watched made her wonder if there was any chance they were being listened to as well, and she shivered.

"When do you want to leave?"

# 16

Night had fully fallen, and she could hear Asher prowling around downstairs. Hannah had left the shotgun with him and gone up to her room to pack a few things. Even though they weren't planning on leaving until daylight when it felt safer and the snow had slowed, she wanted to be ready.

The house that had always seemed safe to her felt like a rickety prison now. The woods she'd hiked and camped in, never fearing anyone worse than Mother Nature, had turned menacing, and it felt as though the trees were tightening around the borders of the yard, creeping closer when no one was looking. Hannah was afraid if she pulled aside the curtain she would see branches pressed against the window glass.

Leaving the bedroom light off, she stuffed a few things into an old backpack by the light from the hallway, shying away from making a lingering silhouette through the curtain. She leaned the bag at the ready outside the bedroom door then grabbed a change of clothes and locked herself in the bathroom.

She looked longingly at the jar of pale pink bath salts and thought about how good a long soak in the tub would feel, but she turned on the more expedient shower instead.

Not that it was much more expedient. Hannah lingered under the spray until the knot between her shoulder blades loosened a bit and the hot water started to run tepid. The worst of the pain from her fall off the bridge was mostly gone, an allover dead-tired stiffness was all that remained. She was looking a little less beat up too, the swelling around her eye subsiding, the bruises faded to patches of lilac and yellow around the thin line on her cheek where the skin had split. Hannah had always healed quickly; it was a bonus when you were prone to clumsiness. She had shins that seemed magnetically attracted to sharp corners.

Water dripped from the bottom of her braid as she looped an elastic band around it. She took a quick last look at herself, at the drawn cheeks, the sunken eyes, the batch of leftover bruises, and sighed.

Hannah followed her nose downstairs, backpack slung over her shoulder.

"Those look amazing," she said.

Asher was hunched over the stove, head crammed under the vent hood, meticulously turning over a perfectly browned pancake. She was beginning to notice he tended toward the robotic, his movements spare and efficient. Maybe when you lived long enough you boiled everything down to its more precise parts. There was coffee in the pot, and she poured herself a cup. It was too late for caffeine, but it was a long time until dawn, and she had a sneaking suspicious that she wasn't going to be able to sleep anyway.

Hannah would have complimented the chef, but her mouth stayed way too full for anything so unimportant as talking. She was halfway through her third enormous pancake when she stopped for a breath and some coffee. Asher was watching her with amusement—he was one to talk, having already demolished a mountain of pancakes nearly a foot high—and she stuffed another giant forkful into her mouth.

The sleeve of her sweater was dangerously near the maple syrup, and she shoved it up to her elbow.

The fire in the wood stove had burned to ashes and they hadn't built it back up, intent on leaving. With its old single-paned windows and lathe and plaster walls, the house was drafty. Without the heat to beat it back, the cold was quickly stealing in. Even though she was dressed in a long sweater, jeans, and thick socks, Hannah was just tolerably warm enough.

"Aren't you cold?" she said.

Asher was in a T-shirt, having left off the ever-present flannel shirt for once. It emphasized just how big his chest and arms were. Hannah dove back into her coffee.

"Cold? No, I rarely am cold. Benefit of my condition, I believe," he said, a wry smile on his face.

"Are there other benefits, besides being warm and not worrying about death being a permanent condition?" She tried to sound flippant, but Hannah was by nature annoyingly curious; there were a thousand questions she wanted to ask.

Asher let out a big breath and got up to refill his coffee.

"There are a few. But unlike many of the others like myself, I do not really accept that this is a permanent condition. All things eventually come to an end." He sat back down with his mug, frowning. "And while I return to life, I still have to die each time. Having your life come to a close is a terrible thing, no matter how it happens. And one of these times, I believe it will be final. I will have to meet my maker and account for what I have or have not accomplished with the many lives I have been given."

"I'm glad to see there's something you have to share with us boring old one-and-done humans. Seems reasonable." She joked, but having had a brush with death of her own so recently, she could understand how having to repeat it constantly could be less than fun.

"Very true. Why should I be excluded from the fear of death?" His eyes crinkled at the edges, his lips turned up at the corners. He started laughing to himself.

"What?" she asked around a mouthful of pancake. "It wasn't really that funny."

"It was not that. You just made me think of something. There was actually one time that it was not so bad." He added cream to his coffee and stirred it, still grinning in a way that told her he was stalling for effect. "This was actually not that long ago, maybe a hundred and fifty years past."

She rolled her eyes at him.

"I was in Italy with an acquaintance of mine, another who is like me. We were staying in a small town known for its grappa, and there were several local gentlemen who believed there was no way an outsider could handle the local distillation like the men who made it. My friend begged to differ."

The grin on Asher's face was mischievous, a smile that reached his eyes. "We drank and we drank, and they drank, and they drank more, and we drank more. Just by size I have a greater than average tolerance, and as time goes by I think it has only improved. But even that has its limitations, it seems. Things grew hazy as the night progressed, and the last thing I recall was my friend marrying a local woman. She was twice his age and already married, but it seemed like a good idea at the time, and we toasted their union with yet more of the grappa, of course."

"What happened after that?"

"That I daresay no one will ever know. Certainly not me. To my confusion, I woke up naked in the middle of a field miles and miles away, on an entirely different island. The truth is, to this day I have no idea whether I died and came back there or if I was still alive and somehow ended there in that state as a result of my inebriation."

Hannah snorted as she mopped up as much syrup as possible with her remaining bite of pancake.

"And the other benefits, besides not being cold and super-human tolerance?" This was the weirdest conversation ever. "Flight? X-ray vision? Telepathy? Please tell me you don't have to drink blood or anything like that."

This time it was his turn to roll his eyes. "No, no, no, and heavens no, that is disgusting. There are no extraordinary powers, no rules or requirements," he answered. "As far as I know none of those things exist, but given my personal experience, I guess nothing is out of the question. But really, I was born just like anyone else, and when I died for the first time, I was the same as any other man. I am still very much as I was, except for subtle changes over time."

"Like what? You're getting better with age?"

He frowned. "I do not know that I believe I am growing any better. I am just slowly becoming something different. I feel as though now I am only an echo of the person I was, beginning in that very first life. I am growing less distinct by degree, I think, smoothing out and losing the original edges as I travel farther and farther from the point of origin."

She looked at his unnaturally smooth skin, the exceptional beauty of his face, the sheer size of him and wondered if that was true. What had the very first Asher been like?

"Were you always enormous?" Hannah blurted out rudely before she could catch herself.

He laughed out loud, and she couldn't help but smile.

"Enormous? By the standards of the day I was certainly larger than average, but yes, that has followed the same pattern as every other trait or ability I was born with. Each time I have come back, I have come back just a tiny bit larger. A little faster as well. Not inhumanly—not faster than the fastest man—but fast. I am stronger and I have more endurance. My hearing is better than the average man's. So is my vision."

That explained why he could pick out the figure in the woods before she could, even though her own eyesight had always been perfect. She wondered if he would continue growing more attractive, because she wasn't sure that was entirely possible. Hannah blushed, then mentally smacked herself in the back of the head. Thank goodness she didn't share his perfect pale-gold skin, which would have made it immediately obvious.

"How old are you? Not how many years, but ..." She wasn't sure how to phrase it, so she wasted time taking down a nice glass from the cupboard above the refrigerator, or rather trying to. "Biologically, I guess, how old would you say you are?"

She was about to pull over a chair to stand on when he reached over her and took a glass down from where her fingertips couldn't quite reach.

"My god you're hot," she said.

She smacked the heel of her hand against her forehead because it was too late to bite her tongue completely off. "I mean temperature wise. You are unusually warm."

He was laughing at her, in a good-natured way. "I think that is why I so rarely feel the cold, because I am unusually hot, as you put it." She was certainly warm enough now, burning with embarrassment. He opened the refrigerator door and poured them each a glass of wine.

"Interesting temperature for red wine." He handed one glass to her and motioned her back to her chair.

She took a sip and winced. "The flavor of this particular vintage isn't improved by being served at room temperature. It would probably not be improved by much other than a trip down the drain, but waste not, want not." She raised her glass in a mock toast.

"You want to know my age?" he asked.

Hannah nodded.

"The first time I died I was nearly twenty-three years old."

"How did you die?" It was a macabre question and it had just flown out of her mouth. Things generally did.

"I do not recall. It was a very long time ago." Hannah watched his face, and she knew he wasn't telling the truth, but she let it go.

"I'm so sorry. You were only twenty-three?"

He nodded. "It sounds a young age to you, I imagine, but it was not terribly far below the life expectancy at the time, especially then, when things were in a state of unrest. I think if I had to hazard a guess, I would say I appear to be somewhere around thirty now, give or take. There really is no way to know for certain, I suppose."

She bought that. He didn't look older than that certainly.

"Why is that?"

He laughed out loud again, mouth open, perfect teeth bared.

"Why? I do not know why. Why are your eyes brown and your hair so dark?" He squinted at her a little, a thought forming in his head that showed in his brow. "I do have a theory though. You know I am not the only person that is like me?"

She nodded.

"One of us, he lived to be an old man, a respectable, mature age even by today's standards. For his time, though, it was an advanced span of years. Keep in mind, this is according to him, but my acquaintance was by his guess sixty-five years old when he died for the very first time. He has never managed to string together as many years in one go since then, but by the time I met him I would have put him at thirty-five years old at the very most. He swears every time he comes back he is a little younger and more physically perfect."

He looked at her, waiting for her response.

"Doesn't seem any more unbelievable than any of the rest of this, so why not. But why is he getting younger if you look older than you did when you died the first time? Will he keep going? Do you think he's eventually going to end up in diapers?"

He rolled his eyes at her.

"I think it is more a matter of everything growing toward the center. I think it may be that my kind all move slowly toward the same age because it is a sort of prime, an ideal point for life. Or maybe it is a reflection of mental maturity. I find that most adults, no matter how old, still feel as though they are of the same age on the inside."

She leaned back. "Well that's something to look forward to. Knowing I've got a couple of years before I hit my prime and start going downhill." *So, this is as good as it's going to get,* she thought, getting up with her plate.

Washing it and standing it up in the rack, she resisted the urge to pull aside the towel over the window and look out, sobered by the thought that someone, maybe even his sister, might be out there.

"You have a sister. Are you all related?"

He shook his head.

"I do not believe any of us are linked to one another in any way, save for my sister and I. We are the only two of our kind to share blood that I know of. It may be because we are twins. We had siblings, but none of them were as we are. Other than the two of us, it seems we have been scattered through time and across the world."

"So, what do you call yourselves? Immortals?"

He shook his head in amusement.

"Call ourselves? I do not think we call ourselves anything. Certainly I do not. It is not a club, Hannah." He shrugged. "And I would surely not use that word. I am just a person who after my life expired was for some reason gifted with another. Thus far. Any time could be the last."

Hannah dried the dishes and put them away quietly, gently closing the cupboard. When he went silent, she asked a question, hoping he would answer.

"If there's more of you, and all this is true, then how are you a secret? Why isn't it common knowledge? I mean, some people know, you said, but how come they haven't told everyone? It seems a little unbelievable that I've never seen a news story leading with 'man has been alive for three hundred years,' especially if there isn't a super-secret club full of repeat offenders like yourself out there protecting your identity."

"Repeat offender." He chuckled. "I like that. It is strangely appropriate. The truth is we have been hiding in plain sight all along. Consider that before modern transportation and communication, before photography or even comprehensive record keeping, if one of us died in battle, out hunting, anywhere out of sight and was never found, it would not be extraordinary. Life was dangerous, and on any given day one might walk from their door and never return."

"But you did return, you do," Hannah said. "And what, no one noticed?"

"Oh, we returned. But consider the time. Imagine if you died in front of a witness and vanished. It would be assumed you were either whisked up to heaven or were a witch, demon, whatever explanation was most acceptable based on the belief systems of the time. At most you might become a local legend or a cautionary tale. On the off chance you came back on the same continent and could find a way to return to where you came from, it would be seen as a miracle, or a curse. I am sure people like me have returned to their homes only to be burned at the stake or drowned for witchcraft, or best-case scenario, proclaimed a miracle and sainted. That has actually happened more than once. No one would attribute it to anything else, especially in the past."

Hannah plunked an ice cube into her now warm but equally crappy wine and sat down across from him.

"Okay, I'll buy that. But that was then. Now technology allows you to get right back to where you came from, if you wanted to, and probably prove with DNA or something that you're the same person. Why hasn't someone done that and, I don't know, taken over the world or convinced people they were a god? Or at least gotten really rich and famous for not ever dying."

"But they have and they do. Can you not think of at least one person in history to vanish and come back from the dead and amass a powerful following?"

"No way? Really?" Her mind was a little blown. "Wait, but where is he now?"

Asher laughed out loud. "Who knows. Still trying, probably. Hoping to have another go round. That problem is exactly what I am talking about, and it actually makes it easier for me to live in peace. The further people have come into modernity, the less willing they are to believe things that are right in front of them. Consider your own case."

It was true. She'd seen him die and disappear with her own eyes and come back more than once, and she still hadn't believed it.

He cocked his head toward the computer. "Hiding in plain sight. If you go online, there are entire websites of old photos side by side with pictures of modern celebrities, meant to be amusing. You cannot imagine how many of them are correct. And those are the ones I know of, the ones who have chosen to be in the public eye. How many am I not aware of? People have made the connection and they do not even believe it."

Hannah's hand was twitching toward her laptop. He shook his head no, and she sighed. Maybe later.

Asher continued. "Many of us have managed to accumulate great wealth and power in this day and age, with what we are as a tool, but never directly because of it. Humanity now will not accept something that so clearly must be impossible. You could put together a suitcase full of proof that a person like me has walked the earth for hundreds of years and hand deliver it to any major news outlet, and at best they would send it over to the *National Enquirer*."

"What about the—"

Hannah jumped from her chair and tipped over her wine, a trail of red snaking its way to the floor. She ducked down below the level of the table.

"Get down, something just went past the window."

Asher was down almost as soon as she spoke, though less successfully out of the way. She was certain she'd seen a dark shape silently pass by the narrow border window to the left of the back door.

Hannah grabbed the shotgun from where it was leaning against the wall and snicked off the safety.

"Stay here," Asher hissed. She reached up to flick off the light, then hesitated. He shook his head no. Whoever it was might not know they'd been seen.

Another shadow passed by, then a third in quick succession. Asher motioned her down into the corner, where the end cabinet met the wall and made a small, less vulnerable space, then held out his hand for the gun. Hannah started to hand it to him, then paused, relief dawning on her face.

"Deer."

"What?" he hissed. "Give me the gun."

"It's the deer," she said. He paused, then nodded in understanding.

"Give me the gun, let me check," he whispered. She relinquished it unwillingly and stayed down, but she wasn't frozen in fear now.

Asher moved silently to the back door, staying low, then eased aside the window covering to look out. He let it slide back into place and turned around.

"Deer," he confirmed with evident relief.

She uncurled from the corner. "I haven't seen a single animal since you got here. Usually I have that whole group roaming the yard all night. They like to eat the grapevines and dig under the snow at the edge of the wood, especially when there's a lot of snow, since it's not as deep under the trees."

"There have not been any deer lately?"

"Not a single one." She grabbed a rag and started to clean up the stream of wine that had made its way across the table and was puddling on the floor.

"I think that means our company is probably gone for the moment. We should go."

Hannah looked at him, then the rag. She realized how relieved she was that it was only deer, and how terrified she'd been until she knew otherwise. Hannah tossed the rag overhand into the sink.

"Let's go."

# 17

Asher stomped on the gas, barreling up the last few feet of the driveway, using the momentum to crash through the deep pile of snow that had been plowed across it. They fish-tailed through the turn, skidding out almost to the opposite ditch, but he deftly corrected at the last second, bringing them back into their lane on the slick road. He drove with the lights off, using only the sliver of moon to navigate by; she hoped his eyesight really had improved with age, because she was struggling to make out much of anything through the windshield in front of her.

"Where are we going?" Hannah grabbed the handle above her head and braced when he made another quick turn a few minutes later. He didn't answer, driving with his eyes fixed on the road. Suddenly they turned again, and sharply, the car bottoming out as they squeezed through a nearly invisible space in the trees. They were on the washboard surface of a narrow lane Hannah didn't recognize. If she had to guess, she'd say they were somewhere off the dirt road that wound between her property and the steep hilly land beyond it, except in all the times she'd driven it, Hannah had never noticed another road coming off from it.

The road shot steeply upward, and he flicked the headlights on, cutting through the pitch blackness under the tight-knit branches. It was a close fit, hemmed in by the pines on both sides, and she winced as branches scraped against the doors of her car. They snaked through several more quick, tight turns before the road suddenly opened up in front of them. The narrow slice of moon was visible again through fat, falling snowflakes, and she caught a glimpse of a log cabin before the headlights winked out.

"I had no idea there was anything up here. How'd you find this place?" she said.

"Airbnb."

She couldn't tell if he was joking. Shaking the snowflakes off her head she followed him closely on the stone path around to the front door, hand on the back of his coat to guide her. They stopped, and she heard him unlock the door and open it.

"Wait here." His warm bulk disappeared and Hannah waited impatiently, ears straining for any sound. She jumped when his voice sounded out somewhere in front of her. "Come in. I am going to hide your car in the garage. I will be right back."

Sliding across the icy stoop, she made it inside and stood stiffly on the doormat in the dark. Just when she'd decided to start fumbling around for a light switch, Asher melted out of the darkness and turned on a table lamp, throwing a pale-yellow ring of light across the room. It illuminated a pair of overstuffed couches around a coffee table made from a giant, solid square of rough-hewn wood. Beyond them were walls of solid peeled log, and at the far end of the room, a great bank of windows that came to a peak far above her. The panes were black in the darkness except for the moon perfectly framed in the highest triangular pane. She'd grown disoriented in the dark, but the moon in the window meant they looked out toward the valley they'd just come from. If they were as high up as she thought they were, they might even look out over the rolling hills and scattered lakes between here and the mountains.

Walking back to Hannah, Asher reached over her shoulder and punched a series of numbers into a keypad.

"Stay inside. Keep the lights off out here where the windows are not shaded. I will be upstairs, in the loft. There is a bedroom past the kitchen you can use."

"Wait, what if someone—"

He flicked off the lamp and disappeared into the dark, leaving her alone, her boots dripping melting snow onto the doormat.

Clouds drifted over the moon and blocked out what little light there had been. Hannah shuffled toward where she was fairly sure the kitchen was, not making it very far before one of her knees made contact with a table she hadn't seen coming. She swore loud enough for it to echo off the bare walls. Asher could see better in the dark, and she hoped he heard better too, since most of the profanity was aimed at him and his not leaving a light on for two more minutes.

The first door she came to past the kitchen turned out to be a small half bathroom, the second a closet. Then another encounter between her shin and a piece of unseen furniture. This one brought tears to her eyes, and not only from the pain. She was running scared from her home, and it had landed her in a strange place, stumbling around in the darkness all alone. *What was I thinking, leaving my house and coming here with him? I let fear get the best of me, and here I am, just as scared. At least at home I knew where I was.*

The third door was finally the promised bedroom. She fumbled for the light switch then shut the door behind her, turning the lock and leaning against it, taking a deep breath. She was here, she'd come here of her own free will, whatever that brought her, and right now she had no other choice but to deal with it.

The room was as foreign as the rest of the house, dominated by a large bed with a headboard made from a half-moon-shaped slice from a massive tree, tawny colored and sanded to dull smoothness. Hannah reached out and ran her hand down over the hundreds of rings, the subtle color changes marking countless years of growth, down to where they were blocked by a mound of pillows. They looked so inviting. Letting her bag slide to the floor, she sat down, just to rest for a minute. She was so worked up there was no way she'd be able to sleep, not here in this strange place, not knowing who might be looking for them and where they might be. But she was so tired. She just needed to sit for a while. Hannah leaned back against the fluffy mountain of pillows, just to rest, just for a minute.

———•◦••◦•———

The sound of footsteps over her head woke her. Hannah listened as they clomped across the room. She heard another door open and close again with a squeak, then the house returned to silence.

Rolling over and getting up, she unlocked the door and peeked her head out. "Asher," she said. "Hello." When there was no reply and no Asher, she decided it counted as permission to rummage around his cupboards.

Hannah took her tea to stand in front of the bank of windows she'd seen last night. They opened onto a wide porch, and over the heavy beams of the deck railing she could see the storm had finally snowed itself out, and a thick blanket of white had washed everything clean and softened the edges of a tumble of boulders at the edge of the yard. Past them the land dropped off and a magnificent view opened up; the entire valley below with the town nestled at its base, the river wrapped around it like a lazy, coiled snake, and beyond them the mountains rolling off in waves.

"I believe an author built this. Writes books about vampires and werewolves, all sorts of supernatural nonsense."

Hannah jumped when Asher spoke. He was pulling a sweater over his head while he walked down the stairs from the loft. He looked amused, breaking into a smile. His mood was as sunny this morning as it had been dark last night. Maybe he had just been tired. She tried and failed to recall actually seeing him sleep since they'd met, whereas it seemed like she was always either passing out or nodding off mid-sentence. Maybe grumpy from lack of sleep applied to people who had been alive forever too.

"Nonsense? Wait, there aren't any werewolves?" Hannah sipped her tea and tried to pick out landmarks she knew from the land below. "I wasn't aware anyone famous lived around here."

"I did not suggest they were famous. Prolific though, based on the library. In any case, I do not believe the owner spends a great deal of time here. This place did not seem much used when I took it over.

When I decided to extend my stay, they were happy to oblige me for as long as I wished."

He came to stand beside her and looked out over the valley, where white wisps of fog drifted by, covering and uncovering the town below.

"My house would be just over there." She pointed her finger toward a small clearing far below them in the distance. He followed the direction she was pointing and nodded.

"How long have you been here? The whole time, since the accident?" She wasn't accusatory, though part of her prickled, knowing that for at least part of the time he'd been here, watching from the shadows while she struggled to find him. And it was a little creepy.

"In this house? For some months. I was not sure what was going on, or why I kept returning to this area. I am still not certain about that. In the beginning I was staying in a rather disagreeable motel outside of town, but after I found out you could describe me and were still looking for me, I felt it best to retreat to somewhere less visible. I was struggling to blend in there anyway. Going unnoticed would be difficult for me in a town this small even if there was not a drawing of me on every telephone pole."

He was smiling at her. This Asher's face was less angular and tense than she'd seen so far. Definitely better rested.

"And you still don't know why you're here?"

He nodded, then turned toward the kitchen. "I have theories and ideas. None that make sense. But I have long since come to terms with there not always being a logical explanation."

"How long do you think we'll stay here?"

Hannah had followed him to the kitchen and was rummaging through the refrigerator, deciding what to make for breakfast. Asher offered to fend for himself, but she shooed him away. He might be perfectly able to cook, but she didn't get the impression he enjoyed it, not nearly as much as she did.

"I went out before dawn and looked around. Our tracks were covered and the snow in all directions is undisturbed, so I have no reason to believe we have been followed here. This house is secluded and has an adequate security system. I would say we will stay for at least a few days, maybe more."

She nodded in resignation. Maybe it was all nothing anyway, and no one had been able to follow them because no one was trying to, but it was better to be safe and not afraid. As much as she would rather be in her own house, in her own bed, this place felt like its own little fortress on top of the mountain. She hoped it was as secure as it felt.

"You think we're safe here?"

He nodded.

"For now."

⁕

Asher disappeared as soon as he'd eaten, and for lack of anything else to do, Hannah went to sit in the large, open living room. The couch where she sat faced the wide bank of windows that looked toward Barclay Mountain, the highest of the knobby peaks in the distance. She thought about the last time she'd been there, standing on the sheared-off cliff. The spot was visible from here, a faint scar near the summit. *If I was there on a clear day would I be able to see this house? Was it here staring at me when I went up to spread Joel's ashes, right before my entire life morphed into a horror movie?* As if in response the sun brightened and flashed across the glass, brightening the room. The cabin must look like a point of light from far away when the sun reflected off the massive windows, a daytime star sitting on a neighboring peak. She might have seen it that day if only she'd picked up her head and looked.

Finally forcing herself to look away, Hannah tried again to settle into the book she'd chosen from the wall of shelves in the office.

She turned a page but then flipped it back, not remembering anything she'd just read. It was failing to pull her in the way a book usually did, and she thought about going and choosing a new one, but she had a feeling it wouldn't interest her any more than this one. The books here were strange, all by the same author—the cabin's owner she supposed—and all so new the spines cracked when she opened the covers. She would have traded all of them for one of the worn-to-shreds paperbacks from her room.

"Is there anyone who would report you missing?"

She jumped, and the stiff book snapped shut when it hit the floor. "Missing?" Hannah picked it back up, fingering the thin crinkled line where the spine had broken, before laying it in her lap.

"Is there anyone who is going to come looking for you if you are not home or if you miss too many phone calls?"

She shrugged. "The sheriff seemed satisfied, so I can't imagine he'd be worried." She opened the book back up and tried to look like she was reading it.

"Anyone else?"

"Nope. No one else."

Hannah didn't look at him and she kept her tone cheerful, because she didn't want to see a look of pity. It wasn't necessary. Her life had always been full enough and happy, until recently. She had friends scattered across the country, across the world even, in all the places she'd lived. Maybe they didn't talk every day, or even every month, but they kept in touch in varying levels of regularity. She just didn't have a great many people in her life that were there every day. It was the price paid for living in a town this small, especially since she hadn't grown up here.

The couch dipped on the other end when Asher sat down. Out of the corner of her eye she could see him looking out over the valley, the surface of the river so still and reflective it was as if it gave off its own light.

"And you have no other family?" he asked.

She shut the book again with a clap and put it down, giving up on the pretense of reading.

"No family. My mother died right after I was born. My uncle Joel raised me." A patch of sun drifted onto her legs and made a warm rectangle, and she held her hand over it, to feel the heat of the refracted light. "We moved around a lot when I was a kid, but then he retired from active duty to be a consultant. We moved here, I finished school, went to college for a couple of years, and after that I came back and stayed."

Not that she'd stayed because she liked it here so much. She'd stayed because Joel was here. Hannah owed him so much and couldn't bring herself to pack her things and leave him by himself, even if it would have meant a better job and not being buried in snow for half of the year. He didn't have to raise her; he had only been married to her mother's sister for a little while when both women were killed in an accident. Hannah didn't have any other family, and there was no one to take her, so he'd brought her up. It couldn't have been easy for a single man bringing up a girl by himself through every awkward, infuriating stage from the terrible twos to the even more terrible teens.

Joel had never married, never even went on a single date as far as she knew, just took care of Hannah. Every time they moved, he made sure they had a place to live that was a home, where she felt safe and normal. Then finally, after the hard part was done, he'd gone and gotten himself killed.

Hannah thought of the ashes in the canister in the kitchen window at home. They might be his, but that didn't keep her from expecting him to walk back through the door. Even here it felt like she could turn her head and he might be sitting there next to her.

"What about you?" she said.

"What about me?" Asher didn't turn to look at Hannah when she spoke.

"Will anyone wonder where you are? I mean, except your sister?"

He shook his head. "No. She is the only one. The only person who will seek me out is the last person I would wish to find me. The last person I would wish to find either of us."

# 18

"**R**eally?" Hannah gave him a suspicious look, eyes narrowed. She refilled his bowl but didn't hand it to him, holding it back in exchange for an answer. He reached up and pulled it easily from her hands, righting it before the contents slopped over the side.

"Really." Asher stuck his spoon in the food, but looked up with a grin on his face before he took a bite.

"Did you ever do it?"

He shook his head. "No, but I know several who have, some more than once. It has become a bit of a long-running joke amongst my kind. Also useful if one should need to disappear conveniently. If your plane goes missing in the Bermuda Triangle, no one is really surprised when the body is never found."

"I don't believe you."

Asher raised an eyebrow. "Probably just as well. It will save me a great deal of talking if you are not interested in history as I am aware of it. I was going to tell you about Amelia Earhart, but now, I will not waste my breath."

Hannah shook her head in amusement while he went to work on the stew, wondering how many other unexplainable disappearances might actually be a little less mysterious than they appeared.

This had been part of their strangely comfortable routine over the past few days. In between questions Hannah basked in the sun streaming through the windows or threw together meals from the contents of the giant refrigerator and pantry. Asher prowled the woods or sat bent over the laptop on the desk in the library.

It was mostly comfortable. Asher abruptly went silent sometimes, eyes growing cloudy, his expression becoming distant and stony. She steered a little clearer of him then. Not because she was afraid of him, or because he was at all threatening toward her—he was unfailingly polite actually, in an old-fashioned, courtly sort of way—but because there was something so alien just under the surface of silent Asher that it made her shy away. Hannah didn't hold it against him, though. She had been known to go dark herself sometimes.

And they weren't on vacation, anyway. It was more a surprise they weren't both wrapped in doom and gloom more often.

For the most part, Asher was plenty talkative. He had lifetimes upon lifetimes of stories, and she had a million and a half questions. If she asked, he answered, though not always completely, Hannah suspected. If her questions became too personal, he would politely but firmly steer the subject in another direction.

"So, you always come back, but how long can you go in between?" He raised an eyebrow, and she thought for a second, then tried to rephrase it so he knew what she meant. "Not like how fast do you come back; I know that part. I mean, what's the longest someone like you has gone before dying, do you think?" Even if you were decently sure you'd come back, dying was still dying, as he'd said, and she wondered how long it was avoidable. "Do you just keep living forever, or would you die of old age first if nothing happened to you?"

He shook his head. "At most I live the same number of years I lived the very first time. I have never made it longer than that. None of us do, I believe. That is how I originally came to be in this area. It was my time. I was sitting on my porch waiting for it, and after, I ended up here."

"Do you age in the time between when you die?"

He shook his head. "Not a bit. Only in the instant between one death and the next, and very slowly."

Asher was looking at her strangely as he answered. He'd begun to do that, she'd noticed, but probably because she asked crazy questions. Maybe he was beginning to wonder what he'd gotten himself into, being stuck here with her, but it didn't slow Hannah down. The more she found out about his strange life, the more she wanted to know.

"So, your friend who lived to be in his sixties before he died the first time, he gets to live longer than you do then?"

"Yes. I have no idea why, but that is how it is. I suppose there are rules over everything under the sun, no matter how inexplicable."

He shrugged, then his brow furrowed as a thought crossed his mind. He didn't share it, just froze for a moment, deep in thought. Asher had a small dimple on one cheek when he was pensive that she'd just noticed. She felt herself blushing.

The oven dinged—perfect timing—and she hopped up gratefully. Pulling the apple turnovers out of the oven, Hannah poked at the buttons to turn it off, growing frustrated as she accidentally set the clock blinking, turned on the vent and every light, and fired up all the burners. Asher got up and leaned over her, turning everything off and resetting the clock while she stood there feeling inept. It wasn't her fault; she was just used to a stove closer to his age than hers, not this shiny metal spaceship.

"Do you ever get tired of keeping up with technology? Because I damn well do." Hannah set the pan down on the counter with a clunk. Right now she was ready to kick the stove back to the stone age.

Burning her fingertips, Hannah pushed the turnovers onto a plate and set it in front of him. He nodded in thanks and picked one up and took a bite, oblivious to the lava-hot contents.

"Do I grow tired of keeping up with the world? Very, and more so now than ever. Things change so quickly. But it is better to embrace it, because it is even more difficult if you fight it," he said. "Though it is tempting, to withdraw from the world and let it pass by. Then one does not have to watch everyone and everything fade away again and again." He paused to take another bite, and the only sound was the clink of the bottle against her wineglass as she refilled it. "I have tried, but it is impossible to escape from the world forever. One finds it too different to fall back into it seamlessly, when everything has changed while you were gone. And people are not meant to be alone."

His glass was empty and he nodded when she reached to refill it.

"I try to keep up now, no matter what happens," he went on, "in case I let too much time pass me by and return to the world a fish out of water."

Hannah sipped her wine, saddened by the thought. It hadn't occurred to her before that living forever meant losing everything and everyone over and over again.

"Well, I'm glad you found your way back to the present," she said. "You're better at it than I am anyway, and I have no excuse. Your knowledge of kitchen appliances is way better than mine, and you have a solid grasp on the lingo. Except for the whole never using a contraction thing, you seem to be doing a bang-up job." She leaned back, pleasantly warm from the wine and the fire burning in the giant fireplace.

He chuckled.

"So quick to criticize my grammar. Do you have any idea how many languages are bouncing around in my head? And the English I grew up speaking has changed so much it is practically a dead language now. Besides, it pains me to butcher it on purpose."

"You have my sincere apology." She smirked. "You do an altogether perfect job of passing for a functional modern human. Above average by age."

Apparently he didn't find her that amusing. In fact, he stopped smiling, though she wasn't sure what exactly she'd said wrong. Maybe she was going a bit far in flippantly teasing the giant sitting across the table. If her mouth had gotten her in trouble it wouldn't be the first time.

"I'm sorry. What did I say?"

He waved her off. "It was nothing you said, but it made me think of a sad story. Not everyone like me manages to assimilate as well." Asher pushed his empty plate aside and leaned away from the table. "Until fairly recently, infant mortality was abysmally high. When I was young it was not unusual for parents to lose several children. It was more unusual if they did not. Reaching adulthood was more of an achievement than a given, though whether by accident or design, all of those like me managed to survive that far. All save one that I am aware of."

Asher was looking past her while he spoke, staring at the fire but not seeing it.

"This particular individual," he said, "Roman, he is called, was born at least six hundred years ago. He died the first time when he was only a few years old." Asher blinked back to reality and looked soberly at Hannah. "Imagine what it must have been like, dying so young, then waking up in an unknown place. He was far too young to care for himself, and we sometimes come back in dreadful, inhospitable places, so I can only imagine he must have passed again frequently and often painfully." He shook his head sadly. "At best he might have been found and cared for, but even then, it would never be for longer than those few short years."

"But he didn't stay a child, did he? You aged some. So he grew up?"

Asher didn't reply for a moment, and they listened to the crackle of the fire.

"He grew up, but changing slowly, as we do. For a very long time he would have been too young to work out what was happening or why. By the time he did, it was too late."

"Too late?"

Asher nodded. "Too late for him, on the inside at least. He was alive and eventually matured, but living the way he had, thrown across the world so many times, had broken his mind. Losing everything and everyone, never forming any meaningful relationships, never being loved for long, his humanity was stunted, any morality twisted. And life meant nothing, because all he ever experienced was death."

"But there's more of you out there. Didn't someone find him and explain it to him?" Hannah said.

"Eventually he did find others like himself," Asher said, "at least like him in their ability to return after death. Maybe they explained the rudiments, their own experiences, or tried to express to him he was not alone in his condition, but the damage was long done."

"So what happened to him?"

"He continued on. He still does, acting only as his own desire dictates. Roman is an unbridled being who has killed a horrifying number of people for no reason other than that he wished to. He has never stopped. He never will. How can man be safe from him when no cell will ever hold him for very long? Even death cannot contain him." Asher paused, looking up at Hannah. "I still catch glimpses of him from time to time. I can trace him out when I read about senseless killings and heinous crimes with no rhyme nor reason. Or when there are strings of brutal murders only an unimaginable evil could have perpetrated. He is out there, shortening the already short lives of people who do not have the chance to return as he does."

They sat, the room silent except for the irregular crackle of the fire. Finally, Asher continued.

"I am telling you this because I feel I have made too light of what we are, with all the amusing stories. He was given what I was given, but it only served to cripple him and create an everlasting monster. And while he may be the worst of our kind, he is not the only one who chooses to do evil. Some of us are demons hiding behind human faces, living side by side with an oblivious population."

She thought he would tip over into dark Asher and shut down, but instead he finished his wine and looked at Hannah with a sad smile.

"It is interesting, that in all your searching you actually did find me once, and it was through Roman. I saw the clipping in your kitchen. How you turned it up from amongst all the photos scattered across the internet, I cannot imagine. He was at his evil work once again and as I was nearby, I thought to step in and put an end to it, though it would only be temporarily. Someone beat me to it. At least there are some trying to lessen the burden of guilt our population carries. It grows heavy."

When he got up Hannah stayed at the table, turned the empty wine bottle around in her hand and watched the dregs roll around the divot in the bottom. She thought about that accumulation of guilt. Not how Asher felt it was his to carry, but about the other side of the coin, where there was none at all, where conscience didn't come into play. His sister, Roman, and how many others for whom human life carried no importance. The thought gave her a shiver. The world was filled with beautiful monsters that would live forever, without a care for how many human lives they snuffed out.

———

Hannah tossed and turned that night, haunted by dreams of a tall, gaunt man with a giant mouth full of razor-sharp teeth. He picked up screaming people and stuffed them one by one into his mouth, like the devil swallowing souls in *The Last Judgement*. She jerked awake bathed in sweat, gasping for breath.

Afraid to go back to sleep, she got up and threw the blanket around her shoulders. Walking silently in her socks out through the great room, she navigated with a care for her shins around the furniture. After turning off the alarm, she slid the glass door open then shut it behind her noiselessly.

The wide porch stepped down into a clearing that curved gently downward. A small group of deer looked up at the crackle her feet made when she walked out from under the shadow of the roof, but they didn't move, returning one by one to nosing under the soft layer of new snow for clumps of grass. They treated her like she wasn't there, as animals generally did, and Hannah walked forward, tipping her face toward the moon, letting the crisp breeze cool her flushed face.

She jumped when the deer scattered around her, one brushing against her blanket as they bounded down the hill, tails bobbing like beacons.

"You should not be outside alone. It might be dangerous." Asher stood on the porch, watching the last white tail disappear into the night.

Hannah's feet were getting damp and she shivered a bit, so she didn't argue, just turned and walked back to the house. Asher locked the door again behind them.

"Tea?" he asked. She nodded and he turned on the light over the kitchen island, its bulb casting a green glow over him as he filled the kettle and set it on the burner. She left her damp socks by the door and padded over the cold floor to join him.

Waiting for the water to boil, Hannah sat at the bar while Asher took down the mugs and tea. When he set a mug down in front of her and looked at her for a moment in that intense way he had, she raised an eyebrow. It was too late and she was too tired for the fixed stare or blushing embarrassment.

"What?" She tucked her chilly feet up under her and wrapped the blanket around her knees.

"Nothing." He smiled. "I heard you slip out and followed you to find a fairy child communing with a herd of deer. A charming sight. I was sorry to disturb it. They ran the moment I stepped out the door."

She shrugged. "You're big and scary."

"I knew another woman once who could talk to the animals. She had a menagerie of every wild creature you could imagine, and they stayed close to her, without a fence or a cage. They would eat from her hand, and I rarely saw her without a bird on her shoulder. 'They whisper their secrets into my ear,' she would say."

"What happened to her?" Hannah fidgeted with her empty mug.

"She died. Many years ago."

Hannah wasn't sure why she'd thought he was speaking about a being like himself. She wondered how many people he might have watched grow old and die in his lifetimes. The burden again of so many lives, the same stories playing out again and again.

The kettle whistled, forcing them both out of their own thoughts.

"Well, the animals weren't whispering any secrets to me, that's for sure. Animals don't like me, actually," Hannah said.

When Asher looked over, Hannah continued, glad he had accepted the bait.

"They don't, I swear. The deer weren't standing there because they like me. It's because they don't even care enough to bother moving. It's always been that way." She never could have been a lion tamer or dolphin trainer because they would have rolled over and taken a nap

146

from sheer boredom. Maybe she should have been a dog catcher; the dogs wouldn't have even bothered trying to run.

"We had animals when I was growing up," she said. "My uncle was old school, the live-off-the-land type. We had ducks and chickens, and they'd follow him around everywhere. It made me jealous, so he used to sneak chicken feed into my coat pockets when I wasn't looking so I'd think they noticed me. It worked until I got warm and took my coat off and they all stayed there pecking at it when I walked away. We had a cat for a while too, but I got so sad because she wouldn't play with me that Joel finally gave her away. I'm not a freak of nature, I'm so freaky nature doesn't even know I exist."

"Yes, well, if we are having a contest, I still believe I win." He smiled at her and her heart thumped automatically. Its growing inability to behave itself upset her. Taking her tea, she went to stand in front of the glass doors, watching the sun that was beginning to rise in streaks of peach and orange over the mountain.

It looked like it might be clear again, another sunny day that seemed miraculous after so much winter gloom. Days like this made it seem like spring might actually be a possibility. Only one lazy gray cloud drifted low across the valley, like a small patch of dirty fog.

"Asher. Ash, come here."

He turned back halfway through the office door.

"What is it?" he asked, coming to stand beside her and looking out across the valley.

"Is that smoke?"

The lazy gray puff was definitely moving upward, and it didn't look like fog now, but it was still dim outside and her vision wasn't as good as his. His eyes tracked the direction her hand was pointing.

He looked back at her, wide-eyed.

"Asher," she said, "that's where my house is."

# 19

"Stop. Hannah. You cannot go there. If there is a fire at your house then it is most definitely a trap."

Hannah took a deep breath, staring at the smoke and picturing everything she knew turning to ashes, her house being swallowed by angry orange flames. She willed her eyes to work better, squinting to see if she could tell from so far away if it really was her house burning.

"I have to do something," she said. "I can't just stand here and watch."

Asher was a half step behind her when she flung open the door to her room and yanked on her socks and boots, then spun around to find her coat.

She collided with him, slamming into his chest on her way back out the door.

"Move. Get out of the way."

He moved, but to widen his stance, filling the doorway completely.

"Move!" She slammed both fists against his chest, her eyes tearing up with frustration.

His arms closed around her shoulders like iron bands, pinning her arms against her chest. She struggled against him, but she could hardly breathe, let alone get away.

"Hannah, stop." Asher spoke evenly into her ear, not letting her move. She kept fighting him, angry at being restrained, scared of what might be happening to everything she had in the world.

"Shhh," he said. "Hannah, stop."

She finally gave up, going limp, and let a few hot tears soak into his shirt before sniffing and forcing herself to get it together.

"You can let go," she mumbled into his chest. He loosened his grip, just a little, and she took in a deep breath. He pushed her away to arm's length, keeping hold of the tops of her arms.

"Can I at least call the fire department, or the sheriff, to find out what's happening?" she said. "I understand running down there wouldn't be smart, but I can't just sit here. What if it *is* my house and someone goes in there thinking I'm inside and gets hurt?"

Hannah thought about Sheriff Morgan. He wouldn't hesitate to run in there if he thought she was inside. The firefighters wouldn't either, if there was a chance someone might be trapped. She squirmed herself out of his grip and tried to squeeze past him.

"Let me through. I'm just going to look out the window. Are there any binoculars here?"

He stepped aside, stopping to rummage through a shelf in the coat closet while Hannah ran to the window.

Asher didn't hand the binoculars to her but looked first at what was now a long, dark snake of smoke slithering skyward. He lowered them from his eyes and held them out, but didn't immediately let go when Hannah tried to pull them away.

"It is either your house or the barn. I am sorry, I cannot see which one. There is too much smoke."

Holding up the binoculars, she couldn't tell either, but she knew he was right, that something on her property was on fire. It didn't matter which, because if it was one it would soon be the other as well, they were so close together. Opening the sliding door a crack, she listened, hoping the wind would carry the sound of a siren to her ear, but she couldn't hear anything. When she pulled the door shut Asher reached over and pushed down the lock with one hand, holding a phone out with the other.

"Call the sheriff on this phone. Keep it brief. Tell him something, maybe that you are out of town and a neighbor called you and said they saw smoke. Get them to send the fire department, though chances are if we saw the smoke, someone else has as well."

She tried to take the phone, but he held on with two fingers and she looked up at him.

"Hannah, this is not a good idea. This has to be a trap."

Yanking the phone from his hand, she turned it over, tapping the screen to wake it up.

"I know that. But if someone is burning my house down to get my attention, they must have assumed I'd be close enough to see it. In that case, how long until they find us anyway?"

The phone screen went dark. She looked at the charcoal-colored smoke, thinning in the wind as it drifted over the trees and toward the town.

"Is there any safe option?" she said. "What else can we do?"

It killed her to just stand there, watching from a distance while her whole life burned. She pictured the canister of ashes, melting in on itself, mixing with the charred remains of everything else she had. And those were just the things. She prayed no one was right now putting themself in harm's way because of her.

But it was reckless to rush in blindly, and she was afraid, frightened of what might be outside, who she might be faced with if she took the bait. And it had to be bait. She had no more illusions about whoever had been slinking around her property being unconnected to Asher's appearance; the fire had convinced her it wasn't a coincidence.

Asher ran his hand through his hair, standing the front on end.

"There is nothing we can do. We should not even be here," he said. "I should have taken you out of this area the first chance we had, the day I pulled you out of the water. Or before even that. But it is far too late now. Even if we leave this instant someone may be watching the roads, waiting for us to make an appearance. If it is my sister, we can assume she has every base covered. I do not think they know precisely where we are, but they will if we make a move. I think that we should—"

A ringing interrupted him, and they both started.

"Hannah, is that your phone?"

She nodded, wide-eyed. "I turned it off. You know I did, in the car when we were leaving. I haven't touched it since. It's still in my bag in the closet."

He looked at her with accusation in his eyes while it rang on.

"Asher, I did not touch that phone. I didn't turn it on." It went silent, and she went and fished it out of the bottom of the bag. It began to ring again the moment it was in her hand.

*Sheriff Morgan*, the display read. She silenced it and handed it to him. "It was off. I know it was. Besides, it was almost dead then, still is. If it'd been on all this time the battery would be completely toast."

He took it from her, looking at the screen. Suddenly his eyes widened. He turned it toward her, and she saw the preview of a text come across the screen.

*Pick up the phone, brother.*

Asher stared at the phone, frozen. It began to ring again.

"It's coming from the sheriff's phone. We have to answer it." Not that Hannah wanted to, especially now that they knew for certain who they were dealing with.

Asher slid his finger across the screen. He held the phone to his ear, then immediately lowered it and touched the screen, holding it between them.

"Yes, that's right. I want her to hear this too." The woman's voice was silky and low. "Since I've had to truncate my carefully crafted timeframe, I've been forced to employ some alternate measures so we can get back on track. Toward that end, why don't you say hello to nice Mr. Sheriff."

"Don't do anything she says! Call the state—" Sheriff Morgan's garbled voice was silenced with the sound of a thud, followed by a cry of pain. The woman's voice—Amara's voice—on the other hand, was as level and sugary as when she first spoke, not at all affected by the tortured sounds she was squeezing out of the sheriff.

"Now that I have your attention, we're going to meet up a little sooner than I planned. I was hoping we could all have a nice family-style sit down in your ugly little kitchen, but since it's well on its way to being an ash pile we'll just have to adapt."

Hannah looked at Asher desperately, but he was staring stone-faced at the phone screen.

"You can meet me behind the house in half an hour. I won't be hard to find. Just park behind the sheriff's car and follow his lumbering trail through the woods. We'll have a great view of the house, even better than you have now." She paused. "Oh, and brother, don't bother trying to run. I know it's what you do, but resist the urge. If you even try I will slowly and painfully kill the man you just heard, every person in those firetrucks about to roll in, and anyone else who happens to wander by. If you still aren't here, I'll start calling the police and firemen from the next town. And on and on, you get the idea. Do you want that on your increasingly guilty conscience?"

The screen went black.

Asher and Hannah stood still in shock, then so quickly she almost didn't see him move, the phone flew across the room and shattered against the stone fireplace, bits of electronics and glass raining to the floor. She backed away from the expression of rage on his face.

"We have to go, we don't have much time," Hannah said very quietly, edging toward the door.

Asher spoke, standing like a statue again. "We can try to flee. She can only be in one place at a time. Even if Amara has help, the focus will be on where she thinks you will go, which is to her." His voice was low and eerily calm.

"Asher, she said she'll kill the sheriff and anyone else who turns up. Do you think she's kidding?"

He shook his head. "No, I know that she is not. She will do as she says. But if we do go to her, she will kill them anyway. And then after you have watched her end the lives of those innocent people, she will slowly and painfully kill you. When I have seen her do that, one more time she will end me. We have danced this dance before, many times, she and I."

Finally Asher moved, stopping Hannah from opening the door.

He stood in front of her, hand wrapped around her wrist, fingers overlapping, making her meet his eyes.

"Hannah, I would save you. We can run, and there is a chance we can make it away from here. You can have a little more time. Some more of this life. I would not have you die today."

She placed a hand on each side of his face and considered it closely, because she could and she might not have another opportunity. Her hands felt cool against his fiery warm skin.

"I don't want to die. But we can't run if there's a chance of stopping her hurting them. You know it."

He looked at her, his eyes sad. "I know."

———————

Flying down the driveway in daylight was even worse than barreling up it in total darkness, though Asher maneuvered the sharp turns deftly in the big black SUV. Hannah's compact had looked like a sad little clown car next to it in the garage, and she wasn't sure it would have survived a trip down at this speed, skiing around corners, not pausing for ruts or potholes. They burst out onto the road, fishtailing across the single lane, then slamming to a halt. Asher threw the SUV into park and turned to her.

"I do not know what to expect. I wish I could tell you I have a plan, but Amara will have covered every possibility. She is smarter than I, more ruthless, and utterly without mercy. If you have a chance, run. Promise her anything." He grabbed Hannah's arm, gave her a jarring shake. "Promise her anything. Do anything, do you hear me. If you have to kill me to distract her, do it if you think you can get away. Put a bullet in my heart."

"Asher, I can't—"

"Hannah, listen to me. Amara will be ready for me. I have no doubt she will consider my every move. But you? She will underestimate you, because she believes you beneath her. If you can, use it against her. It may be your only chance."

He let go of her and opened the console, pulling out a pair of ugly black handguns. "There is no safety. Just point and shoot. Do not hesitate to take her out. Do. Not. Hesitate. Killing her will put her far enough away long enough to give you a chance to run."

There was nothing to dispute, and she nodded dumbly, taking the gun from him. Copying him, she jammed it down the back of her jeans and hoped she didn't shoot her ass off.

"Whatever happens, if you can get away and I die, when I come back I will find you, without fail."

He held her eyes until she looked away, trying to breathe, trying to think. He put the car in gear and they drove the rest of the short way, every foot bringing them closer to Amara.

Hannah knew what she hoped she would do when the time came. If she could prevent Amara from harming the innocent people involved, be selfless and willing to sacrifice even herself, she would have accomplished something in her short life. She wanted to be brave; she hoped she could be. But being brave and putting away your fear was one thing in theory; reality, she knew very well, was very different.

Asher parked on the little widening of the road where the sheriff had looked for the inhabitants of the white SUV. Sheriff Morgan was in danger because he was doing his job, had gone above and beyond it looking out for her. Hannah sent up a brief prayer that he would make it out alive.

She took a step toward the embankment, but Asher pulled her back.

"Take these," he said, putting the car keys in her coat pocket and zipping it shut. "If something happens to me, I do not want them to disappear with me." She nodded woodenly. "If you can get away, take the car and drive, fast and far. Everything you need is in it."

He went ahead, taking the step down the small incline, then reaching a hand up for her. He didn't let go of it immediately but paused to look at her, nodding with determination. She knew how naive she was to hope this would end differently than they imagined. Asher's face told her she was walking to her end.

# 20

There was a haze in the air and tendrils of smoke were curling through the trees. The smell of char was heavy even this far from the house, and Hannah thought she could hear the fire, a low crackle behind the sound of their feet. Her home was settling into ruin. Not long ago it seemed so important. It felt like a meaningless detail right now. Chances were she would never see it again anyway, so did it matter if it stood?

They were only a few yards from the small clearing behind her house where the creek lay like a frozen snake across the snowy ground. They hesitated a moment, Hannah behind Asher's broad back, before stepping out into the open space.

Two bodies in the familiar green of the sheriff's department uniform lay neatly side by side on the ground, unmoving.

"Run," Asher hissed. Hannah turned but was stopped before she could take a step by a figure appearing on the path in front of her.

"I shot the sheriff." The woman laughed melodiously. "Might be my first one. I've been wanting to say that since nineteen seventy-three." She paused then added as an afterthought, "The deputy I strangled."

Asher grabbed Hannah with one hand and pushed her squarely behind him.

Amara smirked. "So gallant. You always did have a protective streak when it came to the fairer sex. And you have a little incentive in this case, even more than your usual sentimental garbage." Amara took a step toward them and Asher walked backward, pushing Hannah as he moved. She had no idea what Amara meant, and she couldn't see Asher's face to gauge his reaction.

Hannah could see Amara though, just barely, through the small gap between Asher's arm and side. They were twins; there was no doubting the connection when you saw them together. Her honey-golden hair exactly matched his, and was long and as shiny as burnished metal, falling to the middle of her back in waves. She was tall, statuesque—though where Asher was broad and muscular, she was gracefully curvy. The only real difference was in their faces. Their features were similar, and both were unusually beautiful, to be sure, but her face was not softened by anything like human emotion. Her eyes were the same strange shade of blue-gray as Asher's, but flinty and cold. She had a face that could match any woman in the world, but her perfect lips were marred by the twist of her sneer.

"Nothing to say? No surprise there," Amara said. "Hannah dear, my brother never was the sharpest tool in the shed."

Amara reached inside her jacket and swiftly pulled out a small, snub-nosed handgun. Asher stiffened and shifted slightly, blocking Hannah's view again. Hannah reached back and fingered the gun wedged against her own back, ice cold against her bare skin.

"Step aside, brother. I'd like to see your new little friend face to face. You really can't take a person's measure as completely from a distance," Amara said. "And she's been rather shy of late; you both have. That tart from the grocery store didn't have any idea where you went, despite how intimately attached she claimed you were. Changed her tune pretty quickly though. Couldn't take the heat." Amara flicked her eyes toward Hannah's house and laughed at her own joke. "The poor little sheriff didn't have any better idea. Funny he ended up being so useless when he's the whole reason I was able to find you in the first place. Between that police sketch and the accident photos in the paper, he might as well have called to give me directions to town." She nudged the still form with the toe of her black leather boot. "Granted, neither he or the little boy deputy here knew where you'd run off to. Their little fireman friends didn't either. Necks like twigs." She sighed dramatically. "They really don't make them like they used to." Amara laughed, a sound like fingernails tapping at a wine glass. "I knew you had to be around here somewhere and probably could have found you in five more minutes, so telling me where you were wouldn't have helped them anyway. I just wanted to make sure you understood the seriousness of the situation and didn't do anything silly like trying to run. My brother is a coward by nature, so I'm sure he made you that offer first."

"Sister, you always did talk too much." Asher's hand whipped behind him before the words even left his mouth. Two shots sounded in quick succession.

Hannah looked at Amara. She stood calmly, both of her hands on her gun, legs wide, smoke drifting upward from the muzzle. She'd fired so quickly Hannah hadn't even seen her move, drawing the gun before Asher had even reached his.

There was a groan, and Asher crashed to the ground in front of Hannah.

"And you always were far, far slower than me." Amara lowered her gun and walked coolly toward them as Asher rolled over, both of his legs shattered and useless, the flesh shredded over shin bones that were separated into wet red splinters.

"He's not bright, Hannah. I know he probably seems rather impressive at first, but you haven't had much by way of comparison. I honestly can't believe he even managed to find you." She nudged her brother's writhing form, then stepped on his shoulder to pin him down. "Did you think you could take me out, Ashy-boy? Just for that I'm going to keep shooting my way up until you're just a big ugly head."

Hannah backed up a step, then two. Amara whipped her gun back up to stop her. "Not so fast, little girl. You stay right there while the grownups talk."

"Run, Hannah," Asher gasped. She could see his hand trying to work its way under his back for his gun.

"I wouldn't do that, Hannah." Amara turned back to Asher, moving her foot from his shoulder. "You are ridiculous, brother." She pointed the weapon down and fired a shot into each of his shoulders. Hannah retched at the sight, his arms nearly severed by the bullets.

Amara sighed. "Pathetic." She put one more in his chest.

Crack! Crack! Flowers of red bloomed on Amara's shoulder and arm, and she flew backward. Hannah was shaking so hard she dropped the gun she'd just fired, fumbling to pick it up before she covered the steps to Asher.

"What are you doing? Run!" Asher's voice was gurgling, a bloody bubble erupting from his lips. It was like that first night all over again, the beautiful face covered with blood, color draining from the skin. "I will find you. Run ..."

He didn't finish, but Hannah knew he was right; she needed to go. His head rolled off toward where his sister lay. Or where she had been lying. Now there was only blood on the snow. Amara was gone.

Hannah looked back at Asher. He had gone silent but was still there, somehow hanging on to life by a thread. She turned and ran.

Trying to keep the gun in front of her, scanning side to side, she retraced the path toward the road. She was shaking so badly she stumbled, going down hard, knees painfully ramming into the ground. Rolling over on her side, pushing herself back up, Hannah looked behind her desperately, waiting for Amara to come crashing through the branches after her. When no one appeared, Hannah pulled herself to her feet and kept moving. If only Amara was injured badly enough, or would just go ahead and die, then maybe Hannah could stay ahead of her and make it to the car.

She thought she heard something. Stopping abruptly, Hannah threw herself down again and listened, waiting for the sound of pursuit. She didn't hear anything, but she knew how stealthy Asher had been; she had to assume Amara was at least as silent. She wished Amara was dead silent, from the bullets Hannah had managed to put in her, but she wasn't foolish enough to bet her life on it, without knowing for sure. There had been blood on the snow where Amara had fallen, and that meant she had gotten up off the ground. There was a good chance she was out there somewhere.

Trying to be quiet, Hannah started again, then quickly stumbled over a hidden branch and did a full somersault, crashing against a tree. Cursing, she staggered to her feet. The gun had flown out of her hand, and she scrabbled around in the snow, trying to find it. Where the hell was the gun?

An unbearable searing pain ripped through her right arm just as she closed her hand around the gun, the bullet catching her a split second before she heard the report. Almost instantly her entire side was slick with blood. Forcing herself to her feet, Hannah lunged forward and scrambled up the last bit of trail, over the ditch and up the embankment to the car. She almost made it.

"Oh. Very nice try. Almost, but not quite."

Hannah spun around, pointing the gun one-handed at Amara, who was standing in front of her in the middle of the snowy road, her weapon raised. Her jacket was shredded from the entry of the two shots Hannah had fired, the shirt underneath slick and pasted to her body with blood. It was running down through her pants and off her boot into the snow, traceable backward in a trail of red and pink footprints into the woods. Despite her wounds, Amara stood upright, coolly evaluating Hannah.

"Now I know I'm supposed to deliver you alive, but alive is a pretty broad term, and I'm beginning to care less and less about what condition you're in when you get there. Too bad my idiot brother didn't make it. I'd rather give him the pleasure of watching you squirm a little. Oh well, he'll be back again soon enough. I have nothing but time." She smiled. "Unlike you."

Hannah pulled the trigger again, but the shot disappeared into the air. She struggled to level the gun for another shot. Amara didn't even flinch.

"Dumb luck the first time around, just as I thought." She leveled her gun at Hannah. "My turn. I think I'll shoot your feet off, one at a time, just to see how far you can get. I'm sure I can find something to cauterize the stumps with before you bleed to death. Maybe your house."

She lowered the weapon toward Hannah's feet and her finger

twitched on the trigger. Amara took one more step forward and smiled an evil smile. Then her head exploded into a fine, red mist.

Hannah looked in the direction the bullet she hadn't fired had come from, then back to where Amara had been standing. She was gone; there wasn't a drop of blood or a shred of clothing, just a trail of footprints in the snow that stopped abruptly in the middle of the road.

Taking a step back toward the woods, Hannah started to open her mouth and call out to Asher, but she froze. Asher was dead or near to it. There was no way he could have made it from where he had fallen and fired that shot. And the way Amara's head had disappeared, it hadn't been done with the handgun Asher was carrying. That meant there was someone else out there with them in the woods, someone with a very big gun.

Maybe the sheriff or his deputy hadn't really been dead. Maybe someone had heard all the commotion and come to her aid. Whomever it was, Hannah was grateful for the favor. But she didn't intend to wait around to thank them. Hannah held her tongue and stepped backward, then turned toward the car. Because there was also a chance the shooter had been someone with the same intentions as Amara. Dazed, dizzy, and bleeding, Hannah threw herself into the car and tore away, swerving, down the empty, snowy road.

# 21

Hannah was positive not a single person that made an action movie had ever really been shot, because they had it all wrong. On film a person takes a bullet and still manages to not only avoid bleeding to death, but continues to barrel around like nothing happened, all without crying or puking or fainting. She was alternating between all three, the pain in her arm like nothing she'd ever experienced—and she'd fallen off a bridge a few days ago. *And you thought that was as bad as it could get.* Hannah laughed at herself a little crazily, then shook her head, fighting to stay conscious, her one working hand white-knuckled on the wheel. She was trying to put as many miles as she could between herself and the town before she couldn't go any farther.

That, it turned out, was not nearly as many miles as she'd hoped. Her vision went fuzzy, and Hannah drifted away for a second, veering into oncoming traffic. She jerked the wheel and swerved back into her own lane just in time to avoid a dump truck. While the angry blast of the horn faded away, she gave up and pulled over to the side of the road. It was a terrible place to have to stop, exposed and visible to every passing car, but she didn't have much choice.

She hadn't yet looked at where the bullet had struck her, and she didn't want to. It felt like a red-hot poker was being plunged into her arm every time her heart beat. After she did look, she didn't feel any better.

From what she could tell—which wasn't a great deal because her eyes swam with black spots whenever she turned her head—the bullet

161

had just managed to catch her on the top side of the arm below her shoulder. It hadn't gone deep enough to strike bone, but it had been too shallow to pass through cleanly either, instead biting off a great chunk of flesh. She toed off her boot and pulled off one of her long knit socks, wrapping it around her upper arm and tying it semi-securely with the help of her teeth. Then she leaned back and closed her eyes, breathing against the pain.

The SUV rocked in the wind every time a truck blew by, reminding her how visible she was here on the road. Keeping her eyes laser-focused on the lines, Hannah pulled carefully back into the traffic. She couldn't keep going forever, but she needed to keep it together just a little bit longer. Hannah had an idea of where she could stop for a while.

The familiar road sign made her sigh with relief and she exited carefully. Finding a place in the farthest corner of the busy Walmart parking lot, she locked the doors and passed out.

---

It was the freezing cold that woke her instead of the pain. Confused and disoriented, Hannah jerked upright, smacking her head against the glass next to her face. The car window was opaque where her breath had created a skin of ice on the glass.

Her entire body felt numb and locked in ice, the way it had felt when she'd woken up after being in the river. Except for her arm. The pain might not be what had woken her, but it was still there and returning with a vengeance, her arm throbbing and refusing to move. A viscous trail had flowed down her sleeve and made a slushy puddle like a cherry icee in the space between the seat and door. At least the bleeding had stopped. Closing her eyes, Hannah rejoiced that she had woken up at all.

She reached forward to start the car. It took her a couple fumbling numb-fingered tries before it purred to life.

"... one tonight with a low of twenty-two. Current road conditions are looking good, though if you're traveling on back roads, keep in mind crews are still working on digging out from that last snowfall. Expect a delay unrelated to the weather if you're going to be traveling in the vicinity of Milltown on fourteen or any of the surrounding roads. We have reports coming in about a dwelling fire resulting in multiple fatalities. Police have the roads ..."

Slapping at the dials, Hannah finally got the radio to turn off. It seemed to take forever for the heat from the vent to feel warm against her good hand, and even longer for it to penetrate her skin. As the frozenness inside her began to thaw out, tears did too, starting with a trickle, then streaming down her face. She thought about the sheriff, Sheila, the deputy, and god knew how many other innocent people who just happened to be in the way. She pictured their bodies scattered across her yard, mowed down in a ring around the charred remains of her house. All dead, all for nothing.

Wiping her tears away, wishing she could wipe away her memories as easily, Hannah tried to figure out the why. It bothered her as she replayed the events in her mind. She and Asher had been wrong, it seemed—not about who was after them, but about her motivation. This was more than Asher's sister tormenting him. There was another reason, and if Amara was telling the truth, she wanted Hannah alive, and for someone else. Hannah was someone else's target. That made less sense than anything. She was just a random unwitting piece in Amara's sick never-ending game with Asher, wasn't she?

*And where are you now, Asher?* How much time had he spent lying on the snow, clinging to life and suffering before melting away? Chances were he hadn't lasted much longer. She hoped not, then thought how strange to sit there hoping someone died quickly, in the midst of all this death. But for him it would mean he was alive now, healed and perfect. *I know you're out there. At least there's that. But where?*

He'd said he would find her, but if he was smart he would go far away. What was the point anyway? She might not survive the gunshot, let alone successfully evade Amara much longer. She wanted Asher to escape. She wanted Asher to find her. She wanted a handful of pain medication and a warm bed. She didn't know what she wanted.

*Everything you need is in the car.* That was what he'd said. It'd better be, because Hannah had nothing left—no home, no wallet, no phone, no ID. If she was going to have any chance at all, she needed to get patched up, get over the weepy self-pity, and get on the road and disappear.

———

The sound of her blood-soaked coat sleeve peeling off the leather seat was almost as nauseating as the pain that came after it. She looked around, hoping the loud cursing that accompanied it hadn't drawn any attention. There was hardly anyone around, only a few late-night shoppers far across the parking lot.

Giving herself a moment to recover, she quietly opened the door and stepped out into the freezing air, then slipped into the back seat. She was quickly disappointed. There was nothing there, not in the seat pockets or on the floor. Again she got out of the car, this time opening the hatch to find a spotless empty space. Feeling around with her good hand, she found the tiny loop she had hoped for and lifted up the flap to the compartment that held the spare tire. There was a black bag in the space next to the jack, and a triangular emergency roadside kit jammed underneath it. She grabbed them both and gratefully locked herself back into the warm front seat.

It took a minute for the dots in front of her eyes to fade, but as soon as she could see straight, she tore through the bags. The emergency roadside kit came first out of necessity. She could feel blood beginning to trickle down her arm again, warmer than her skin and making its way toward her hand.

There was a surprisingly large number of items packaged like a puzzle inside the hazard triangle, most of which were of no use to her right now. Setting the pair of canvas gloves sealed in plastic and the roll of duct tape aside, she tossed everything else into the back seat.

Getting out of her clothing was slow and agonizing. Her coat and the sweater underneath it had dried to her skin, and pulling them off felt like being shot all over again. She pressed the folded gloves over the raw wound, hoping whatever they were made of was at least remotely sterile, then wrapped the duct tape around her arm several times to hold the gloves in place. She tore the tape with her teeth and tucked the edge under her arm.

Time for the backpack. The zippered front pocket held a phone charger, a pen, and a small flashlight. Zipping them back up, she opened the main compartment where she found a change of men's clothes, a small leather toiletry bag, and a black jacket of windbreaker weight. There wasn't anything else in the main compartment, but the bag was obviously heavier than it should be, and Hannah ran her fingers around the bottom until she found a small recessed zipper.

First, she pulled out a small, thick envelope. Inside was a stack of passports, US, British, Canadian, French, Israeli, followed by driver's licenses from states across the country. All had pictures of Asher with different names. Interesting, but absolutely useless. Next was a brick-shaped package wrapped in black plastic, taped tightly. She slit the side open with her nail and sighed with relief; a brick of cash, all big bills, all US dollars. *Thank you, Asher.* Finally, she pulled out a stack of credit cards. Hannah turned the inch-thick bundle of plastic over in her hand. She took off the rubber band and thumbed through them.

She almost missed it. One felt thinner than the others, and when she flipped it over she found a business card, the cheap glossy kind you design online and have shipped to yourself five hundred at a time. The edges were rounded at the corners, trimmed to match the shape of the credit cards. One side was blank, shiny black, the other with generic clip art of a bar, mirrored and lined with bottles. The white type was difficult to decipher, but she eventually made out "The Next Whiskey Bar" 12 Main Street, Falder, Alabama.

That was all.

----●+●●●----

She was still a bloody, woozy mess, but she covered it up the best she could, changing into Asher's clothes, the rolled-up pants mostly covering her bloody boot, black jacket with the hood up on top of her mangled coat. Pushing the cart through Walmart, she kept her head down, picking up what she needed most desperately as quickly as she could. She tossed a tube of antibiotic cream on top of the mountain of first aid supplies. Under all the gauze and bandages were cheap slip-on shoes, a change of clothes, and whatever food had been on the end caps of the aisles.

"Are you okay, dear?"

Hannah jumped, backing into an aisle and sending an avalanche of cereal boxes to the floor. The speaker was a stranger, a bundled-up middle-aged lady pushing an overloaded cart full of food. She wasn't looking at Hannah, but down on the floor. There was a snail trail of blood dribbling from the sleeve of her coat. Hannah traced it back around the end of the aisle and out of sight.

"Goodness. That doesn't look good. Let me call—"

"It's nothing. I must of …" Hannah didn't bother to finish fake explaining. She darted away, plowing her cart through the scattering of boxes, and tucked the end of her sleeve up to stop the blood.

Checking behind her, thankful the woman's concern hadn't gone far enough to make her follow, Hannah threw in an armful of bottled waters and energy drinks from the cooler and awkwardly used the self-checkout, paying with a crisp hundred dollar bill from the stack. By the time she made it across the parking lot to the car she was shaking and light-headed from the blood loss.

Washing down a handful of pills with a tall can of tinny tasting energy drink, waiting for both to kick in, she tended to her arm a little more thoroughly. Biting her tongue against the burn, she smeared the wound with a gob of ointment, taped down a thick layer of gauze, and wrapped it all up with an ace bandage. Then she cleaned herself up as best she could and finally pulled on the new clothes. It was an unfortunate looking sweatsuit, pastel and tacky as hell, but clean and dry at least. If she could find a gray wig, maybe she could hide from Amara in a retirement community somewhere.

She reached out and poked the button for the radio.

"… unfolding. The newest reports have increased the number of fatalities to at least eleven, and so far none appear to be related to the fire. Fire departments from as far ..."

Hannah wasn't safe by a long shot, and she wasn't certain of anything, except that she couldn't stay here. In a normal world she could drive back the way she'd come and turn herself in, explain what had happened, ask for help, for protection. Maybe they'd put her in the hospital. Maybe they'd put her in a jail cell. But Hannah didn't think for a moment there was a cell that would keep Amara out, or that she would hesitate for even a second to pile up a mountain of bodies, if that's what it took to get to Hannah.

So there was no turning back. Pulling out of the parking lot, she followed the signs heading south, trading sips of energy drink with scoops of peanut butter from the jar. It was better to be moving. Hannah wasn't safe but she was alive. She had food and gas and money, and at least a direction in which to drive.

She hoped it was the right direction. Maybe Asher had been to the bar on the card once and crammed the piece of paper in with his credit cards, swiftly forgetting about it. Considering the neat bundles and organized bag, Hannah doubted it. He said everything she needed was in the bag, and while she couldn't claim to know him well, she didn't think he did too many things without intention. He said he would find her, and hopefully this was how.

*Was this what you meant? Are you going to be there when I get there, Asher?*

———◆•◆•◆———

There was plenty of time for wondering. The angle she was driving across Virginia made it seem endless, and by the time she crossed the border into North Carolina, Hannah was desperate for rest. She'd been riding a wave of caffeine and sugar through the state, but the crash was coming. Things were appearing in the rearview mirror that weren't there, making her slam on her brakes for phantom police cars and swerve to miss something that looked like a llama but disappeared as she passed by.

At a rest stop Hannah found a corner as far from the facilities as possible and parked, grateful the windows were heavily tinted against prying eyes. She fell asleep instantly, but the rest was fitful and short, ending when her arm began screaming for attention. The over-the-counter pain medication barely made a dent in the pain, but it was better than nothing, and she quickly chewed another handful, choked down the bitterness, and got back on the road.

It occurred to her that someone could be tracking the car. The thought bothered her, but there wasn't anything she could do about it. Hannah considered stealing a different car, but even on the slim chance she managed to pull it off, there were just too many ways that could go south. Buying one without drawing attention wasn't a much better idea, and she wanted to conserve the cash, hoping to be alive long enough to need it. Hannah toyed with some other options, places she could go to disappear, cutting all ties to where she had come from, but none of them seemed completely safe. As far as she could tell, she didn't have a better option than to keep going, driving toward some unknown bar in Alabama.

*Almost there. If this was a bad idea and I'm about to drive a stolen car full of fake IDs and a brick of unmarked bills across yet another state line, you need to give me a sign.*

Nothing. No light from the heavens, no sudden rainbow.

But there was a sign. It was green and white and it said *Welcome to Sweet Home Alabama.* Better than nothing. She watched it pass, finally disappearing in her rearview mirror.

The hills had flattened out into large tracts of featureless land and sunshine reflecting through the window. When she stopped outside Birmingham for gas, Hannah stood for a moment, letting the sun warm her face. She unzipped the jacket and started to take it off, then pulled it back on over the red and brown mess seeping through the arm of her sweatshirt. She hoped with frequent smears of antibiotic cream and flat-out good fortune that she'd managed to avoid getting an infection, but the wound was still mostly open and wept bloody fluid that soaked the bandages and glued the gauze painfully to her skin.

The GPS in the car could only tell her where her destination was on the map, and the most she could gather was that it was in a wide swath of commercial properties on the outskirts of a town called Falder. Unless it was located in the middle of a war zone, she was going to have to do something about her appearance.

# 22

Catching a glimpse of herself in the window next to her, Hannah decided she was acceptably disguised, barely resembling the person who had driven into town four days earlier. She certainly felt like an entirely different person.

"Do you want another one?" the waitress asked. Hannah nodded, sliding a ten-dollar bill under the empty mug in front of her and pushing it to the end of the table where it was swiftly replaced with a full one. The screen of the tablet propped up against the sugar went black and she tapped it with her index finger to bring it back to life. It was mostly there for window dressing, open to the first free ebook she could find after fighting the urge to look at the news from home.

Hannah had no idea who besides Amara might be trying to locate her, and she had no idea how sophisticated their means were, so she resisted searching for her own name or any of the people who were continually crossing her mind. Maybe she'd seen too many high-tech espionage movies, but out of caution she stuck to the most visible headline news and worldwide stories.

The brutal murders of every resident of an apartment building in Buenos Aires made her think of Asher and the story he had told her of Roman. The story about the unexplained deaths of an entire volunteer fire department and several other residents of a small town in Pennsylvania made her cry, the drops making pale circles in the artsy leaf swirled onto the top of her drink.

The shape of a man getting out of a truck and walking through the door of the dive bar across the street made her pause for a moment. Nope. Too small. She adjusted her hat, snugging it down a little more, pulling the strands of her wig in front of her face.

"Thanks," Hannah murmured, but she didn't make eye contact with the waitress as the woman dropped off Hannah's change.

Her scalp was sweating and scratchy, and she thought about taking off the hat, but resisted. She wiggled a finger up into her hairline and itched irritably instead. The hat had enough brim to hide her face fairly well and helped disguise that the dishwater-blonde wig was, on close inspection, cheap and plasticky.

The backpack was propped up on the chair beside her, but everything else that had traveled south with her was in the trash can of a truck stop bathroom. Staying in one place waiting for Asher to show was risky, so she shed everything that might identify her.

At a crowded outlet mall she'd done her best to melt into the crowd and purchased jeans and a shirt more appropriate for the nicer weather, and dark, so it wouldn't show blood from her still-seeping arm. She also bought the cheap tablet and an insanely expensive pair of leather boots. The money in the bag wouldn't last forever if she had to keep running, but she might not last that long either. When she considered the boots might be her last pair, she let her guilt slide about the cost.

Her next item of business, at a truck stop off the interstate, had not been at all what she expected; these places were definitely not getting the credit they deserved. Hannah bought a ticket from a machine and wolfed down a smoking hot burrito while she waited for her number to come up.

After days of sleeping in the car, encrusted with blood, being able to lock herself into a private shower with an unlimited supply of hot water was a blissful experience. She let it wash over her, dissolving the blood and dirt, stinging as it ran over the wound in her arm. For the first time she saw it completely in the light; it was angry and deep, though there were no telltale streaks of a spreading infection. She stood under the spray until the heat began to make her light-headed.

Stuffing the clothes she had arrived in deep into the trash can, she re-bandaged her arm and put on her new clothes. She bundled her braided damp hair into a knot at the back of her neck, crammed it up under the wig, pulled the military-looking soft cap over the top. When she reluctantly left the steamy comfort and privacy of the truck stop shower, Hannah was a stranger from the woman who had walked in.

Since then she had quickly settled into a schedule of vigilantly watching the bar while it was open—which turned out to be most of the time—and fitfully sleeping in the back of the SUV when it wasn't, waking up to park it somewhere new periodically to avoid notice. Today was going to be different, she finally decided. If she didn't see Asher walk into the bar, she was going to go in and scope the place out. Then she was going to leave. To where, she hadn't decided.

It was Friday night and the quiet weekday street was marginally busier, though not as busy as Hannah would have liked. There wasn't anything that resembled a crowd to blend into, but that might change. It was early yet, not quite dark. Parked up the street and across from the bar, she had a clear view of the front door, which swung open and shut to let early evening drinkers in and out. She hoped she was invisible behind the tinted windows in the half light.

Her stomach grumbled, and she wished she'd had something more than a muffin and an obscene number of lattes today, but she tamped down her hunger. She could wait, and besides, this might be it. She might have to make a run for it soon. The thought tightened her stomach and her wallet.

Speaking of her wallet, a big man with a shiny bald head and a leather vest with no shirt on underneath dragged a bar stool outside of the door and planted himself on it. Guess she was stuck paying the cover charge. It was appropriate really, she mused, paying the charge to get into the bar, because cover was exactly what she needed.

Hannah kept her head down, hat on, until she came to the door. This was going to be the hard part. She didn't have an ID, so all she could do was hope she appeared as old as she felt right now, which was closer to a senior citizen. Taking a deep breath, she willed herself to look confident instead of guilty, but she was pretty sure the look on her face just came across as deranged.

"Ladies night. No cover for the gals," the bouncer said, looking to the next person in line. It was almost disappointing.

It was fuller than it looked from the outside, and Hannah pushed her way into a wall of music. She quickly ducked out of the entry and then had to scoot away again, out of the middle of a game of darts she'd blundered into. Trying not to do anything else to draw attention, she wove her way around the clutches of people and deeper into the bar.

The four-top tables along the left-hand wall were all taken, with people filling the spaces between them and lined up in front of the bar that ran the entire length of the opposite wall. The back of the room opened up like the top of a T, where a band was pounding out southern rock at a deafening level.

After carefully threading her way the length of the room, Hannah slid into the small space where the bar made an L against the wall, between two guys with shot glasses in their hands and a busty brunette trying to use her assets to get the bartender's attention.

It wasn't working. The girl leaned further across the bar with an exaggerated huff. Hannah scanned the crowded room, not seeing any familiar faces, which she expected, and not seeing any turned her direction either, which was reassuring. She looked up in surprise as a glass on a round cardboard coaster slid in front of her.

"Hey!" the brunette whined.

"Lulu, I know you aren't even close to twenty-one. Now get out of here before I call your father." Lulu's eyes widened, and she melted backward into the crowd.

"Now I asked him what you drank and he didn't think that was pertinent information, but I take you for a vodka girl."

Looking up in surprise, Hannah saw the bartender smiling at her with kind, faded blue eyes. His wild chocolate-brown hair was curling down in front of one of them, and he flipped it away with a practiced toss of his head, grinning impishly.

"I've been wondering how long you were going to sit and window shop before coming in," he said. "I was about to step across the street and get you myself."

Hannah started to back slowly away, hemmed in by people on all sides.

"Don't worry, Hannah, the big guy warned me you might be coming. You're safe with me. I'll keep your glass full and you just stay put until I close down this madhouse."

"Hey dude, dude." A loud young man wearing a backward baseball cap was standing on the rail, waving a twenty.

The bartender sighed with a mock beleaguered look and went back to work, deftly popping the caps off bottles two at a time, pouring drinks without seeming to pay attention. He managed it all effortlessly while chatting up flirting women with a roguish glint in his eye.

Before the space vacated by the underage Lulu was squeezed shut, Hannah slid onto the cracked black leather bar stool, still scanning the crowd. This could be the opposite of what it seemed to be, but if Amara or the bartender or anyone else was a part of this and that far ahead of the game, then Hannah was trapped and screwed. She might as well enjoy what could be her last drink.

Besides, the bartender was right. Apparently she was a vodka girl. Who knew? Sipping from the deliciously sweet drink in front of her, she tried to will away the feelings of unease and claustrophobia, find something enjoyable about the music in all its off-key, rowdy glory.

A fresh drink replaced the unfinished one in front of her, this one an artificial turquoise color with a flashing plastic ice cube in it, making it turn purple then back to blue at a steady tempo.

"They aren't poisoned. Promise." The bartender winked, leaning an arm on the bar. The noise was all voices now, laughter and loud drunkenness while the band took a break.

It had crossed her mind. But if it was drugged or roofied or whatever you could put in a drink, it was slow acting. She felt fine, except for being the slightest bit buzzed from drinking on an empty stomach.

"I'm Gabe, by the way." He smiled and was gone again, catching up the impatient queue at the bar while the band pretended to tune up before their next set.

The flashing colors were hypnotic, and the new drink was so delicious that she'd drained half of it in one long pull, watching it shift from color to color as the level dropped. There were scattered dots of flashing drinks all over the bar, held above swaying hands on the dance floor, sliding across the bar. One of them was flying.

The glass sailed through the air and shattered against the wall. A human wave surged toward the dance floor as a man grabbed another man by the shirt and took a wild swing at his head. Someone slammed into them from behind, the fighters quickly growing to three then to six as the brawlers' friends lunged in. The leather-vested bouncer pushed his way through and launched himself into the fray, then went down, disappearing into the pile and not emerging. Bottles were flying, one smashing into the line of whiskey bottles behind the bar. Gabe ducked another projectile glass, then, pushing off on one hand, gracefully cleared the bar and jumped into the middle of the melee. It didn't appear to do much good. Even the band stopped to enjoy the entertainment.

Suddenly the fight surged in her direction and she tried to squeeze herself out of the way. There was nowhere to go but into the wall. A body hurtled toward her, and she cringed to avoid the impact.

It never came. Instead a human form flew in the opposite direction, the people closest to her falling back, shoved clear.

"You cannot stay out of danger anywhere, can you?"

# 23

Hannah clung to Asher for a full minute, unembarrassed, not caring at all if he stood still as a statue. He had picked her up and bull-dozed his way through the crowd, putting her down in the small office through the back, the chaos from the bar now just a dull roar behind the closed door.

Asher was here, in front of her. That she was relieved was an understatement. That she was slightly intoxicated was not, but it wasn't enough to completely dull the pain that made her whimper involuntarily when he grabbed her by the shoulders to look at her.

"What it is?" He looked concerned, drawing back.

"Nothing. Gunshot. It's fine, really. I'm so glad you're here." She threw her arms around his waist again, and he patted her back awk-wardly. After tolerating it for a moment, he gently unclamped her arms.

"Let me see." He sat her down on the desk and motioned for her to pull up her sleeve.

"It's fine."

"Do not act like a child. Let me see it. Maybe Gabriel can find a physician that can be trusted, if we need to."

"Fine." She slid her arm painfully out of her sleeve and hiked one side of her shirt up over the bandage.

"My, my, not here for five minutes and already the clothes are coming off." Gabe stood, hands on his hips, leaning against the door-frame. Hannah pulled her shirt down quickly and tried to stuff her arm back in the sleeve, wincing with the movement.

"Don't stop on my account." He threw her a naughty smile.

"Gabriel, she has been shot, for mercy's sake. And when I arrive I find her about to be crushed in a bar brawl. I was hoping she would find her way here and you would look out for her." Asher was glaring at Gabe, who looked no less amused than he had a moment ago.

"Relax, Asher. She seems fine to me. In fact, she's been in town for a couple days casing the joint. Maybe longer, since she's been rather sly and I didn't pick her out first thing. I'm looking forward to seeing what's underneath that wig." He grinned at Hannah. "Anyway, she seems very capable of taking care of herself."

Asher sighed and shook his head, turning his back to Gabe.

"I'll leave you love birds to it then, before the natives tear the place down. Apartment's open." Gabe threw Hannah a wink and headed back to the thumping bass of the bar. Hannah managed not to wink back, since Asher was staring at her disapprovingly.

The apartment turned out to be directly above the bar, the exposed brick walls and wood floor doing little to muffle the band's final number below. Hannah was holding carefully still while Asher unwrapped the ace bandage from around her arm, pulling it gently, trying not to hurt her.

"How did you do it?" He stopped unwrapping where the bandage was firmly crusted to her arm.

"Do what?" If he meant bandage her arm, poorly was how, based on the way it was cemented to her skin.

"How did you get away?" Asher crossed to the kitchenette that made up one wall of the room, then ran warm water into a bowl and threw a dish towel into it.

She told him the story while he dabbed at her arm, loosening up the gauze.

"So I take it that means it wasn't you?" she asked.

He shook his head without looking up, the bandage sopping, water dribbling down to her fingers.

"I wasn't sure. I didn't wait around to find out."

177

"Good. Because I was still on the ground at that point. The last thing I remember ..." He paused for a moment, turning away to rinse the rag in the bowl of pale pink water. "The last thing I remember is staring down the barrel of my sister's gun, knowing I was going to wake up to find I had failed to protect you."

If she hadn't been so distracted by the swift and painful removal of the last layer of gauze, she would have sworn he was choked up. Or maybe it was because he caught a look at her arm, because when she looked at it, she felt a little uneven herself.

The wound might not have been life-threatening, but just because it didn't look gangrenous right now didn't mean it was going to stay that way. There was definitely what was shaping up to be a permanent depression in her upper arm, a gouge that was currently a raw, open mess. There was an angry looking red ring around it that didn't look too promising, and the whole area felt numb and clumsy. She wondered what muscles and nerves might be permanently damaged, what feeling and movement she might never get back.

"Jesus, Hannah." Asher sat back on his heels beside where she lay on the couch.

"Is he here too?"

He shook his head, unamused. "Do not change the subject. This is very bad."

"Tell me what happened after that," she said.

"After what?" He was still staring at her arm.

"After you died, what else? I found your clue and got out of town almost a week ago. Where have you been?"

Hannah pulled her shirt back on over her uncooperative arm without putting a new bandage on it, letting the wound get some air, and to get him to stop staring at it and start talking.

"I woke up in a field across from a big store," he said. "I do not know why, but for some reason I ended up nearly forty miles from where we last were. Unfortunately, before I could manage to make it back to find out what had happened to you or track down my sister, I was hindered by law enforcement."

"Hindered by law enforcement, what does that mean? Did you get arrested?" She leaned back against the arm of the couch and raised an eyebrow at him. "And why were you 'hindered'?"

"Public indecency. Anyway, it took some time to sort out the situation and by then—"

Hannah laughed out loud, then slapped her hand across her mouth. "Public indecency? Wait, did you get picked up for streaking? Please tell me there weren't any kids around."

Asher didn't look as entertained as she absolutely was. "As you know, the nudity is one of the perils of my lifestyle."

"Where do your clothes go?"

He looked at her like she was crazy. "Of everything that is going on, this is your biggest concern?"

She snorted. "Maybe not my biggest, but I know you don't leave them behind, and you keep coming back without them, so where do they go?"

He shrugged. "I have no idea. For all I know there is a patch of wallets, watches, and men's briefs floating around in the vastness of space."

"That's sad. What if you had something important on?" She stretched her tired legs out on the couch, turning over to lie on her good side. It was nice to not be scrunched up in the car. Hannah yanked off her wig and hat and shook out her hair, itching her scalp with relief.

"One learns quickly never to carry anything of great value. In this day and age, I have certainly learned not to carry both sets of car keys on me." He had pulled out a cell phone and started to type, then he hesitated. "I feel like you should see a doctor, but I would hate to risk revealing our location. I trust Gabriel, but I know no one around here. There is a person I can try to make contact with, but I cannot be sure if they are in a location or position to help."

She waved him off, sleepy and relatively comfortable, her arm only throbbing dully thanks to the help of the vodka. "How do you know Gabe? He's one of you, isn't he?"

Asher nodded at her, leaning back tiredly against the loveseat that sat at an angle to the couch. It was good to see his face. The shadow of stubble on his jaw he was scratching at mindlessly had grown long enough to look soft, a reddish-gold beard darker than his hair. He looked as exhausted as she felt, though the shadow under his eyes lent gravitas to his face, rather than the haggardness it did hers.

"Gabriel is like me. I wondered if you would pick up on that. I have known him for a great many lifetimes, and he is one of very few people I believe I can trust. He is also the biggest Lothario in the history of womanizers." He smiled. "He will tell you he was the inspiration for Don Juan, and I am not sure he is lying."

Hannah yawned hugely, unable to catch herself, covering her gaping jaw with her hand.

"You should get some sleep while you have the opportunity. There is no way of knowing how long it will be advisable to stay here."

She blinked herself awake and shook her head. "Not until I hear what happened. I believe you were naked and under arrest?"

Rolling his eyes, he grabbed a neatly folded blanket from the arm of the couch and threw it over her.

"Fine. As I was saying, I found myself in the parking lot of a large store. Sadly, I was noticed by some shoppers, as those horrendous places are open all hours, and apparently buying Gatorade and corn chips in the middle of the night is sometimes a necessity. Given my state of undress it was assumed I must be under the influence and someone called the local authorities. It took some time to convince them I had been robbed. I had to invent some armed assailants, file a police report about a nonexistent stolen car, explain why the assailants had needed my clothing, and waste a perfectly good identity. After I was released, I had to find a replacement for the prison jumpsuit I was given and get someone to take me all the way back to Milltown so I could find out what happened."

"I was there," she murmured sleepily, struggling to keep her eyes open.

"You were where?"

"At Walmart. I was at that Walmart."

———•◦•••◦•———

The voices were low, speaking in whispers not far from where Hannah lay barely awake on the couch, the patch of sun on her face pleasantly warm.

"Amara wiped out the entire fire department, the sheriff's department, and a number of people who must have been passersby or neighbors who saw the smoke," Asher said. "There are bodies spread throughout those woods the authorities have not even found yet. It is all over the news. At present I am the prime suspect. Hannah and I were both persons of interest until they found a woman's body in the house. I presume it is the woman from the grocery store. It will not be long until they discover their error and make Hannah a suspect again, though that is the least of our concerns." He paused then quietly added, "I thought she was dead. Until you called, I could not imagine she would have escaped my sister."

The other voice murmured something unintelligible.

"If there was any chance she still lived, I imagined it was as a captive of Amara's," Asher said. "The car was nowhere to be found, and I was so far behind I never could have caught up with them, even if I knew what route they were taking. For all I knew I was sending my sister right to you. By the grace of god Hannah evaded her, found the card, and chose to come here instead of setting out on her own."

Gabe chuckled. "I called you as soon as I saw her and that she was alone. I'll admit that was a bit of a disappointment. I was looking forward to a go-round with your sister. Wouldn't be the first time she succumbed to my charms."

"It would not be the first time she removed several of your extremities either. I still cannot discover why she is set on Hannah. After I got your message, I thought about trying to shortcut it down here so that I could get here more quickly, but you know how unpredictable that can be. That is how dire the situation has become."

There was a pause. Hannah was fully awake now, listening intently.

"Too unreliable," Gabe said, "and besides, that's never been your style, taking the nonstop flight. I don't know why not, though, it's ideal for getting out of tough scrapes. I poisoned myself once just to get as far away as possible from a woman in Paris. You remember Deirdre?" Gabe laughed softly, then grew serious. "Anyway, why the fuss? No matter why Amara wants her, it's going to be a dead end. You can never save them, and you know what a pit bull your sister is. It's the same every time. Amara is relentless."

Another pause. Hannah was about to feign waking up when Asher continued.

"How hard do you think it would be to track down Mena?"

A laugh rang out. Asher shushed it.

"Sorry," Gabe whispered. "I had no idea you were that desperate, crawling back to the one who got away. I can try. No telling where she might be off to, saving the world. And even if she's in the country, you can't really think she could walk in here without drawing attention, though."

"Why?" Asher asked.

Gabe chuckled. "You haven't turned on a television in a couple of years, have you?"

"Best not then. It is just hard to imagine Hannah could survive another encounter with Amara." Hannah heard Asher let out a sigh. "It would be enlightening to know who fired the shot that let Hannah get away this time, if it was an extant member of the local authorities or a more helpful ally, but I guess we will never know."

"How long are you going to risk staying here?" Gabe said. "I mean, you can stay as long as you want, but how long do you really think you can hide from your sister?"

"Not long. A couple more days if we can avoid attracting attention. Amara will be trying to find us again by now, and I would like to delay the meeting as long as possible, though it pains me that Hannah will have to suffer from the lack of medical care. I cannot tell for sure, but I think the wound has become infected."

"Maybe you should just take her to the hospital," Gabe said. "Get her patched up. If you're being realistic, your sister is going to find her one way or another, like she does every single time. Make sure Hannah is as comfortable as possible. No sense having her be in pain, since she is probably not going to be around that long anyw—"

Asher interrupted. "You are so flippant about the lives of those not as we are. Besides, it is not like that. Not at all. There is something more going on." His voice grew even quieter, more serious, so low Hannah could barely make it out. "That is not what I mean, Gabriel. My sister is not out to break my toys this time. She is not after me. She is after Hannah and at the behest of someone else. Amara does not play well with others, so she must have a good reason. I just cannot determine what it might be. Hannah is entirely human and there is nothing exceptional about her. She is more like an injured animal or lost child. By herself, what interest could she possibly be to one of our kind?"

# 24

"**H**ungry?" Asher walked in with two paper coffee cups balanced precariously on top of a stack of cardboard takeout containers.

"Starving." Hannah had muddled through the morning, silently processing what she'd overheard. Physically the sleep had done her a world of good, and after a blissful shower she had patiently let Asher clean and bandage her arm, then choked down some horse pill-sized antibiotics for good measure. If Asher found her quiet, he didn't comment.

Gabe brought up the rear with a big paper shopping bag in each hand.

"Not that my bathrobe isn't absolutely fetching on you, but if you have to leave my little love nest, these are slightly more presentable." He grinned, and she forced a smile in return. Hannah didn't enjoy being pandered to, having overheard what she had, though she knew it was true. To them she was a temporarily interesting commodity for whatever reason, but ultimately she was far more concerned with pre- serving her relatively short life than they were. They were convinced she wouldn't make it, and that was probably true. But she wasn't quite ready to quit and cash it in yet.

She mulled over her options while she devoured grits drowning in red eye gravy from the takeout container balanced on her lap. She had the car and the money—or at least they were nearby—and she wondered if there was any chance she could slip away and ditch Asher and Gabe, removing herself from the whole situation. They thought so little of her they would hardly suspect her of planning anything other than waiting under their protection until Amara and whoever else was out there showed up.

Washing the last bite of breakfast down with lukewarm coffee, she picked up the shopping bags and headed for the tiny bathroom, nodding to Gabe in thanks.

When he'd said the contents of the bag were more presentable than his bathrobe, he hadn't mentioned by whose standards. She considered putting back on the dirty clothes she'd been wearing when she arrived but decided it would lower their suspicions if she was accommodating.

The jeans were more elastic than denim, with a crisscross pattern up the side that showed little diamond patches of skin from the ankles to the waistband. The top had long loose sleeves that hid the wad of bandages on her arm, but the front was cut indecently low and fit tight across her ribcage to where it stopped two inches short of her jeans. Being accommodating only went so far; there was no way she was wearing the shoes, even without considering her natural tendency to fall on her face. Hannah threw the high wedge heels back into the bag and zipped up her leather boots.

There was no one in the small apartment when she made her grand, slightly drafty entrance, so she headed downstairs into the bar. It too was empty, and pausing to listen, she didn't hear any noise from the kitchen or the office. Spurred on mostly by self-preservation, and a little bit by anger, she made a split-second decision and quickly slipped out the door and down the street to the car. Inside she shot the locks and started the engine, throwing it in drive and cranking the wheel. It was now or never.

Two giant hands slammed down onto the hood and drove the front end of the car downward, the sudden halt throwing her forward. Apparently, it was never. She briefly toed the pedal and considered hitting the gas and running Asher over … again, but the thunderous look on his face made her put it in park. With a sigh she slumped back against the seat.

"Where were you going to go? Have you lost your senses?"

Hannah felt like a child being scolded, sitting on a bar stool, keys surrendered and swallowed up by his massive hand.

Seething was the only word she could think of to describe the look on Asher's face. Over her shoulder she could see Gabe behind the bar laughing silently. Hannah was too incensed to want to deal with either of them, and didn't even crack a smile at Gabe's salacious look as he walked out the back to the kitchen.

She raised an eyebrow at red-faced Asher, crossing her arms over her chest in a display of attitude, and to cover the gap in the fabric, which she was pretty sure was the last thing Gabe had looked at.

"Do not do that again, Hannah. There is no way to know if someone is outside, just waiting for you to surface." He glowered down at her.

"I'm not sure why you're so bothered. 'What interest could I possibly be to your kind?'"

He was silenced. She wasn't. "I'm not an idiot, Ash. I know what you are and what I am without needing to be babied. You aren't in any real danger here. Maybe I don't want to put my life in the hands of someone who's only interested in me for the sake of his conscience. At the end of the day, it's all just temporary for you. It's my life, and I only get one, so I'd like it to last a little bit longer if you don't mind."

Fists balled, she stood up, facing him nose to nose, or rather nose to ribcage. Staring up at him, she held her hand out for the keys. "Give them back. It's no big deal for you, but it's kind of a big deal for me."

"You are wrong." He put his hand around the wrist held out toward him, encircling it completely, holding her back when she tried to jerk away.

"About what?"

"Nearly everything," Asher said. "There is a great deal more going on now than when you and I first met. I will tell you everything I know, or suspect I know, but you need to stay with me, at least for the time being. Besides, you are in no shape to be on the run." He un-manacled her wrist, moving his grasp to her hand. "Please, do not leave without me again."

"Yes, Hannah, please, please don't go. Asher will pout and there's nothing more disturbing than seeing a man his size cry."

Asher dropped her hand and glared at Gabe.

"And you, Gabriel, you are far too cavalier. I need to locate some things. Do not let her out of your sight until I return, or we will see where you wake up next."

———————

Hannah sat at a round table in the empty restaurant in a snit. She wasn't enjoying being on lockdown, but at least her babysitter wasn't hovering. She wondered how fast he would notice if she walked out the front door, not that she would get far without the car keys.

Gabe walked in from the back with a round tray balanced on one hand.

"If you're going to make a run for it, at least don't go until after lunch. I make the best fried catfish in the history of the universe, and I want someone with actual functioning taste buds to experience it. Our friend here has zero judgment in anything but women." He blew a kiss toward Hannah.

He wasn't exaggerating about the catfish. The appetite she'd been mostly without for the last few months was back with a vengeance. When she finally decided there was no way she could possibly fit in another bite of food, she popped one last hush puppy in her mouth for good measure and leaned back in contentment.

Gabriel smiled. "Told you. It's an honor for a catfish to die to be a part of a meal this good."

"What about the puppies?" Hannah smirked.

"We use artificial puppy in our hush puppies. Or at least that's what I tell people."

It was funny how much more easily Gabe passed for an average person. He was still inhumanely attractive, but there was an easy way about him Asher hadn't quite mastered.

"So how long have you known Asher?" she asked, stifling an unattractive belch semi-successfully.

"Oh …" He stopped to think. "Since around sixteen twenty something or other. I met him in Oslo, where it was then." He tipped his head and thought for a second. "I don't think it's in the same place now, or at least isn't called the same thing. Anyway"— he shrugged—"that was the first time I ran into Asher. I imagine he was there to blend in. The population is unusually tall and light complexioned, so someone like Asher didn't stick out too much, as long as they didn't stay overly long or do anything to draw too much attention. Of course, I was there for the women. Second to none." He rolled his eyes heavenward and sighed.

"It was purely coincidence that we actually met. We might never have, except it was an old city made of mostly wooden buildings, and someone started a hell of a fire. It was ripping its way through the streets, everything going up like kindling, people running around, trying to get out of its path. That's what I was in the process of doing myself when I saw this man running into a burning building without a moment's hesitation. He came out with a person across each shoulder, dropped them, and ran right back in. Then he charged into the house next to it."

Gabe sat back and shook his head, amused smile on his face. "You don't see too many people without extra lives blindly running to their death, so I was fairly certain of what he was. Of course, I was also instantly shamed into doing the same thing." He threw his head back and laughed, tossing his hair out of his eyes. "You should have seen us, Hannah. Burned to a crisp, not a hair or a piece of clothing left on our bodies. And it hurt like the fires of hell. I headed to the outskirts of town, figuring I'd throw myself in the river and drown myself or something, anything to get myself back to one piece. Who do you think I found there? There he was, but he was just lying there in the water, bald as a baby, burned down to the bone in some places. It had to hurt like you can't even imagine." Gabe looked at Hannah with a little more seriousness. "He didn't do anything, just stayed where he was, and I thought I'd been wrong, that he was just an amazingly brave or stupid average man. But he knew what I was too. He rolled his head over and said 'What if this is it my friend? Only a fool thinks something can last forever.'" Gabe smiled. "I wished I had the strength of will, but the pain was unbearable. I walked into the water and let the current do its work. But when I came back I tracked him down. We've been getting into trouble ever since."

Hannah sat thoughtfully while Gabe opened a bottle of beer for each of them. She had known there were depths to Asher she couldn't begin to understand, but she was happy to find her instincts about him had been right. He'd done more with his extra time than he gave himself credit for.

Taking a long drink and wiping the foam from her lip, she asked a question she'd been holding in since the morning.

"So, who's Mena?"

"Eavesdropping? I like you more by the minute." Gabe chuckled, putting down his beer. "If you think Asher is a paragon of virtue, well Mena is a saint. Literally, I believe. You really don't hear enough about the good ones among us. Less exciting news probably." He leaned back in his chair, balancing his bottle on the tip of his index finger. "Anyway, Mena's made it her personal mission to fix the world. She's a real goody two shoes, that one. Crazy smart too; there aren't many who can match her when it comes to intellect. Unlike yours truly, she hasn't squandered her lives." He gave Hannah an impish smile. "I won't deny it, I've spent most of my lives in the most dissolute of pursuits, worrying primarily about having a good time. What's the point of eternity if you can't enjoy it?"

"You told him she's too noticeable? Why would she draw attention coming here?"

He laughed out loud. "Mena wants to save the world, but people as a whole tend to be uninterested in helping with that. Unless you can get their attention. And what gets the most attention these days?"

"Wars? Terrorists?"

Gabe made a buzzing sound. "Wrong. Celebrities. So dear, sainted Mena made some movies, did some other carefully calculated things to draw attention, and then used it to get people to pay attention to the causes she wants to see supported. But it does makes her stick out. Obviously, an A-list starlet walking down the street here wouldn't go unnoticed."

Hannah shook her head. As if she didn't feel inferior enough already.

"So, she was the one that got away?" She imagined Asher with a glamorous creature, an Oscar-wielding Mother Theresa, someone his equal, and a being that would be there forever. It made sense, the tiny jealous monster inside her hated to admit.

"They have a great deal in common. Decency, compassion, not much fun, absolutely no sense of humor, all topped off with the belief that all this is too good to be true. All that touchy-feely stuff. No wonder they spent so many lifetimes together."

Gabe finished his beer, deftly flipping his bottle upside down and catching it by the neck. He pushed back his chair and got up.

"What happened?" Hannah asked.

He shrugged. "Forever is a very long time. Maybe they just wanted different things. Mena wants to save the human race. Asher just wants … well, honestly, I have no idea what he wants. Or maybe they got bored. They're both pretty boring, compared to me." He set the empty bottle on the bar with a smile. "But who knows, maybe they'll bump into each other again. Bound to happen when you live as long as we do."

Gabe's ear turned to a sound Hannah couldn't hear. Then he spoke loudly to the empty doorway.

"And that, Hannah, is why you should run away with me now, and I'll really show you what you're missing. We can travel the world, visit every exotic destination, walk hand in hand down the most stunning nude beaches."

Asher walked in shaking his head.

"Hannah would have been safer with me after all."

———◦•◦◦•◦———

She felt like a new woman. Asher bandaged her arm with a new layer of material that he swore wouldn't stick and gave her an injection of antibiotics followed by another of pain medication. The painkiller was responsible for the majority of the way she was feeling.

"Where did you manage to dig this stuff up?" She couldn't imagine much of it had been over the counter.

"I broke into a veterinary practice."

Great. Pet painkillers. The dog tranquilizers were working at least.

Feeling pleasantly floaty, she followed him down to the bar, enjoying that—for what felt like the first time in ages—absolutely nothing hurt. Gabe had closed the bar for the day, and it was empty and warm, the jukebox playing a familiar song quietly in the background. Whatever Gabe was whipping up for dinner smelled delicious.

"Country fried steak and fried pickles. And french fries and fried okra. Fried everything. I might even fry something for dessert. Oreos, or maybe cheesecake. Or Oreo cheesecake. Thank heavens I lose the accumulated weight every time I die." He patted his stomach, which was flat as a board.

After they ate, she wished *she* had instant magical metabolism. Her stomach was visibly distended, but she was thinking about asking Gabe if he'd been joking about frying the cheesecake.

The bottle without the label was a different story. It was filled with an oddly green moonshine a friend of Gabe's made outside of town in an illegal still. Over and over Gabe and Asher had tossed off a couple fingers each with no ill effects as they compared notes on the situation. Asher filled Hannah in on events that seemed far away from the quiet dinner they'd just had.

"We know Amara is after you on behalf of someone else. There are a finite number of reasons she would do anything for anyone, and none of them would be without proper incentive," Asher sat back and thought for a moment. "It would not be for financial motives unless it was on a scale that would alter world markets. Amara has no need for it; she has amassed a fortune over the centuries. And even if one *could* tempt her financially, she would do nothing for a regular human. My sister would find that beneath her," Asher said. "And truly, power is the only currency she recognizes. What she is doing must be for one of our kind, and they must be offering something appealing."

He tossed back another inch of moonshine. Gabe refilled his glass while Asher continued.

"I reached out to someone I know who keeps herself appraised on the actions of many of us out there," he told Hannah. "She sometimes knows about the ones who are a threat to the general population."

Gabe laughed out loud and topped off Hannah's still mostly full glass, then pushed the bottle toward Asher. "Please tell me you didn't get ahold of Leandra? You did, didn't you?" He turned to Hannah. "Leandra might be the craziest being in existence, human or otherwise, and that's saying something. I mean, some of us get a little"—Gabe circled his ear with a finger—"woo woo after all this time, but she's on a whole different cosmic plane."

Asher drained his glass, then refilled it, shaking the empty bottle for the last dribble. "Gabe just thinks that because after three hundred years of attempts, she still will not sleep with him."

"Isn't that proof she's crazy?" Gabe said. "Anyway, Leandra believes she and everyone else like us are actually fallen angels or something like that, put here on Earth for some divine reason she hasn't quite figured out yet. Where is she these days?"

"I did not ask." Asher tipped back his glass and set it back down with a clink. "Though most recently I heard it was somewhere in South America."

"Yep. Still at it then," Gabe said. "Last I knew she had a giant doomsday cult going down there, tons of people, all hippy-dippy Earth-child types. It's the usual gig—not even that original." He turned to Hannah. "She kills herself so she can disappear and pop back up a couple days later, proving to all her groupies that she's immortal. Does it to build up a huge following, a real army of people willing to do whatever she wants so they can be on her team when the end comes." Gabe drained his glass and eyed the empty bottle. "Leandra is also super suspicious of others of our kind because she's convinced there's going to be an epic battle between good and evil or some nonsense. She has her people all over the world keeping tabs on all the eternal types she knows about, because when the time comes, Leandra believes the winners are going to get sucked back up to heaven or inherit the earth or get a big shiny pair of wings or something. Whatever she thinks is going to happen, she wants to know who's on her side when it does."

Asher interrupted. "Leandra is a little different, but she is a useful sort of different. And she has information when others do not. I put out a message to her before I started down here, on the off chance she knew anything. She did not have anything definite— only rumors, mind you—but she told me what she heard."

He looked at Hannah, who was sniffing the moonshine, debating whether or not to finish it. Asher shrugged, and she knocked it back. It burned so badly her eyes teared up and she coughed until Gabe pounded her on the back.

"Leandra told me there has been some information drifting back to her about Michael," Asher said. "Apparently he has popped up again after a hiatus. He is looking for someone."

Gabe's eyebrows rose, and he got up, taking the empty bottle. "If that's the case, we're going to need another one of these."

Asher nodded, running his hand up through his hair the way he did when he was thinking. It was longish in the front now, and it stood up like a cock's comb under his fingers.

"Who's Michael?" Hannah asked.

When Asher opened up his mouth to answer, the bar exploded.

# 25

She couldn't hear the noise, but she could feel it. The air around her vibrated with a wave of unbearable heat and she could smell her own flesh cooking, feel it as it contracted and crackled. Hannah opened her mouth to scream and found she was already screaming, deaf to the sounds coming from her own body, only feeling the stripped rawness in her throat.

Hannah was running out of air, fighting for breath against an intense pressure against the center of her back, losing against whatever was pinning her facedown to the ground. Only one of her hands was free, and she groped blindly around with it, struggling against the weight on top of her. It was soft and gave when she struck at it. It was a body. She pounded at it feebly, but there was no response.

Trying to turn herself over wasn't working, with so much dead weight pressing down on her. She couldn't move and she was still on fire, the odor of burning hair filling her nostrils and choking her. Hannah opened her eyes, but the smoke was so acrid it turned everything into a stinging haze.

A blast of cold white caught her in the face, blinding her entirely.

"There you are. And underneath Gabriel. Just where he would like you, I'm sure." Another gust from the fire extinguisher hit her. "He always was a sucker for a damsel in distress. Or a damsel in a dress. Or a damsel without a dress. Or with an address. Anyone really. Never was too picky, this one." The silky voice cooed, and the weight on Hannah's back disappeared.

Pushing herself up on her forearms, Hannah was slammed back down to the floor by a foot between her shoulder blades.

"Now don't get up on my account," the voice said. There was a girlish giggle Hannah would know anywhere.

"Amara." Hannah coughed.

"Oops, and there he goes again. So soon, and I didn't even get to say goodbye. Oh well, no big loss there."

Hannah sucked in a desperate breath only to choke on the smoke and ash in the air. When she tried to roll over, Amara's foot struck her in the temple, and she lay still while the pain ricocheted back and forth between her ears.

"Now where is that useless brother of mine? You'd think he'd be a little tougher for as big as he is, but I swear to god, he dies every time you breathe on him. Did you know he actually died from a cold once? Who dies from catching a cold?" Hannah tried to roll over and sucked in a desperate breath. "Don't tell anybody," Amara said, "but I admit I might have gone a little heavy on the C-four. Any more and you'd be toast—literally. Just imagine the fuss if I brought you back a crispy corpse." The metal fire extinguisher hit the ground with a thunk. "Oh well, all's well that ends well-ish."

Hannah heard herself scream this time, when she was dragged to her feet by her injured arm. Her entire body protested, and she immediately fell back to her knees, only to be jerked back up just as painfully.

"Oh, get up, Hannah Banana. Don't be such a baby. I'm not going to kill you right now. We have places to go, people to see, and time is a-wasting. Your dear old daddy is most anxious to meet you."

Amara pulled Hannah through the smoking remains of the bar. She tried to make herself dead weight, but fingers dug into the gunshot wound in her arm and forced her to her feet. The air was mercifully less smoky as she was dragged outside the burning remains of the bar, and she sucked in ragged breaths to ease the tightness in her lungs.

A siren wailed not far off and someone screamed. Hannah heard the sound of running feet, then she was suddenly released and shoved face-first to the pavement.

Shots rang out, deafeningly close. Hannah managed to roll over in time to see Amara casually squeeze off another shot at a bystander rushing toward them to help. Near the sidewalk, just feet away, a familiar figure in a barista's apron lay crumpled in the street. The feet were now rushing in the other direction.

"Nope. Nope, nope, nope. Just where do you think you're going, missy?" Amara planted a boot on Hannah's ankle, and when Amara twisted her foot and ground down, Hannah screamed at the crunch of her own failing bones. Then Amara reached down and dragged Hannah back from where she had been trying to scramble under a parked car. "Cute pants. And in we go."

Hauled up by her hair, Hannah was shoved into the passenger seat of a car. Amara paused to fire off a few more shots in the direction of two police officers who ducked between cars. One disappeared, falling backwards and out of sight. The second crumpled sideways, clutching his side.

"Stop struggling." An open hand cracked against the side of Hannah's head as she tried to shove her way back out of the door. Before her head stopped ringing, her hands were locked into handcuffs, the chain looped through the grab bar above her shoulder.

Throwing the car into drive, Amara whipped away from the curb with a squeal of tires. Hannah pulled down so hard against the bar above her that she felt the skin around her wrists tear against the metal cuff.

"Don't make me knock you out."

Without warning the window beside Amara's face exploded in a hail of glass. The impact of the truck against their car threw Hannah into the door, yanking her handcuffed arms so brutally she felt the bone being pulled from the socket. Her vision had gone fuzzy from the pain, but she saw hands reach through Amara's empty window frame. Caught off guard, Amara didn't react quickly enough to stop them, and they locked around her neck and squeezed. Her eyes bulged like a cartoon frog until there was an audible snap. Then she was gone.

Hannah's door opened and the bar her handcuffs were looped through was ripped from the roof. The hurt was just so bad, and things were growing hazier, but she tried to stay awake. It got harder when she started bouncing painfully. Letting her head fall, she watched the road roll by below her, a yellow line in the middle of the black. Then everything was black. It was black and it was night and she was flying. Flying, flying, through broken glass, and the wind was stinging, nipping at her skin, and she was being pushed through the sky, the stars passing by like blurs, one after the next.

"Come on, love. Hannah, come on." Something gently patted her cheek, but it felt like fire and her eyes teared. When the liquid rolled down her cheek, that stung as well, and then the steady stream of tears was a trail of acid running down her face.

The stars kept flying by, but they changed and found their shape and she gradually realized they weren't stars but street lights. They flew by where her head was leaning against an open car window, the speed stretching them into elongated blobs.

"Ow." She closed her eyes against the passing lights that were making the inside of her skull ache.

A choked laugh rang out.

"Ow? I would say ow does not begin to cover it." The stinging hand patted her face again. "Hold on, Hannah. Just hold on a little bit longer. Just stay with me until we can stop."

She rolled her head in his direction, blinking her eyes to clear them enough to see.

"You're naked."

———◆◆◆———

Waking up to unbearable pain seemed to have become a regular thing. She'd managed to live her entire life up until recently without it and would be happy to go back to a normal, pain-free existence as soon as possible. Unfortunately, it wasn't going to be today.

But somehow she was alive, and if waking up feeling like this was the price, so be it. Hannah took a deep breath and as she carefully moved her limbs, she tried to accept every single twinge, each burn and hurt, and embrace the pain. Embracing the pain did exactly jack toward easing it, and only some body parts responded, her right shoulder and left ankle useless. She remembered the crunch and the agony when Amara brought her boot down.

"Here, try to drink this."

A hand behind her head gingerly lifted her forward, and a cool glass was placed against her lips. She choked a little on the water, sputtering it back up and feeling it run down her neck. Able to squint one eye open, she could see a cloudy Asher in front of her. Even though she knew his sister couldn't permanently damage him, she was relieved to see him sitting there, whole, next to her on the bed. She laughed a little, and it hurt from head to toe.

"What is it?" His voice sounded concerned.

"Nothing." She was remembering the last time she'd seen him. She was pretty sure she remembered sitting beside Asher in a car that had been traveling down the road during the night at breakneck speed. And that he had been naked. It might have been a hallucination. Then again, probably not if her recent life was any indication. "Where are we?"

"Somewhere safe. What hurts?" he asked.

She squeezed her eyes shut tightly and when she opened them again, her vision was clearer, though the eye that had been slammed against the window of the car was definitely not fully cooperating. Damn it, she hadn't even been able to get rid of the last black eye.

"Everything." She shifted to try to sit up a little, and he put an arm behind her to lean her forward, propping her up with fat, soft pillows.

She was dressed in a too-long white T-Shirt—his, guessing from the size. Hannah was past being embarrassed at the fact that he must have had to undress her. It wasn't even the first time. Below the hem, her legs were a boiled-looking lobster red except for a bizarre, charred pattern down the sides. The damn trashy jeans Gabe had picked out. She hoped he woke up in a briar patch and two hundred miles away from a woman.

There were bandages around her wrists and one arm was strapped to her side with gauze. Her left ankle was fat as a sausage, colored in shades of green and purple. Looking at it made her stomach turn, and she choked back the urge to vomit. She looked away from it and at him instead. Asher looked nearly as tortured as her ankle bones.

"I am so sorry, Hannah. I was able to put your dislocated shoulder back into place while you were unconscious, but I think your ankle may be broken. With everything that happened, the gunshot on your arm has opened back up as well, and the lump on your head is massive. And the burns …" He trailed off and looked at her, shaking his head. "Yet again you need medical help, but if I call the wrong person, it would lead her right back to us. She is finding us so fast, and if we have to run again, I am not sure …"

"No doctor," she rasped, trying to shake her head and failing. "If we have to run, I won't make it." Hell, if she had to use the bathroom she wouldn't make it. Thankfully she was too dry even for tears. "More water."

"Here." He tilted her up again. "Open your mouth." She felt him push some chalky tablets past her lips. "They will not help that much, but it is the strongest thing I was able to find."

She swallowed them gratefully. Then she remembered something.

"Amara, she said …" Hannah's throat felt so hot and scratchy, she paused to swallow painfully, and tried to sit up.

"Do not speak. You should rest," he said, reaching forward to gently push her back against the pillows.

"No, wait," Hannah said. "Amara said she was going to take me to see 'dear old daddy.'"

Asher's hand paused in midair.

"Your father?" he asked. "What do you know about him?"

"Nothing." Hannah shrugged, wincing with the effort. The very little her uncle had known was the only information she had.

"I did not discover anything either," Asher said. "I tried to look into your background after the fire, but there was nothing. Your birth record is not real."

"What do you mean it isn't real?" Hannah suddenly felt light and floaty.

"I mean your name is on it, the date, the location, but it stops there. All of it is fabricated. None of the information goes deeper than the ink on the paper."

She closed her eyes, clearing her foggy head and enjoying the lessening of the pain. "What do you think Amara meant?"

Asher took up her hand gently, and for a moment she watched him examine it, looking at every line, the bruises, the thin fingers with their cracked burned surface. He looked at everything but her face.

"I had hoped I was wrong, but if that is what my sister said, then it may be as I feared. I may know who he is. Do you remember what we were talking about, before the explosion?"

Hannah nodded.

"Michael is arguably the most well-known amongst our kind. He is an anomaly amongst the anomalous." He stopped abruptly. "Hold on, I will be right back."

The side of the bed popped up without his weight and she fought to stay awake, drowsing, the pain medication taking effect with merciful speed. She was enjoying feeling the burning pain float away when freezing cold on her leg jerked her back awake.

"For the swelling." Asher settled a bag of ice wrapped in a towel over the distended skin on her ankle. "So, Michael." Asher paused, gathering his thoughts. "He is different from the rest of us, than those like me. You recall us speaking about Leandra?" Hannah nodded. Cult leader type, somewhere in South America. "Leandra and Michael share similar delusions of grandeur. Michael believes that because he is the only one of us that can reproduce, he is destined to create a world populated by his descendants."

Hannah forced her eyes open. "Wait, the rest of you can't ..."

He shook his head, removing the ice pack from her ankle, poking at it gently, then replacing it.

"None of us. Not even in our first lives. When Michael discovered his death was not permanent, he proceeded to set himself up as the god he believes he is. Word of him eventually spread; imagine Leandra's surprise when she heard of him and learned he had any number of children running around. She took this as a sign something was changing, that his offspring had to be more than human, and creatures like the two of them were in their ascendency."

Asher looked at Hannah, his eyes serious. "If Leandra knew what he would come to be, I do not believe she would have encouraged him in that line of thinking, that his children would be ..." He shook his head sadly. "Hannah, Michael slew every one of his children to see if they would come back. Every single child he murdered. Not a single one lived again. They all proved to be perfectly human."

"He killed all his children. Oh, Asher that's—"

"It was not enough for him," he said, cutting her off, closing his eyes wearily. "It was not enough that he killed his own children to see if they would come back. When they did not, Michael kept trying, and on an even more horrific scale. He amassed a whole group of women, convinced them he was a god by arranging for his death, disappearing and reappearing again to prove his divinity. He gathered these women, promising them children with an unlimited span of years, who would be gods among men."

His voice was low and quiet, and Hannah fought to stay awake, not wanting to miss the rest.

"Michael waited until every woman there had a baby at her breast or clutching at her skirt, all of them awed by the prospect of their god-children. They were overjoyed to hold children who would never see death, who would grow to perfection and remain that way, as Michael did. They nursed sons who would grow into great soldiers, who when felled by the sword would ever rise up again. Their daughters would never perish in childbirth. They had born the future kings and queens of this world. Had they all not seen their husband die only to have him return to them, perfected, a living god?"

Asher said, voice mournful, "Again Michael was not patient enough to wait even until his children grew to adulthood. When they were old enough to stand without a hand to steady them, in a great ceremony he bade the women cut their children's throats, offer up their blood, so they could watch their bodies melt away and be reborn to live again and again, eternally.

"None did. Not one. In a fit of rage, Michael killed the women while they wept, stunned over the bodies of the children they had slain with their own hand. He dispatched them one after another, berating them for being unfit to carry his seed, or whores, all of them, for would not his children be gone, reborn if he was their true father? When every mother and child was dead, he stepped over the bodies and disappeared to start again."

Asher did not look up at Hannah but continued to sit perfectly still, the only sound the shifting of melting ice, until he continued.

"It is a story he has repeated throughout history, across the world. The bodies of a great many women and children, all killed, no explanations. Sometimes a string of children, spread across a country, missing, seemingly unrelated unless, if you look more closely, you find the father always seems to be a ghost."

Hannah was aghast, horrified, and also confused.

"But why keep doing it, if they don't come back?"

Asher shook his head. "Some like Leandra and Michael are always focused on a future time, when whatever ineffable plan that made them what they are comes to fruition. Why would they be so clearly set above the average human if not for some great reason? Maybe Michael thinks it just was not the right time, or maybe, like Leandra, he believes once he reaches the threshold, has died enough times and is utterly perfected, it will work. Maybe, like my sister, his soul is irrevocably damaged and he enjoys causing pain and death. Probably only he knows."

Hannah reached for the glass. Asher picked it up before she could and held it to her lips. She didn't bristle at the nursing, too beat up to be bothered by her own weakness.

"And you think he's my father?" She shuddered at the thought. Why would he think that? In Hannah's mind her biological father had always been a foggy picture of a possibly violent figure, but pathetically human, easily substandard compared to the man who had raised her. Not frightening to her.

"How badly does it hurt? I want to take a look at your arm. I will need to get something stronger for the pain and a real antibiotic." Asher rose to cross to the other side of the bed, ignoring the question.

"Ash, why?"

He sat down next to her, making Hannah groan at the movement, and busied himself pulling up the sleeve of the T-Shirt from where it hung down to her elbow, hitching it over the wad of bandages.

"I am not sure, not entirely. But Amara would not have had any thought you would manage to escape her, so for her to say anything as a method of diversion would have been pointless. And it is not her way," he said. "However badly she hates me, the truth is, we know each other very well. Violence is her method, not dissimulation. She has never had the patience for the long game, has never needed it, and is too assured of her own success to spend time in subterfuge. Whoever your father may be, he has something that has made my sister willing to retrieve you for him. Amara would not do anything as a favor, so whatever she is getting in return is not going to be something of small value, of an importance confined to a single human lifetime. Since Michael is the only being like us who could even have offspring, it seems at least feasible."

Hannah was distracted by the pull of gauze against her arm. So much for not sticking. Could modern medicine not come up with something that didn't cement itself to dried blood? The arm was once again a mess. The fragile new skin and scab that had begun to form had been shredded, and around the gunshot was a new ring of dark purple and angry red. She remembered the feeling of Amara's fingers digging into it and the wound twinged, as if it too recalled the brutal treatment.

"All of it is irrelevant, really," he said. "That you are being hunted is the pressing matter. Why would be informative, but it would not change anything. No one will bother to wait to explain their motivations before they strike." He rolled her sleeve neatly to her shoulder. "Leave it open for a while. Until I have something to put on it."

She shivered.

"Are you cold?"

She shook her head. "Must be the ice pack."

Reaching over, he started to pull the sheet up over her, but looking at the line of blistering burns running down each side of her red legs, he sighed and crossed the room, opening a pair of French doors to let a gloriously warm breeze roll in.

"Where are we?" Hannah reveled in the warmth, even though it felt like fire on her legs.

"Savannah."

# 26

Hannah dragged herself down the uneven dirt path, struggling to stay on her feet with an ankle that buckled every time she took a step. Both sides of the path were lined with people standing shoulder to shoulder, rigidly upright with their backs turned to her.

"Help me. Help me please!" she cried out, but it was like they couldn't hear her. No matter how loud she yelled, not a single head turned. Hobbling closer she reached out and grabbed a man by the arm. He spun around.

"Oh, thank god. Sheriff Morgan, thank god you're alive." Relieved beyond belief she tried to throw her arms around him, but he shoved her away, the face that had always been so stolid contorted with rage, his uniform shredded with bullet holes and dyed black with blood.

Backing away from him, Hannah collided with another of the still figures. They wheeled around, another familiar face, a woman wearing a coffee shop apron, though the logo on the chest had been replaced with two bloody holes. She threw Hannah to the ground and kicked her savagely in the ribs, then spat at her, a glob of blood landing on Hannah's cheek.

Hannah tried to drag herself away, crawling through the gauntlet of figures, recognizing them as they turned one by one. There were firemen and deputies, EMTs, and police officers, Sheila and sweet old Betty from the Shur Shop, her uncle and Gabe and Asher. They were burned and shot and torn to pieces. And they were all angry—all angry at her. She tried but she couldn't get away from them, couldn't run or even stand. Hannah curled up and covered her head with her arms, giving up and trying to shut them all out. They wouldn't stop. They hissed and spat and kicked.

"Hannah. Answer me, Hannah. Open your eyes."

She was being shaken, roughly enough to make her head flop back and forth. Her eyes opened, and to her immense relief the hand closed around her arm was Asher's, the real one, not the angry, hazy one from a moment ago.

He loosened his grip slightly. "What it is? Are you okay?"

She nodded. Her head felt like her brain was sloshing around inside her skull. "It was just a dream. A horrible dream." She shuddered at the relief of reality.

Letting go of her arm, Asher stood his hair on end with his fingers, and exhaled with a whoosh. "I thought you were having a seizure."

"Sorry I woke you up. I don't know where that came from." That wasn't quite true. She'd been having all sorts of crazy dreams since she'd gotten here. The things that weighed heavy on her mind in the daylight tended to crawl into her head while she slept. It was a lot like after she'd hit him, but with an expanded cast of characters.

"You look like you have seen a ghost. I will be right back."

He disappeared through the door. Hannah sank back into the mountain of pillows and waited for her heart to slowly return to its normal rhythm.

"Here, drink this." Asher appeared at her elbow with a cup. She took it and drank it off in one motion, then sputtered and choked, eyes watering.

"Holy crap. Was that gin?"

"It was meant to be medicinal."

He sat down and swung his long legs up onto the bed, coming to rest shoulder to shoulder with her. His bulk was comforting, and she was happy to sag against him and feel the rumble of his deep voice like a cat's purr when he spoke.

They sat there in silence for a moment watching the clouds shift in the sky outside the open doors, bellies showing sherbet orange and pink as the rising sun caught them.

"Better now?" he asked.

She nodded. "Better now. I'm fine. I swear."

It was true, especially compared to where she'd been a few weeks ago. When she'd seen herself for the first time after she arrived, Hannah wasn't sure how she'd even made it this far. It looked like she'd been set on fire and thrown off a cliff.

She shifted her leg to look at the burns that had been raw and weeping then, but were now covered in crackly looking scabs. In another month all that would be left of them were scars, a permanent geometric pattern of diamonds to remind her of those horrible damn pants.

All the other parts of her were healing tolerably too. The dislocated shoulder only troubled her if she lifted her arm over her head, and the assortment of cuts and abrasions had been replaced with new, tender patches of skin that were shiny and tight. Her ankle still hurt—it had most certainly been fractured or even broken—but the bones were at least in place. She could move it gingerly, and if she didn't try to put too much weight on it, the pain was bearable.

"How much longer do you think we're safe here?" she said. "I'm healing pretty fast, but I could use a little more vacation time before I can even think about another go-round with your sister." The air was still cool from the night, and she leaned against Asher's arm and laid her head against his shoulder, enjoying the warmth that rolled off him. Closing her eyes she thought about all the battered parts of her. Her father might not be a regular human, and Hannah might heal a little quicker than most, but really she was just a regular, badly banged-up person who wouldn't be in fighting shape for a little while yet.

When she turned her head, still waiting for his answer, he was looking down at her.

"What?" she asked.

He shook his head. "Nothing. You are a particular woman, Hannah."

She'd been called worse. Maybe he meant peculiar. His grammar was a little wacky.

"While we have been here, I have seen nothing to make me believe our location has been discovered. I think we are safe here for the time being, as safe as I know how to make us. Had I known what was coming, though, I would have come here in the beginning. I am sorry."

"For what?"

"For being selfish. If we had retreated to this place sooner your injuries might have been avoided, but I hesitated because this is my home and I have never brought another person here. It is the only place I have managed to keep hidden from my sister for any length of time."

"I hope it can stay that way. I'm sorry that bringing me here might blow that." She truly was.

He shrugged. "It makes no matter. If this is the last time it exists as such a sanctuary, so be it. But we need some more time, and remaining here is the only way I can think of to buy it."

———◆◆◆———

Hannah plopped down onto the bench and leaned uncomfortably against the stone back to catch her breath. She could make it down the stairs by herself now, but it wasn't pretty.

Almost since she'd arrived Hannah had been hobbling to the bathroom and around the bedroom, embarrassed at having to be carried around. She'd started by shoving a chair in front of her for support, until Asher had hacked an improvised cane from a gnarled branch for her. It was a kind gesture, though it may have had something to do with the trail of scuff marks she'd made across the tile in her bedroom.

But he'd had to continue to bring Hannah out here every day, carrying her around the long stretch of balcony, down the stairs, and out into the brightness of the courtyard. She loved the open space that was so warm and sun-lit, with a big, graceful fountain splashing and flinging sparkling droplets into the air. Twisting trees in giant pots reached from the corners up to the railings that wrapped around the second story, their wrought-iron scrollwork embroidering intricate shadows on the red tile of the floor.

Shifting in an attempt to get comfortable against the pointy carvings behind her back, she looked over to the fountain where a bird had swooped down and landed. Hannah watched in amusement when it ignored her and began to splash at its reflection in the fountain. Its mate soon joined it, perching on the edge to watch, head cocked at the display.

The pair abruptly shot away, darting back into the sky. She turned to see Asher stepping out through the doors from the kitchen.

"I do wonder what goes on between you and the animals," he said.

He handed her one of the glasses he was carrying and Hannah had to make an effort not to break into too great a smile. It was difficult; Asher was so abnormally attractive no normal person would be able to ignore it, let alone her, and here it was even more difficult.

It was harder because Asher was different here, though she couldn't quite put her finger on any one reason why. His looks had changed, but only slightly; he had shaved, his hair was longer, falling over his forehead, and he hadn't stood it up with frustration in days. He was growing more tan, and in the full noonday sun over the courtyard, his eyes leaned decidedly toward blue, the skin at the edges crinkling when he laughed or smiled.

Maybe that was the difference. Here he never went dark. This Asher nearly always laughed and smiled.

"Do you like it?" He nodded toward the glass she'd forgotten in her hand.

"Not another one of your medicinal beverages, is it?" Hannah took a sip from the glass. This drink was delicious and icy cold. She wasn't sure exactly what it was, but she tasted lime, and dark, sweet rum.

"I like it." She turned to set it on the side table, swearing when the bench dug into her back. Asher burst out laughing.

"It wasn't that funny." She turned to frown at him, but failed to look properly put out, because he was doing it, grinning and laughing a big, genuine laugh.

"I am sorry. But you surprised me by coming down on your own today, and I did not get a chance to cover the bench with the pillows and blankets. Now you will be able to see it was not solely for your comfort."

Hannah turned around and looked at the bench she'd been sitting on every day for weeks now. For the first time, she saw the carvings in detail.

"Ugh, good lord." She shook her head. "If I had known what was poking me in the back …" The carvings were very well done, of men and women in the midst of all sorts of activities. The utmost attention had been paid to every anatomical detail. No attention had been wasted on clothing. "Did you have this made to your specifications or did it come with the house?" she said.

"When I bought this house twenty years ago, the realtor told me some elaborate fairy tale about how it had been originally built as a retreat for monks, as a place for them to come for reflection and prayer. The realtor was remarkably creative, giving me the details of every nook and crevice." He laughed and said, "I did not bother to correct her, but it was hard to keep my composure as she went on and on, knowing there was not a bit of truth to any of it. I knew this because although I was buying the house, it was not for the first time."

"Why would you need to buy your own house more than once?"

"I sell it to different people every once in a while to retain its secrecy. Aliases are never foolproof, and everything leaves a trail if you know what to look for. By removing it completely from my possession every so often I can sever the link, making it nearly impossible to tie to me. Plus, it leaves the improvements to someone else. Saves me a fortune in renovations."

"What if someone doesn't want …" Hannah had turned slightly to talk, and now there was a tiny carved body part poking her between the ribs. "Never mind. This bench?"

"I am getting to it," he said. "The bench is from one of those periods where I had sold it temporarily. It has been inhabited by some interesting people."

"More interesting than you?"

"Vastly. Once it belonged to a smuggler who used it to move things in and out through the swamp that backs up to the property. He added the tunnel that leads down to the water so he could come and go, poling his goods in and out unseen. It was a speakeasy for a time, and the same tunnels were used to hide illegal alcohol. It was once a school for young girls."

"I'm guessing they didn't put in the bench?"

"Of course not. I made use of the tunnel then myself, moving it there for safekeeping. The bench is from the period before it was a school, when this house was a bordello."

Hannah leaned away from the back of the bench. "That is gross. I've been lying on this thing for weeks."

He laughed at the look on her face. "I admit I did not sell the house on that occasion knowing what it was intended for, but you do have them to thank for the fountain. Gentlemen would arrive and the proprietor would seat them on this bench—a piece of work she brought with her all the way from France, a gift one of her lovers carved for her. The men would throw coins in the fountain for the ladies to go splashing after until their gowns were thoroughly soaked, making it easier for the men to see what they were selecting."

She shook her head, not as amused as he was.

"*That's* why you kept the bench?"

"No. I kept the bench because of the artist; he is one of my kind. He is still creating, though I think he did his best work in his first couple of lives, when he was painting cathedral ceilings and sculpting saints and religious whatnot. And women." He looked at Hannah and grinned. "His ability to capture the likeness of a woman was incredible, and he never missed a chance to paint a nude. But in any case, can you imagine the value of this bench, created by a man who is in reality four or five of the greatest artists to ever live? It is not particularly comfortable, I will give you that, but it has to be one of the most valuable pieces of art on the earth."

Hannah laughed, amazed and amused by the story, and by him. Asher was happy here, and she could see why he loved the house, with all its layers of history. It really was a sanctuary, tucked away from the world at the bottom of an endless crushed-shell driveway between a border of live oaks. Tall trees hid it from the world, clinging close to the walls, dripping Spanish moss over the roofline of the mission-style house like hanks of witches' hair peeking into the courtyard.

It was also silent. The immense quiet here had initially felt strange after so much chaos, but she quickly came to appreciate the value it, of the world outside that was so distant no man-made sound could break through and reach them.

Her satisfied smile faded. Because they could be reached. Eventually they would be found. A shadow passed overhead at the same time it passed over her features, thinking about what was out there, beyond these silent walls. This bird circled but flew away without landing.

# 27

"I'm glad you're tall." Hannah yanked down the shirt she was wearing as a dress, tugging it back down from where it had crept up when she reached up to open the cabinet. She wasn't thrilled with the clothing situation, but she didn't have anything else. At least his gigantic shirts were long enough on her, if a little breezy.

Asher stepped behind her and reached up, taking the bowl she was trying to put away and placing it in the cabinet. She swatted him away.

"I can do it."

She felt him laugh against her back before he stepped away.

"You are incredibly stubborn."

That was true. Especially about doing everything she could in the kitchen, since it was the only thing she could contribute. Glaring at him good-naturedly, Hannah propped her cane against the cabinet and washed and dried the plate from the mountain of pancakes he'd just demolished. She then limped over to sit beside him where he was making his way through a pile of no-bake cookies. The man could eat, there was no doubt about that. It made her feel good about her cooking skills, because he seemed to like everything well enough and he never turned down a second helping. He hadn't complained about breakfast for dinner for the fifth time either, even though it was starting to wear a little thin on her. Then again, it was possible he had absolutely no taste buds, like Gabe suggested. Maybe those didn't improve with age.

"These are very good. I do not think I have had them before. What are they?" he said around a mouthful.

"The only other thing I know how to make with oatmeal."

He put away a couple more as she picked hers apart, taking a small bite here and there, but mostly smooshing it into pieces. Asher shot her a raised eyebrow, and she took an exaggerated bite.

"Hannah, we have discussed this. I need to go, and some distance from the house. I cannot risk being seen near here. It would be too dangerous."

She frowned. This wasn't a new conversation, but she hadn't quit hoping to change how it ended.

"Then let me go with you. I'm pretty much on my feet now. And you stick out more than I do. I can go inside and you can drive the getaway car."

The problem was, they needed supplies. The house had been fairly well stocked with nonperishables when they arrived, but they were quickly running through the contents of the cupboards. There were some canned goods and dried things left, but those wouldn't last much longer, especially at the rate Asher ate. He was planning a trip out to resupply and Hannah had been steadily trying to dissuade him, or at least convince him to take her with him. He refused to consider it, insisting on going alone since she was still recovering. Hannah saw the sense, but didn't relish the idea of being left alone.

"What if we wait? We can stretch what's here a little bit longer, until I'm off this cane. Just a couple more days?" she wheedled.

Asher shook his head. He wouldn't budge. "I am going tonight." He finished the last cookie and got up. "But there is something I want to show you before I leave. Just in case."

He waited patiently as she maneuvered up the stairs, then went through the door into his bedroom. Hannah paused just outside. She clomped her way pretty freely around the house, but she hadn't been inside his room before.

"Come in." Asher waved her over the threshold. She crossed the room, her cane heavy against the painted terra-cotta tiles on the floor.

Each one was a small piece of art, and it seemed like a shame to cover a single one with the rug and the vast bed with its heavy posts of twisting wrought iron.

Beyond the bed, past a fireplace and a comfortable looking over-stuffed chair, Asher opened a door and waited for her to follow him into the cavernous closet. At the far end he pressed a hand against the coffered wall and the whole thing rotated noiselessly.

An "ooh" she couldn't contain slipped out. He nodded in agreement. Behind the cleverly hidden door was another closet of a sort, like the one they had come from, though similar only in size. In features it was more like a bank vault.

"If something should happen and I do not come back as planned." He pulled out drawer after drawer. Money, in any number of currencies. Gemstones and gold coins in plastic tubes the size of half-dollar rolls. A rack of keys to various vehicles, their locations written on the tags. A stack of thin drawers holding deeds to properties, titles, documents.

And weapons. He handed her a compact black handgun.

"You can manage this?"

She nodded and took it, turning it over, taking notice of how to drop the clip and where the safety was, knowing she could use it, hoping she wouldn't have to.

"I have never really needed to worry about security here as there has never been anyone to protect but me. The building itself is solid and secure, but there are no alarms, no cameras. If Amara or someone else wants to find a way in badly enough, they will."

"I could come with you."

He shook his head at her final stab at getting her own way. "I hope to come and go quickly, and until your leg is fully healed you are safer here. This is just a precaution."

He turned toward the door, but instead of leaving he pushed the wall they had come through shut and cranked down on a lever, shooting two thick bars into slots on either side of the door.

"Come in here if you hear anything out of the ordinary. Even if you just have a bad feeling, trust your instincts. Come here, lock yourself in, and wait. Stay inside as long as you can." He opened one of the lower cabinets wide for her to see inside. "There is food and water enough for a week at least, if I am delayed and need to stay away to ensure I do not lead my sister back to you. If anything happens, come in here, stay hidden, and I will return without fail." His voice was intense. The room behind the closet seemed smaller now, overwhelmingly hot with the two of them bolted inside. He was stern and serious, and he filled up the space. She imagined being trapped in here and it made her heart accelerate. Perhaps he heard it, because he released the bolt and pulled the door open.

---

That night, after he had left under cover of the cloudy sky, Hannah tossed and turned in a futile attempt at sleep. Giving up, she did what she normally did when she couldn't make her thoughts stop racing.

She started with the kitchen, wiping down every surface, polishing off invisible fingerprints and straightening the contents of every shelf. After awkwardly sweeping the floor she moved to the living room, dusting every piece of furniture, straightening objects a millimeter here and there into perfect alignment. She did the same in the dining room, working her way around the house, only avoiding the courtyard where the gaping square of sky overhead was like a hungry open mouth, the moss whispering eerily against the roof tiles in the breeze. She listened intently for movement, the darkness and quiet in the house ominous without his presence.

By the time she limped her way upstairs and around the promenade, cleaning her way through an office crammed with books and the other extra bedrooms, streaks of pink and coral were beginning to show themselves.

Less edgy in the beginnings of the day, she made her way back to the doorway of his room. She brushed her hands down the rows of perfectly hung clothing on either side of the closet, shaking her head at the perfect gradient of shades starting with whites and pale creams by the door, darkening to black near the false wall. Hannah was amused by his fussiness, and because she did exactly the same.

It took a couple of tries probing the back wall to find the right place to push until the door unengaged with a click. Once unlocked, the door pivoted on its center effortlessly.

*I'm not being nosy; I'm just being prepared. If I hadn't come in and figured out how to open that door beforehand, I might not have been able to do it under pressure,* she told herself. That might have been partly true, but Hannah felt a twinge of guilt when she began opening the drawers one by one.

She couldn't begin to imagine the worth of it all as she peered at her hand through the transparent shapes on thick stacks of money from Canada and Australia and admired the beautiful colors of the Brazilian reals and the fierce painted dragons on Chinese renminbi. Hannah ran her fingers over the row upon row of coins, surprised by the weight of one when she picked it up. Turning it over she looked at it in the low light, seeing the unmistakable luster of gold.

Below the newer money were thick stacks of larger, older coins, individually housed in acrylic cases. Many were worn nearly smooth with time, and she tilted them sideway to better make out the faded images of emperors and animals.

In a long, thin drawer she pulled out a lumpy bag, tipping the contents out into her palm, a rainbow of gemstones tumbled into her hand. Another drawer lined with dark velvet held more stones, gems big as robin's eggs rolling around loosely against jewelry in heavy, old-fashioned settings.

The next shallow drawer she pulled out made her pause. Compared to the others it was bare by comparison, the only thing in it a single necklace, a teardrop-shaped silver pendant the size of a half dollar on a slim chain. The metal was smooth and dull, the raised design worn away and indistinct. The edges of the pendant were not quite symmetrical, oddly beautiful in their irregularity.

Letting the chain trail over her hand, she fingered its surface. It weighed heavy in her hand, and she could almost feel the enormous age of it. She stared at it, examining the barely visible pattern.

"Hannah."

The pendant hit the ground with a thud and she nearly followed, backing into a cabinet knob painfully. She righted herself to see Asher framed in the doorway.

She blushed furiously at having been caught rummaging through his things. Hannah reached for the necklace, but he got there first, picking it up.

"You're back sooner than I'd hoped," Hannah said, looking down, feeling too guilty to meet his eye. Even though he had shown her the room, she had most definitely been snooping. Hannah wished she had been caught in the gun cabinet at least.

He was holding the pendant, small in the center of his hand, and looking at her with an expression she couldn't decipher as she made to edge clumsily past him and out through the closet.

"Wait." He undid the clasp carefully with his large fingers and placed it around her neck, then stood back to look at it where it lay against her chest. He reached out and tucked a strand of hair behind her ear, his hand brushing her burning cheek when he did. Her face was hot with shame, and she reached up a hand to touch the necklace.

"It suits you." He smiled at her sincerely but somehow sadly, and stepped aside to let her out of the room, clicking the door shut behind them.

———•◆••◆•———

"How did you manage to get all of this so fast?" Once Hannah had finally been able to subdue the flush on her face, and trying not to constantly touch the pendant around her neck, she helped him put away the mountain of groceries he had lugged into the kitchen.

He shrugged and closed the refrigerator door on the last of the perishables. "I was rather surprised myself. Had I known it would go so smoothly I might have taken you along after all. Did you know it is possible to place an order online for almost anything and someone will helpfully load it into your trunk without even having to see your face?"

"You don't think anyone saw you?" She reached overhead to put a box of pasta in the cabinet, tugging down on the hem of yet another giant shirt at the same time. She winced as her arm protested at having the healing skin pulled taut.

"I do not think so, or else I would not have come straight back."

"Is that everything?" Hannah stuffed the last of the groceries into the cupboard.

"Almost. I brought some things back for you. I put the bags on your bed."

She turned around to speak but just caught the back of him heading out into the sunlight of the courtyard.

There was a neat row of brown shopping bags on the white bed-spread, their twisted paper handles in a perfectly aligned arch across their tops. One by one she unpacked them, feeling worse and worse as she laid the items out on the bed.

Shoes and sandals in the correct size. Soft leggings, jeans, and a pair of rugged, cargo-style pants. A variety of shirts, and two jackets, one canvas with a soft fleece lining, the other light and waterproof. Undergarments and pajamas. Another bag held every toiletry she might need and then some. She was embarrassed at the generosity. Also by the thought of Asher selecting her underwear.

She changed into leggings, happy to be covering the itchy still-heal-ing skin down both sides of her legs, and a soft, long-sleeved shirt, pulling the necklace out and combing her hair down her back. She quickly braided it to disguise the worst of the burned-out chunks at the bottom and went back downstairs.

Unable to find him at first, Hannah wandered through the courtyard until she saw the back door she had never seen unbolted was cracked open. She peeked cautiously through the space.

"Come join me."

Asher nodded toward the other chair and poured wine from a dusty bottle into a glass for her, topping off his own before setting it down.

Hannah picked hers up and pondered the viscous red that clung to the sides of the glass as she tilted it this way and that.

"Thank you, for everything," she said, and looked to where his eyes were focused over a wide swath of green grass, and beyond it to the black water. The bayou was dark as ink under the cypress trees, their gray old men's beards hanging still and unmoving over the water.

He looked at the pendant, then back into the distance.

"When I told you I did not recall how my very first life ended, it was not the truth," he said. "As you knew, I imagine. You see through my falsehoods rather too easily." He smiled, picking up his glass and draining it swiftly, setting it down with a click. "The world Amara and I were born in was very different than this one. We were not free. My father was a serf, at the mercy of the man whose land we lived on. All of us were; my father, my mother, Amara and I, our brothers and sisters. Though I will not glorify an unjust system, I know we were luckier than most. We had a home, enough to eat, and the unrest in the land never came to our doorstep."

Asher paused, drew a long breath.

"Hannah, I am a simple man. I was then and I am now. Maybe I cannot look back from such a distance at the way we lived and say I was happy, but at the time, in the only world I knew, I wanted no more. I would have lived and died in the same manner, forgotten by history and been no worse for it." His face darkened. "But not Amara. My sister thought herself made for more, and maybe she was.

"In appearance she has not changed a great deal." He turned to look at Hannah. "She was as fair then as she is now, and shrewder than any of us; this she well knew. Because of this she might have had her choice of matches, to men above her station, men who would have paid for her freedom and the right to her hand. Amara refused them one after another. She thought to go higher."

He shook his head, picking up the bottle to refill his glass, then setting it back down.

"I teased her about becoming an old maid, still unmarried at the great age of nineteen, having turned down offer after offer. I laughed at her scheming to rise up, to find a way into the manor amongst the likes of those who were so far above our station they might as well be gods. But Amara never wavered. She would have fine clothing, servants, and live in the great stone house, her children carried behind her by their nursemaids.

"This will sound strange to you, knowing what my sister is now, but I was in awe of her the day the son of the manor lord came and took her away. It was not even that she managed to catch the eye of someone so far above her station—that I could understand. It was that the father was convinced to countenance a marriage to someone so far beneath them; it was beyond imagining. When it happened, we simply looked on in disbelief."

He paused for a moment and when she looked over at him his face was in shadow, his eyes far away.

"I went off to fight behind her husband that year, and brought home with me a wife, a widow with two young boys. She was kind and beautiful and we were happy in our small life. Her sons called me father, and I was content."

*A wife. Asher married, children running around him.* Hannah had never thought about him like that, but she could see it. She wondered what he saw. For so happy an image, his face looked haunted.

"As time went by, no more children came. I could not have known what I was at the time, or that the failure was mine. Nor could Amara. For her, it was far more dire. After four years she still had not provided her husband with an heir. What good was a beautiful base-born wife if she was unfruitful?"

His face had gone stony, dark for the first time since they'd come here. Hannah sat back, waiting for the storm to pass. His voice was grim when he continued again.

"My sister had no use for us until then. But one night she came sneaking back home on her fine horse, hidden beneath her expensive cloak. Amara had not returned to see her family, but to seek help from my wife. Sara was a midwife, greatly respected in the village, and an herbalist and healer of the sick. Amara wanted her to make a remedy to bring a child. She had grown desperate, fearing the loss of everything she'd accomplished if she was put aside for being barren. Sara obliged her—what else could she do? She sent Amara away with a tea to help bring a child, and a tonic to make her husband virile."

Asher finally moved, turning his head toward Hannah, but he was still looking past her, through her, as he spoke. "Truly I do not know what happened, though I believe it must have been a mistake, the wrong herb, two roots that looked similar, or an unforeseen allergic reaction. Amara slipped her husband Sara's potion and that same night he suffered a horrible, painful death.

"We heard the bells toll the next morning, but we did not know the reason why until the door crashed in and Sara was hauled out. When I learned what had passed, I feared for Sara's life. The sentence for poisoning was a brutal death.

"Then the father of Amara's dead husband came to us. He offered us a solution that would save Sara's life. If we would deny any knowledge of Sara's part in what had happened, and swear Amara had wanted her husband dead, he would allow Sara to keep her life. He would be free of his son's low-born widow and any dower claims against him, and he would have revenge once and for all on a woman he had hated for her grasping elevation.

"Hannah," he whispered, "I did not hesitate. I gave over my sister as a murderer to save my wife. They tied Amara to the post and put the rope around her neck, to strangle her, then lit the pyre before she was yet dead. I had to stand there and watch, show my support in the condemnation of my own sister, guilty of nothing more than desire for a child."

This time Asher met Hannah's eyes.

"And in the end my betrayal did me no good. Amara's horrific death was only her first. A week later I heard the screams from the field, saw the smoke. By the time I reached our home it was engulfed, my wife, my sons, swinging by their necks while the flames rose around them."

His voice faltered. "Amara made me pay for my sins. And after, she made our mother and father, our brothers and sisters pay. She made her father-in-law pay, and his wife and daughters for looking down on her. And the maids for begrudging her their service, everyone in the town who had ever slighted her or showed her unkindness. Finally, someone managed to pierce her with an arrow, but she disappeared. A week and a day later she returned again." He shook his head. "She came for me. I did not raise a hand against her, let her strike me down like the avenging angel I believed her to be. At least then I would go to my family."

Hannah sat in silence and wondered how a hurt could still feel fresh after so many years. She could almost feel the depth of his anguish and loss, the heat of Amara's rage.

"Asher, I am so sorry." She didn't know what more to say. There weren't any words.

He picked up the bottle and divided the remaining wine into their glasses. The storm had passed, leaving only sadness. Asher looked over, managing even to smile weakly.

"I did not tell you this to bring you sadness, but to remind you of who is out there, to keep you from growing complacent here, lest you forget the depth of my sister's hatred and the danger in her. And more, so you understand my complicity. You are an innocent victim in this, no matter what Amara's motivations for pursuing you. I am not."

# 28

Hannah sat stock still, holding her breath as long as she could, staying entirely silent so she could listen. There was a stiff breeze tonight and it pushed the branches of the trees back and forth against the roof with a whispering sound, one her mind turned into a rope sliding down over the tiles, the knot of the noose bumping on the ridges as it went. She'd left the window cracked, and every breath of wind that blew a strand of hair across her throat was a cord, winding around her neck, waiting to jerk her kicking and choking up into the air.

They were nothing, the noises, just the same outdoor sounds she'd grown used to hearing every night. But they were different now, after Asher's story. She couldn't get the image of Amara standing under the dangling, spasming feet of his family out of her mind.

Creeping out of bed, she tiptoed down the hall and around the corner.

"Ash." She tapped softly on the door. "Asher. Are you awake?" There was no answer. Turning the knob, Hannah pushed the door open a crack and peeked inside. No Asher, bed still neatly made.

He didn't sleep much, and though she'd seen him go into the room earlier, that didn't mean he hadn't gotten up and gone wandering; most likely down to the kitchen.

Padding barefoot down the stairs she found the kitchen empty too; no Asher. Hannah poured herself a glass of water by the green glow of the clock on the stove and headed back out.

It wasn't pitch black, but the clouds across the moon made the light muddy. She made her way mostly by feel back across the corner of the courtyard and had one foot on the stairs when she heard a soft whump.

"Asher, is that you?" She hoped it was, the water in the glass slopping over the edge as her hand started to shake. Squinting in the dark, she didn't see anything or sense any movement.

Slowly, Hannah took two steps forward into the courtyard, then stopped to listen. Nothing. She let out the breath she'd been holding. Nothing, just like there had been every night before she'd let what Asher told her creep into her head.

Turning to go back up the stairs and to bed, Hannah tripped over something and hit the ground, landing painfully on her side, hearing the glass that had flown from her hand shatter across the floor.

Whatever she had tripped over was thick and round, as big as her thigh, and very smooth, like a log. It moved, sliding against her skin, slipping down the length of her leg. She shrieked and clawed her way backward, scrambling to get back up on her iffy leg.

"Hannah!" Asher raced into the courtyard as bright lights came on and blinded her. "Where is she?"

"Over there!"

"Hannah, run!" Asher was almost to her. "What are you waiting for? Go!"

"Right there." Hannah pointed toward the edge of the fountain. Then she looked at Asher. He was naked.

"Oh no! Where's Amara? Is she still here? How did she get you?"

Asher yanked Hannah to her feet and shoved her behind him.

"Where is she?" he asked again. "Where is my sister?"

He stopped, looking around frantically and followed Hannah's finger to where it pointed. His eyes widened and he backed away with a shudder.

"What? Where is she? You tell me. You're the one she just killed," Hannah said.

The python Hannah had tripped over was eyeing Asher warily—though not as warily as he was eyeing it—from where it had gone to coil around the cool base of the fountain.

"Is that what you yelled about? The snake? I detest snakes." He shuddered again. "My sister has not found us?"

Hannah shook her head.

"I didn't see anyone. I came down looking for you and tripped over the snake. It must have dropped down from that tree." She pointed up at the branches trailing down over the edges of the roof. "How did Amara find you? Is she still here?"

Asher furrowed his brow. "No, I heard you yell. I came running immediately."

"She didn't kill you? Then why are you naked?"

He disappeared, suddenly, leaving her frozen, waiting for his sister to drop down from the roof or dart out from the shadows. When he quickly reappeared, he was holding a kitchen towel in front of himself.

"Ash, what's going on?" she said.

He looked Hannah over, where she was standing eyeing the snake that was ignoring her.

"I was in the shower," he said.

When his words sunk in Hannah closed her eyes in relief. She sat down on the edge of the fountain, to hell with the snake behind her heels—it paid her no mind anyway—and put her face down in her hands.

"I thought that …" Hannah started to laugh, from relief.

"Hannah, have a care for that animal."

She looked down at it and shrugged, but got up. Asher was standing there stone-faced. The severe look would have had more effect were it not for the clothing situation, but it was stern enough to sober her.

"What is it?"

He scanned the roofline for a moment, then looked to where the snake still lay curled up lazily. Giving a little shake of disgust, he turned and walked inside, motioning for her to come into the house and leave it safely outside.

———•◦•◦•———

He came to the kitchen a few minutes later fully dressed and sat down at the island. Hannah looked at the clock and shrugged, then began pulling pans out of the cupboard. Asher looked about to launch into something serious, and serious conversations were easier with busy hands. And no matter what time it was, Asher would always eat.

"Is the snake still out there?" she asked.

"I hope not. Though I do not know how it will get out. Surely not as easily as it got in. As easily as anyone could get in."

Hannah threw sausages into a pan, adjusting the heat under them before she turned around.

"But no one did."

"But they could have. If that had been what it seemed ..." He shook his head. "Hannah, you might have been taken before you even had time to cry out. I might have woken in the morning to find you gone, or lying there dead. It is time we left."

She turned away without speaking, chopping her way through the onions so she had an excuse for tears when she had to face him.

This day had been coming, it was inevitable. That didn't make it welcome.

Life had fallen into a rhythm over the last weeks, more regular and comfortable than she ever could have expected. Yes, she'd been hurting and healing, but she had also explored and cooked and read for hours on end in the warmth of the courtyard. They'd eaten together companionably and drank wine from old, dusty bottles on the back patio, and occasionally he would break out into ringing laughter at something he found funny, or tell another story about something that had happened lifetimes ago. He teased her about her habit of cursing under her breath and would magically produce books he knew she would like. He would reach out and examine a stray strand of her hair, marveling how he never saw the red until they were in the sun, then absentmindedly tuck it back behind her ear.

It was a pleasant fiction. Hannah wasn't naive enough to fall too far into it, but she didn't fault herself either for being a little enamored, with this place and with him. There would be something wrong with her if she wasn't. This house felt enchanted, and he was so kind to her, caring, warm as the sunshine in this, his own environment.

No, Hannah wasn't a fool. She was smart enough to see the reality of what she was to him, but she also was selfish enough to enjoy what she wasn't afraid to call happiness while she could.

Suddenly she felt his hands on her shoulders. Hannah jumped, sending the knife spinning away across the floor; she hadn't even heard him get up. He turned her around to face him.

"Say something," he said.

"When do we have to leave?"

"I had thought to wait a while longer, but now, I think we should leave as soon as it is light. We have grown too comfortable in our seclusion; it was foolish of me to delay this long."

"Where are we going?"

She twisted out of his grasp and reached up to take down plates from the cupboard, mostly to hide the expression on her face. Hannah had grown comfortable, that was true. And to leave in the morning? It was just a few hours away. It was so soon.

"I made contact with someone who is going to provide us with some identities. It would be next to impossible to go on for too long without some. It would obviously not be safe to use your real name, and any number of my aliases might be compromised as well. We will leave here and get them, and from there …"

Hannah turned to the stove. Asher didn't finish and she didn't ask another question, just finished cooking. By the time everything was done and she had filled the plates, she was able to turn around dry-eyed and manage a small smile.

"If this is my last meal—here, I mean—do you think it would be safe to eat outside?"

———◆◆◆———

They ate in silence, then sat with their coffee, listening to the anhingas calling to each other and the slap of alligators as they slid into the water. Hannah fingered the necklace absentmindedly while she sat, staring out into blackness that was just beginning to show a faint line of light above the cypress trees.

"Asher, who did this necklace belong to?"

Hannah had been wondering about it since he'd put it around her neck. Asher reached over and picked it up from her chest, running a thumb across the surface.

"It belonged to my wife."

She wished she hadn't spoken. "I'm so sorry."

He let it fall back gently against her skin, and the weight of it pulled down against the chain, heavier now than it had been a moment ago.

"You need not be sorry. But me, I am ashamed. So many years have gone by that I cannot remember her face clearly, or the faces of my sons. What I can recall I question, because time has smoothed away the details as surely as it has smoothed away the surface of that metal."

He turned to her and she looked away, a guilty feeling in her stomach. He reached out and touched her chin, turning her face back toward his.

"Hannah, do not be saddened on my behalf. Sadness after so much time is different. It is a reminiscence, like reading about grief in a book, feeling it but not feeling it truly. It causes me no pain. I struggle to remember them clearly, but I do recall the story of that pendant. Maybe because I can see it and touch it still."

She reached up and ran her finger around the irregular edge of the metal.

"My wife brought it with her to our marriage, as she had into her first, though not in the same form," he said. "It had belonged to her mother before her. Sara learned her skills as a midwife from her mother, who had saved the woman and unborn child of a nobleman. It was an unusually difficult labor, and in gratitude he gave her a silver cup." Asher toyed with his coffee mug, turning it over in his hand, examining the pattern around the rim. "It was a great gift, of immense value, but they were poor and a large family. It was their prized possession, but at some point their need became great and her father shaved off a curl of the silver to settle a debt. A hard winter came and another piece was carved away to buy food. As her sisters and brother were married, a piece was cut away each time to help them on their way.

"Sara was the youngest, and when she went to be married the remainder was given to her, a piece a little larger than you wear. She carved it yet smaller after her first husband's death so she and her children could survive. When we were wed, I bored the hole so she could wear it, and I was proud that we never removed even a sliver from it after that."

Hannah felt weighted down by the silence, feeling the heaviness of his words. She wished she hadn't let her curiosity lead her to open that drawer, and she wondered what had made him pick it up and put it around her neck.

"This was where I was sitting, it was just like this," he said.

It was an unexpected change, and she hadn't followed, her mind still on his story.

"I'm, sorry what? I was woolgathering."

"Did you just say woolgathering?" He chuckled. "You speak like you are a hundred years old sometimes." He was abruptly lighthearted, or at least it seemed that way in comparison to her borrowed sadness.

"You would know," she replied with a forced smile. "What did you say?"

"I said this is where I was sitting. When I died and came back near you for the first time."

"You were expecting it, though, weren't you?"

He nodded. "It was my time again. It is a different feeling, to know you are about to die, even when there is a fair chance it will not be permanent. It is hard to describe what it is like to know a life is coming to a close, but not where you will find yourself when you next open your eyes."

She said, "You mean how almost every other person on Earth feels?"

"I guess you are right," he said. "If I should live out my entire span of years, without meeting my end prematurely, you will be forty-five."

And you will still be exactly the same, she thought. Young and beautiful and perfect. The thought wasn't disturbing. Hannah accepted that she was living on borrowed time, and she was grateful for every moment. Compared to his life, hers wouldn't amount to much. Compared to almost anyone's maybe. But you had to work with what you had.

She reached up and pulled the necklace over her head.

"I think you should take this back." She held out her hand, the chain puddled in her cupped hand. He didn't reach out, and he didn't say anything. "Ash, I probably won't be around to wear it that long, and what if it got lost then, when I die? And I know you say you don't really remember her, but you remember this, and it keeps them close that way. This is important to you."

He reached out his hand, but instead of taking the necklace, he closed his hand over it, and over hers. The metal made a cold core in the middle of their hands.

"You are important to me. It is a gift."

Asher held her hand in his for a moment, fingers wrapped around her closed fist, swallowing it up in his. He stayed like that for a moment, going completely still.

"What is it?" she said.

"I forget how very, very small you are. How very fragile. And I am afraid for you."

He swiftly let go and stood up. "Pack your things. I want to leave before the sun is risen."

# 29

"How much longer, do you think?" Hannah asked. She eyed the little green dot on the GPS that was them, watching it crawl steadily west on Route 16.

"We are about thirty miles outside of Macon, so we should be there around ten."

She looked around, trying to judge if anything felt familiar, but unsurprisingly, nothing did.

"I lived near here for a couple years," she said, "but it was a long time ago." Hannah didn't really remember a great deal about it; she'd probably been all of five when she and Joel had moved. The things she recalled were more snippets of memories, like the cardinal red uniform she'd worn to kindergarten or waking up under the pink canopy in her bedroom.

"You lived near here?" Asher pulled off at a gas station, eyeing the fuel gauge.

"I'm pretty sure I was born here too, or at least in the state, but I don't remember much of anything. Some of that might even be just what my uncle told me. I know he was stationed at Robins Air Force Base for quite a while. The name always stuck because when I was little, I pictured it with the birds all over it. After that we lived in Biloxi for a while, two different places in California, in Japan, South Dakota, and in Alaska. The house that burned down in Pennsylvania is actually the longest I've ever lived in one place."

She sat and studied the people coming and going from the

convenience store while he waited for the tank to fill, all the while keeping his face low, watching their surroundings. Hannah realized she had no idea what day of the week it was. Probably a Saturday or Sunday, seeing far too many school-age children being hurried along by their parents for it to be a weekday.

"If Michael is your father," Asher said once back in the car, "I wonder how you ended up being raised by your uncle. That you survived to be raised by anyone is miraculous. I have never heard of Michael letting any of his children live beyond their first few years."

Looking out the window as they pulled out of the parking lot, she shrugged. "My uncle always said he didn't know anything about my father. I don't think he really wanted to. He didn't sound like a very nice guy, since it was clear my mother moved in with him and my aunt to get away from him. I don't think Joel spent much effort trying to find him, since if he did there was a chance my father might decide he wanted me or something."

They passed a sign for the Macon exit and Asher steered into the turning lane.

"I never really looked too hard either," Hannah said. "I poked around a little online, did one of those ancestry DNA tests where you spit in a tube and all that, but not much else. I never really came up with anything."

"And the DNA test? I considered trying one of those when they first became available. I am curious as to what it would discover."

She snorted. "You're so old it would probably come back with a caveman as your closest relative. Not that I made out much better. They just sent it back saying it was contaminated. I tried two more times and then I just gave up." Spitting in a tube and walking to the mailbox had been the extent of the effort she'd been willing to spend looking for her father.

"Looking for him seemed like an insult to Joel, anyway. He'd done the stand-up thing and raised me, and he wasn't even really my uncle. I don't think he and my aunt were ever legally married. He didn't wear a ring, and I never found a marriage certificate or so much as a piece of paper with her name on it. And the only picture I ever saw was one of my mother and her together."

She wondered more than ever what the truth really was.

Asher looked over at her. "There are a great many unanswered questions. How did they find you now? Why would anyone bother after all these years? It is fortunate it appears you are wanted alive, to be taken to him, but why? My fear is that he wishes to see you dead by his own hand."

Hannah rolled down the window against the heaviness of the conversation, letting the sticky heat of the sun soak into her bones. She watched the scenery fly by on the highway next to the green Ocmulgee River until they crossed it. The remaining distance counted down on the GPS until they turned into the shady green entrance of a state park.

"This is where we are meeting." Asher checked the time, then pulled into a parking lot under a low overhang of trees. "We are early, as I had planned. This is obviously illegal, but I have it from a trusted source that his work is reliable and that he has a total lack of curiosity as long as his price is met, which is equally important."

Hannah nodded. She wasn't thrilled, but she understood the necessity.

"And what's his price?" she asked.

Asher turned and pulled a small duffle bag from the back seat, hefting it in his hand before slinging it across his chest. "You do not want to know. We are meeting him farther into the park, about ten minutes from now. I am going to scout things. Stay here, in the car. Lock the doors."

He got out, tossing her the keys before she could protest. "You have your gun?"

She nodded. Asher slipped into the trees and was gone.

The SUV they had come in was a big, growling beast of a machine painted a matte gun-metal gray, one of three shrouded hulks she'd seen in the garage when they left this morning. It made her wonder what would become of her poor, beat-up compact. What would the owner of the cabin back in Pennsylvania think when they found the sad little car abandoned in their garage?

Hannah cracked open one of the darkly tinted windows against the heat that had descended the minute the engine was turned off. There wasn't a breath of air to move the leaves above, and Hannah reached over to start the engine.

"It is all clear. Time to go."

She jumped at Asher's voice next to her window.

It was cooler outside. Hannah pulled her clammy shirt away from her back, feeling a droplet of sweat sliding down to the gun tucked in her waistband. She probably should get a holster sometime. This whole maybe-shooting-herself thing was happening way too frequently.

"I can see him at the spot we arranged to meet, and no one else appears to be around. Just stay behind me."

She hung back, following him along a narrow paved path, past carved wooden signs with line drawings of the park trails and the track of the river.

"Lincoln?" Asher spoke quietly to the man's back. He was sitting on the bench seat of a picnic table, facing the river in front of them.

He didn't turn, keeping his arm casually resting on the small bag lying on the table.

Asher's arm shot out, stopping Hannah. She had seen it too, the black pool spreading under the table. The man they had come to meet wasn't sitting upright on his own steam. He was pinned in place by a long metal blade like a sword snapped off at the hilt. It ran downward at a sharp angle through his unnaturally opened mouth, emerging from his back where it buried itself into the table. Asher reached forward and snatched the bag out from under the man's arm, shoving it at her.

"Run."

This time she didn't hesitate. Hannah could hear him just behind her as they charged back the way they'd come. Her ankle screamed at the effort, but she ignored it, nearly covering the distance to the tree line before she heard a *thwang*, and then a thud.

She heard Asher grunt with pain. Looking back she saw him reaching over his shoulder, clawing at something.

"Go!" he roared, ordering her ahead, falling in place behind her, though not so close now, moving erratically.

A flash of red zipped by, narrowly missing her face and lodging in a tree. Hannah ducked lower, trying to make a more irregular target, glancing back at Asher who was too big to miss as he doggedly struggled to keep up with her, losing ground.

They finally broke through the trees into the parking lot. She heard a whipping sound, and another grunt. Asher skidded to his knees, then fell forward. Two red darts stood out like flags from his back.

She grabbed his arm and tried to haul him up.

"Hannah. Go." His voice was slurred, groggy.

"Get the hell up!" Hannah yanked him upward with all of her strength, feeling the pop in her ankle, only able to get him as far as his knees. God, he was a tank.

Then Hannah saw her, the lean figure in black striding calmly out from the trees, long rifle casually draped over her arm. Hannah dropped Asher ungracefully and sprinted to the SUV as Amara raised the gun to her shoulder, shaking her head in amusement. Hannah climbed up into the driver's seat and started the car, the gears screaming as she skipped several. On her first try she stalled it trying to get it into reverse. Jamming the stick into place she whipped it backward, then went forward, stalling it again, throwing herself toward the windshield. In the rearview mirror she could see Amara shaking her head again, taking a moment to brush a strand of hair from her face before she took aim. The gears grated and squealed, and Amara came closer, not pausing to even glance at her brother face down on the pavement.

One more stall out, followed by the engine racing in neutral, then grinding as Hannah forced the gear shift forward without depressing the clutch. The engine screamed in protest while Amara stood there, steely eyed. She slung the rifle behind her back, pulled out a handgun, and the back windshield shattered in a hail of glass.

The gears ground painfully. Amara was so close now Hannah

could see the color of her eyes in the rearview mirror. Exactly the same shade as her brother's.

That was when Hannah threw the car into reverse and gassed it, feeling the thump under the tires once, then twice. Being careful not to back over Asher, Hannah put the car in first and did it again. Then twice more, until there were no more thumps.

*Stupid bitch*, Hannah thought. *Like I don't know how to drive stick.*

———●◆●———

Hannah proceeded cautiously, pulling the sweaty handgun from her waistband before she opened the door. There was no sign of Amara. Checking the bumper and tires she was relieved to find no blood, no hair, not a trace of her. She was dead—for the moment. Asher was on the ground, alive, out cold, but thankfully still there.

She backed the SUV up as close to the unconscious Asher as she possibly could without running him over. After trying to move his dead weight she briefly considered shooting him, though if they managed to get out of here she would never admit it to him. Anyway, even if he had come back near her the last couple times he died, there was no guarantee it would happen again. If he died and things went differently this time, she wouldn't know how to find him.

Hannah heaved and hauled until finally he toppled ungracefully into the back seat. He immediately rolled off onto the floor, wedging himself into the space behind the front seats. There was no chance she would be able to un-wedge him from there, so she shoved his feet inside and shut the door, and as quickly as possible, began to drive out of the park.

"Ash. Asher. Wake up." Hannah reached back and poked him, getting no response. "Asher!" She smacked him across the face, swerving a little as she drove. Eyes back on the road, she struggled to subdue the full-body shaking and slowed to a less conspicuous speed. As inconspicuous as an SUV with a shot-out back window and a destroyed rear bumper could be.

There was a groan, then silence.

"Ash, can you hear me?"

Torn between the urge to put as much distance as possible between them and their last known location and the need to get Asher awake long enough to figure out where to go next, Hannah settled on the latter. At the next available turn she pulled off and backed the car as far out of sight as she could behind a shabby strip mall.

Asher was still crammed solidly on his side between the back and front seats, unconscious and deathly still. She gave him a tug, but she couldn't begin to move him, especially with her ankle. She could already feel it swelling inside her boot, and her shirt was wet with blood where her arm had somehow torn open, yet again. That was definitely never going to heal.

Hannah moved the front seats up as far as they would go, then groped under him until she found the lever to move the rear seat, sliding it back until he was at least lying mostly flat. His face was slack and he was drenched with perspiration, his hair plastered to his waxy white forehead.

"Come on, big guy. Wake up. Don't make me do anything stupid." She was bluffing of course. She'd had no qualms about backing over his sister, but on the off chance this was his last get-out-of-dead-free card, Hannah could never do it.

The only thing she could do until he came to was keep moving. Careful not to shut his feet in the door, she climbed back into the driver's seat.

"No ... No. No. No." When she looked over the seat to back up, there was nothing there.

Asher was gone.

She looked around hopefully. Maybe he would just reappear in front of the car. He'd climb in and they'd figure out what to do next. Hannah sat still, waited. Nothing.

Hannah bounced her head off the headrest. Where was he? She'd been right, it was a fluke, and this time—the worst possible time—it hadn't worked.

Now what? She didn't know what to do. Dropping her forehead on the steering wheel, she let hot tears drip down over the leather. But not for long, only for a moment. Picking her head up and hauling in a couple of deep breaths, she made herself pull it together.

Rolling down the window, Hannah took a careful look around, convincing herself that at least she had a while before Amara could pop up again. Maybe if she ditched the car and figured out an inconspicuous way back to Savannah she could get to Asher's house. If she could find it. He'd make his way back there eventually. She wasn't helpless, and sitting here waiting for some miraculous rescue would probably just get her killed.

Something made her ears prick, a sound in the distance. She didn't move, except to pat the console where she'd laid her gun to make sure it was still there.

She heard another scream.

There was a commotion in the plaza she was hiding behind. She fumbled the car into gear, rigid with fear, afraid of the pop of gunshots she was sure would come next. There was no way Amara could have found Hannah and gotten back to her this fast, but she wasn't working alone. Was it the unknown factor, maybe her father, or someone sent to make sure she didn't escape again? If that was the case, it was time to move.

Hannah put the car in drive and started to pull out when a police car blew by. A second followed, this one stopping halfway across the end of the narrow alley. They hadn't seen her, but they were blocking her from leaving her hiding place without drawing attention.

She put the car in reverse and slowly backed it up, scraping against a loading dock with a shriek as she squeezed by. Hannah let out a sigh of relief when the stretch of pavement behind the long building didn't dead end. Carefully, Hannah backed around the end of the building, looking for the police cars, or for worse, who the police were after.

What she saw was a large naked man running across the parking lot of a grocery store, heading for the nearest exit. Tearing out, she sped across the parking lot, pulling up beside him. He looked wide-eyed into the window.

"Get in."

# 30

"I really liked this car."

Hannah nodded in agreement as Asher looked woefully at his mangled vehicle. At least she could meet his eyes, now that they had been able to stop and retrieve the bag with his clothes from the back seat. It had been a good half hour since she'd hopped it over the curb and taken off, and she'd kept her eyes firmly glued to the road—with minimal peeking—since she'd picked him up and told him everything he had missed.

They were sitting on the curb behind the back bumper in the far corner of a busy outlet mall. With the remaining bits of the back window knocked out, the gaping hole was a little less noticeable.

"The darts, that was new," she said.

"Indeed. Amara must be getting desperate. They do not work well on us. It takes a great deal to knock one of us out, so much so that the heart will usually give out soon after the dart fully kicks in." Asher shook his head in consternation. "She had to be wagering it would slow you down. If I was dead and gone you would run, but if I was lying there unconscious you might hesitate." He looked over at her. "Hannah, you should have run."

She didn't respond. It was irrelevant now, and it had given her a chance to wipe the grin off Amara's face with her bumper.

"So, what do we do now?" she said. He didn't answer. "Asher?"

He was looking at the battered car again. Maybe he was regretting driving it, having conceded that they were going to have to ditch it.

Amara had seen them in it, and even if she'd popped back up halfway across the planet, she wasn't working alone. She could have someone looking for it right now; keeping it was too risky.

"What were you going to do?" He looked at her, his lips pulling down at the corners.

"I was going to try to keep you alive long enough to see if you had any ideas. I blew that, sorry to say."

"And after that?"

She shrugged. Honestly, she hadn't had time to worry about the next step in too much detail. "I don't know. I would have kept driving I guess."

"To where, Hannah? Where were you going to go? And when you needed fuel or food, what were you going to do? This is serious." His voice grew sharp, and it felt like he was growing larger beside her.

"You don't think I know this is serious? Why the hell are you getting upset with me? It's not my fault I couldn't manage to keep you from dying from an overdose of elephant tranquilizer."

"I am sorry," he said.

"Yeah, well maybe you should be. I don't need your attitude. We've got enough else going on."

"Not about that," he said.

Hannah looked at him and raised an eyebrow.

"Not only about that. And you could not have saved me. I am sorry for bringing you into this situation in the first place. I took us from my house to avoid being detected by my sister and she finds us within the day." Asher shook his head in disgust. "After this long I should be more adept at predicting my sister's actions. She clearly anticipates mine. I even managed to take the money with me when I died, so you had limited resources to continue with. I have failed to do my duty and protect you properly."

She shook her head at him. "I appreciate all the help so far, but when it comes down to it, I can take care of myself. And anyway, this isn't your *duty.* I know you feel like it's your job, making sure your sister doesn't kill any more poor little helpless humans that you have

to feel bad about"—Hannah looked pointedly away from him— "but
don't beat yourself up on my account. There's no point. She's going to
get me eventually and it'll be just like every other time. If I were you,
I don't know if I'd even waste the time."

"You do me an injustice, Hannah." His words sounded harsh, but
his tone was soft, the edge from a moment ago gone. "You look at me
wrongly, if you think that is at all how I feel. And how can you say I
am not meant to watch over you?" he said. "What other reason can
you think of for my being sent to where you are over and over again?
I know now it has been going on longer than either of us knew."

"What do you mean?"

He shook his head. "I told you about how I had lived out my allot-
ted span of years and died before I found myself in your town for the
first time. It had been nearly twenty-three years since the last time I
expired. Can you guess where I found myself that time?" He didn't
give her time to answer. "I woke up in Macon, Georgia, which means
I was sent to where you were while you were in the womb, Hannah."

She sat back and tried to process what he was saying.

"Time after time I was sent back to you. Even at the Walmart when
you were fleeing after my sister shot you. We must have missed each
other by minutes. And it is happening more quickly and more precisely
every time. What reason for it beyond fate can you imagine?"

He didn't wait for an answer from her, which was fine, because
she didn't have one. Hannah didn't really believe in fate, but she didn't
have a better explanation for why they were being thrown together.

"No more of this. I will not let Amara catch us unprepared again. I
have been alive long enough that I should be fully capable of covering
every possibility, despite this failure. If this happens again, if we get
separated, you need to go back to the house in Savannah. In the—"

"Asher, don't be an idiot." It came out fast, but she mostly meant it.
"What's the point. In the end, she's going to get me." She turned away,
face growing warm. "Truth is, you can plan all you want, but eventually she's going to get me. I'm sure as hell going to avoid it as long as
possible, but you're wasting time making plans in the long term. No

matter what keeps putting us together, it's going to end with me dead."
She stopped and swallowed hard before she continued. "It's going to
end, and maybe if you aren't there for that part, you won't have to live
with the misplaced guilt. Why make it worse than it has to be?"

Getting up abruptly, Hannah walked around the car, out of the
shade to where it was brighter. She was eternally grateful for the protection, but why suffer the guilt of fighting a battle you couldn't win. It
would be better if he walked away and never even knew how it ended.

"You think I would just leave you, that my only lookout is the state
of my conscience? Is that what you think?"

He had come around the car silently to stand in front of her. She
looked up at him, and he stared her down, her back against the warm
metal of the SUV.

"Maybe you should. It's the truth, isn't it?" she said. Asher didn't
answer. He put a hand on the car on each side of her shoulders, then
leaned down and silently rested his forehead against hers. They stood
there for a moment. Then he leaned back and looked away.

"You are wrong. So very wrong. And I am not going anywhere."

Hannah stood there for a moment, trying to understand, wanting
to ask, but she pushed it away. It all had to wait. He was choosing not
to walk away, whatever the reason, whether he should or not.

"So … if you're staying."

"I am staying."

"Then what now?"

What they needed most right now was to put some distance between
themselves and Macon and regroup without being detected. It was
easier said than done without knowing exactly where Amara was and
how many people were working with her, or exactly how anyone was
continually managing to find out where they were.

"My sister has the advantage. She has never been one to hide from
the world, and she is never afraid to use others to do her bidding,"
Asher took one last wistful look at the SUV and began to walk across
the parking lot, hunched in his usual I'm-trying-to-blend-in fashion.
Hannah followed. "She will enlist anyone who can be of use to her, so

you can bet she has some tech-savvy lackey, or more likely several of them, scouring the country for one of my identities to pop up, or for some type of facial recognition to catch us. Amara has always embraced the passage of time and the advancements that come with it. She will always be one step ahead of me in this matter. I have learned to accept the changes, but she courts them."

Hannah stopped. "So, let's pop up."

Asher looked at her quizzically until Hannah told him what she had in mind. After she was done, he stood for a moment, going over it in his head.

"My instinct is to get as far away from here as quickly as possible, but it may be too late to leave unobserved. I feel as though we are being closed in on already. If it were not for that I would not even consider it."

"But you are, since we don't have a whole lot of other good options."

He nodded.

"And because my sister always seems to know what my plans are. It might not occur to her you might have plans of your own."

---

Asher bought a cheap phone from a store in the outlet mall and ordered a ride share for them. After it arrived and they were on their way, he took out the new IDs and credit cards from the forger's little bag and used them to book two tickets to Portugal, with about four different layovers. He had barely finished when they slowed, and pulled to a stop beside a door with a sign for departures. They were out of the car before the driver could put it in park.

Inside Asher disassembled the phone and dropped the body, SIM card, and battery into the first trash can.

"Our new identities were short lived, but hopefully useful. If Amara knew about the meet to obtain them, there is a chance she knew about the identities themselves and will be on alert for them to be used. The credit card is an old alias, so there is a chance she is on watch for it as well."

Walking through the door, they found there wasn't as much cover as they'd been hoping for.

"Should be easy enough to blend in with the crowds here," she said, sarcasm evident. The airport was tiny, four or five gates, a little newsstand and souvenir shop, and a restaurant where three men in suits sat at the bar. Asher and Hannah walked through, stopping at an ATM to take a cash advance from another of Asher's credit cards. They dumped the card in the next can then went to the kiosk to buy her a baseball cap. Finally, they turned toward the security stand under the sign with the arrow for departures.

"Are you ready?" he said. She nodded and they started walking. He followed her past the entrance to security, through the baggage claim, to the doors that led out to the taxi stand.

Asher handed her a wad of cash. "Keep your head down. Do not look back. Take the first cab directly to the bus station, then tell them you changed your mind and have them take you to the hotel. There is a bar in the lobby. Stay there, and I will meet you. If I do not come within the hour, get a cab back to the bus station. Get a different cab from there to the address I gave you. When you think it is safe, go back to Savannah. You have the address memorized?"

She nodded. "Of course, I have it memorized. It was my idea."

"Make sure you are not followed." He put the hat on her head and pulled down the brim over her face. Tucking her hair underneath, he said, "Whatever happens, I will find you, without fail."

She looked up at him and drew in a deep breath, then took a step toward the door.

He pulled her back by the arm just briefly, squeezing it, then pushed her toward the exit. Hopefully Amara would take the bait, anticipating their taking a flight; Hannah would be out the door unnoticed and long gone before it took off. The minute her taxi was away, Asher would go check in for their flight with the passports, discard them, and if the coast was clear, get away and find his way to her. Once they met up, they could start the next part of the plan.

As much as she wanted to, Hannah didn't look back, walking out of the airport and into the cool evening. The waiting taxi pulled forward and she climbed in.

"The Greyhound station on Spring Street, please." She settled into the seat and tried to pick out Asher's form through the glass of the door. She saw the doors open, and he was charging toward her, a look of horror on his face.

"Hello, Hannah."

A familiar pair of eyes looked back at her from the driver's seat before she felt the crack against her temple. *So much for my plan,* she just had time to think before everything swam away to blackness.

# 31

Her eyes opened to fog, then shut again of their own volition. Forcing them open, blinking rapidly to clear the mist, she saw a face come into focus directly in front of her.

"Gabe," she mumbled.

"Yes, yes, there we are."

She tried to get up, but her hands were secured with wide leather bands to wooden arms, like she was strapped to an electric chair. Her head was pinned back by a restraint across her forehead that pressed painfully against her swollen temple. It would be a miracle if she wasn't brain damaged from all the blows to the head. If she made it until tomorrow, that is. Her ankles were similarly lashed down, and didn't give when she struggled.

"No sense wasting your energy. You're snug as a bug in a rug, Hannah darling, and you're going to stay that way for the time being."

Hannah strained against the bonds, futilely. "Gabe, what's going on? Let me go."

He shook his head. "Sorry, my dear. I am under strict orders to keep you breathing, for the present. I would hate to deprive Amara of whatever it is she has in store for you. She's rather cranky when disappointed." He grinned, the smile that had seemed roguish and charming now cruel.

"Why are you doing this?" Hannah gave up straining and instead tried to figure out where she was. Gabe rose from where he'd been seated next to her and strolled casually to the wide window where a slit of sky was visible over a knob of trees.

The room they were in was large, squat and square with a low, dark ceiling. She couldn't move her head, only able to see a long, medieval-looking dining table lined with stiff carved chairs, one of which she was strapped to. The walls were paneled in dark wood, bare except for evenly spaced torchieres that gave off a dim glow.

"Gabe, let me go," she said again.

"Sorry, dearie, really can't. I promised I would keep you secure until she could make it back."

Amara. She was coming.

"Why are you helping her? I thought Asher was your friend. You betrayed him for his sister?"

He turned from the window, eyebrows raised. "Betrayal? Betrayal is only a thing if you actually believe in loyalty. And friendship? Oh no, how about morality, and dare I say, love?" Gabe laughed in the lightest, most nonchalant way. "Not for me, darling. Those are all just constructs of the mortals and the imbecilic, like Asher. The man is as old as time and he still thinks like a human. I can't figure out how that prize pig turned out to be such a pale shadow of the creature his sister is. They shared a womb, and all he got was the size." Gabe leaned casually against a chair. "He got nothing while she got all the intelligence and looks and backbone. While she's ruled kingdoms, wiped out entire armies, brought death to whole cities down to a person, he's done nothing." He shook his head. "Asher is just a pitiful pawn in a game where she's queen."

"Gabe, let me go. I'm nothing to you. Just let me go before she gets here. I don't matter."

"You don't matter? No, not for your own sake, I guess. Nothing about any of you humans does. Amara has the only thing that really matters in this existence. Power. Power is the only thing that lasts."

"You don't need me, Gabe. Let me go."

"Sorry, dear heart. I really do need you. Because Amara has plans for you. I won't ruin the surprise, but this time she's outdone even herself. Now bite your tongue, or I will."

Gone was the beguiling accent, the rascally facade. Gabriel was a beautiful snake, a cold venomous creature, and Hannah was stunned to silence.

He cocked his head at a sound she couldn't hear. "And here she is now," he said. "My darling, that was fast, even for you."

"I didn't want to miss a moment of a party as exciting as this one. It's so very seldom anything really interesting happens," a familiar voice murmured. "I was so anxious to get back I didn't even delay long enough to kill anyone." Hannah strained to turn her head. Someone should delay Amara again by removing her head, even if it was only temporary.

"Tut tut, looking a little rough, Hannah." Amara squatted down level with Hannah's face and considered her with cool, blue-gray eyes, a slight smile pulling up the edges of the perfect mouth. "Though it is the only way I've ever seen you look, so maybe you're just naturally a disaster." She tilted her head to the side. "Yes, I can see the resemblance. Especially with that hair."

With a long, perfect finger she pulled down the collar of Hannah's shirt. Her eyebrow cocked up in amusement. Hannah forced herself not to flinch at her touch.

"Asher, Asher, when will you ever learn. Boy is a hopeless romantic." Amara shook her head and laughed softly. She lifted the pendant up by the chain. "Sentimental fool. I took a rope to the last throat this hung around." She pulled the necklace aside. "Hmm, I thought there would be a scar."

Amara stood up, considered Hannah for a moment, then walked toward the door, pausing for a moment to call back over her shoulder.

"Gabriel, would you do the whole bad guy thing where you tell the entire story? I'd love to, but I need to make a few phone calls, get up to speed on daddy dearest's arrival."

Pulling out the chair next to Hannah, Gabriel sat back and tented his fingers.

"Nice dungeon, Gabe. Is it yours or are we in the basement of a

Medieval Times?" Hannah glared at him, still trying to feel for any give in her bonds.

"Mine? Good gods no, this place is horrible. Just visiting. The real owners got hung up somewhere." He smiled.

She was certain he meant that literally. Straining her head, she tried to get a look out the window, but her vision was limited.

"Looking for Asher? Don't look too hard. He won't find you here, and even if he could, we'd have him boxed up and in a timeout before he even made it to the door. I really think it's just a matter of getting the dosage right. It's amazing the new technology out there, how it's really changing things. You've only seen the fly by the seat of your pants method, but this is a finely tuned operation. Much classier. Plus there's easily a dozen men armed to the teeth out there to keep things from going pear shaped again. You were a little slipperier than expected, but we learn from our mistakes, don't we?"

"Christ, Gabe, get on with it. One of us is getting older here." Hannah was finding out abject fear made her mouthy. She considered making an effort to control it, to avoid shortening her already bleak future, but decided she might as well go down swinging, at least her tongue, which was the only part of her she could move.

"So very sassy. Fine. Let's skip to the part you don't know. Now let me see." He paused to listen for a sound her ears couldn't make out. "Yes, I think we have time for the long version. Amara is bringing your father around, but I can't yet hear his supercilious tones." He looked her over. "The resemblance really is uncanny. Unmistakable really." Gabe picked up a strand of Hannah's hair and eyed it under the light. "Not really black, is it, more of a bloody dark red. Hmm." He dropped it and patted it into place. "Amara can be a little impatient. She blew up my perfectly good bar before I got all the information out of Asher I'd hoped to. However did he manage to find you before his sister did? Your picture popped up in the newspaper, but there was his, right beside it." He shrugged and leaned back against the table. "It was clear your father must have approached him about tracking you down. Why else would Asher be doing anything besides his usual running for a bolt-hole? Why Michael thought Asher would be as equipped to find you as Amara I can't imagine, though somehow that giant oaf managed. I guess Michael was desperate for results and thought two heads would be better than one, even if one of them is empty."

God, what a sanctimonious prick. He was really eating up this villain stuff. As much as Hannah wanted to drag out the remainder of her short life, she wished he would shut up even more.

"It worked like a charm, mostly. Asher was stupid enough to send you to me and follow right behind and stay there, giving Amara time to catch up. Then the idiot called me about getting some documents. Literally handed you to her on a plate."

Hannah's wrists were beginning to bleed from rubbing them desperately against her restraints. Gabe shook his head.

"Don't bother. You're just wasting energy. You know, Asher never did let on how he found out about you, let alone tracked you down. The whole hitting him with the car story is interesting, but what was the point?"

Hannah didn't react. It wasn't true; she didn't believe for a moment that Asher had actually been looking for her before she hit him. But they did. And they had no idea Asher was coming to her again and again for a totally different and totally inexplicable reason. She felt the weight of the necklace around her neck.

"All because of your dear father, with his unique 'gift.' He's ended lives in quantities that would make a genocidal maniac blush. Makes me look like a kitten. It's impressive, considering how many of them he managed to father before he killed them. No wonder he likes to work in quantity when he can. Shame cults are harder to get rolling these days." He smiled with satisfaction. What an ass. "You, however, are the only one that has evaded him. It seems after he impregnated your mother she managed to elude him. Temporarily. Some people get a whiff of fear from us, you know. Like an animal that suspects a predator. A fascinating instinct that sometimes pops up among the lower orders."

Pushing off with her good leg, Hannah tried to get the chair to rock, but Gabe kicked her in the ankle, not hard enough to hurt her, but to remind her she had no choice but to pay attention to him. "While Michael did manage to track her down and dispatch her, he was interrupted before he could finish you. It was the ceremonial garbage that got him, I imagine, all the knives and blood and whatnot. If he'd just snapped your little baby neck none of us would be here right now. Well, you anyway." He gave her a nasty smile. "Whoever rescued you barely scraped by with the win, according to Michael. He had you bleeding in his hands then bam, he's out, and you, gone without a trace. Someone did a masterful job of hiding you for so long. Any desire to share?"

She didn't even blink. Screw him.

"Well, maybe later we can convince you to spill. Amara has a talent for loosening lips. Sometimes completely."

Hannah shifted uncomfortably against the tight restraints.

"Get on with it, Gabe. The arch villain thing is getting lame. You're giving me a headache. If you loosen this thing across my head it might help."

"Don't interrupt, sweetheart," he said, picking right up with his diatribe where he'd left off. "Michael didn't look for you too hard in the beginning, I daresay, or he probably would have found you, but recently he found his need to locate you much more urgent. Can you imagine why?"

"I'm sure she can't, Gabriel," Amara's voiced chimed in. "Why even bother? He's here."

# 32

Hannah closed her eyes and kept them shut. Her father, right here in front of her at the end of it all. Gabe wondered if she could imagine why. She couldn't, and she didn't care to try. There weren't enough minutes left to waste any on something as trivial as the why. The end of her story looked clearly written, so did she really need to spend her final bit of time filling in the gaps? She didn't care to have the last thing she saw be the homicidal maniac who contributed the weird half of her DNA. Instead she thought about what came next.

She wished she could've said goodbye to Asher, and thank him. If there was nothing else, nothing that came after, he would never have to face it, the possibility of disappearing into empty oblivion; Hannah took comfort in that. Knowing you were about to end, seeing the insignificant sum of all your days, the paltry accomplishments and dreams; it was an indescribable feeling.

"Open your eyes. Don't be so dramatic," Amara said.

The strap around her head suddenly loosened, and Hannah's head dropped forward at the abrupt release.

"So, this is she?"

Hannah looked automatically to where the voice had come from, and what she saw was not what she expected.

"Hannah. What a plebeian name."

The man looked at her down a long, thin nose. They were right about one thing. The resemblance was undeniable. Their features were remarkably similar, the high cheekbones, the shape of the jaw, even the

253

arch in their eyebrows. But his face was lined, his precisely combed hair—dark, with the same familiar tinge of red—was touched with gray at the temples. Mature. He wasn't like the rest of them, frozen in time. He was older. How was this her father, a being with supposedly endless lives and youth? He should have been coming closer to perfection every time he died, not farther from it.

"I know, shocking, isn't it?" Amara was standing behind him, hands on her hips, next to Gabriel.

"Give me her blood and then you can have her," Michael said to Amara, glaring at Hannah. "That was our arrangement. I only wish to be restored and continue my mission. When I have finished with her, she is yours to do with what you will, though I desire that it be as far away from me as possible."

Michael seated himself grandly at the other end of the table and held out his arm, all the time staring at Hannah in a manner that was not fatherly or kind, but disdainful. Finally, he sniffed and looked away from her. Amara approached Hannah with a syringe, cracking her across the face with the back of her hand when she thrashed against the restraints.

"Hold still." She clamped a hand down at Hannah's elbow and inserted the needle into the vein, pulling the plunger back. When it was full she eyed it with curiosity.

"Amara, there's gunfire outside. I think we may have company." Gabe was looking out the window.

"Damn it, how does he find me so fast?"

"Or her. Did you check her for bugs?" Gabe asked.

She paused, needle in hand, and looked at Gabriel with an expression that said an idea had come to her.

"Do you want me to go sort it out?" Gabe moved toward the door.

Hannah's father, or Michael, or whoever he was, cleared his throat, still holding his arm out. "Now, before this becomes even more tiresome."

Amara nodded at him.

"Not yet, Gabriel, help me with this first." As Gabe moved toward her, as quick as a striking snake Amara jammed the syringe into his arm and rammed the plunger home, then shoved him across the room, pulling out an ugly snub-nosed handgun. Then she put a bullet between Michael's eyes, which stared open, wide with surprise.

———•••••———

Hannah's ears rang from the deafening sound of the gunshot. Amara's gun was now trained on Gabe, who was on his feet, hand on his own weapon. He froze, unsure, looking at the syringe wobbling up and down where it protruded from his arm.

Amara looked over her shoulder at Hannah. "You see now, don't you, Hannah, or haven't you worked it all out? There was a reason for Michael's exceptional quality. He thought he was creating eternal life, when all this time he was creating his own death, over and over again. A little bit of your blood when he tried to off you when you were a baby and he started aging like a normal man. I wonder how long it took for him to notice. The first gray hair? A little wrinkle? At some point he figured it out and needed to track you down rather more urgently. He was desperate enough to think that if you could undo him, maybe you could put him back the way he was." She cocked her head to where Michael still sat, a thin line of blood making its way down the side of his nose and dribbling from his chin, darkening his precisely pressed shirt. "Guess we'll never know."

His head fell back. He was dead, but not gone. Dead for good.

"Men. All he had to do was keep it in his pants and he could've lived forever." Amara's arm swung toward the movement on her right. "Drop it, Gabriel, or we'll find out right now if she's a one-hit wonder."

Hannah heard a gun clatter to the ground and felt a hand clamp down on her shoulder. The minute Amara's eyes shifted, Gabe moved, not content to await his now-uncertain fate. Instead of attacking, he turned and threw himself out the window in a crash of glass. Amara's arm whipped out and she fired three quick shots into his back, and a rush of cold air hit them the same time as the thud of his body hitting the ground outside.

255

"Guess we'll see what happens," Amara said. "If he follows in your father's footsteps, you and I are going to be spending some quality time together, culling the herd. We are going to make me one of a kind."

She pulled another syringe from her pocket. "Just in case my brother makes an appearance."

Suddenly, Gabe came flying back through the broken window. He crashed into the table, bouncing off it and sliding to the floor in a pile, not moving. He hadn't come back in of his own volition. Amara's gun was still trained on his limp form when another body appeared in the opening. She whipped her weapon toward it with her usual blinding speed and opened fire. A man in a helmet and flak jacket tumbled inside, taking almost the same route as the last body, sliding to a halt on top of the still-present, unmoving Gabe.

Gunfire erupted outside, and Hannah cringed, an easy target strapped to the chair. She swung her head wildly back and forth, pushing off with her good leg, trying to gain enough momentum to rock the heavy chair and tip herself out of the line of fire.

Amara's gun was aimed at the broken window. It shifted when something slammed against the single door into the room. Amara cursed. Another crash, and the door gave. A second black-clad form was hurled through it, slumping to the ground. It could only be Asher, Hannah thought. Hoped. She continued to thrash in the chair, rocking it side to side, trying to tip it over. Maybe she could free herself while Amara was occupied.

"Not so fast." Amara clamped her hand across Hannah's mouth and pressed the muzzle of the gun against her temple. "I know it's you out there. Enough throwing things around, Asher. Show yourself. I have her and I won't hesitate to put a bullet in her."

Hannah had seen Asher in all the ways she thought possible, but this was a giant raging demon of a man. Streaked with gore, seething with anger, he stepped on the body of the man he had just thrown through the door with an audible crunch and came into the room.

"Stop right there," Amara said.

She squeezed the hand covering Hannah's mouth and nose. He

didn't look at Hannah, didn't meet her terrified face. His eyes were fixed on his sister. Amara's hand was closing off Hannah's air, the metal of the barrel cutting into her head.

"Let her go, you evil witch. How many years will you play your vile games, torturing these creatures?" Asher boomed, his voice like the gunshots that had echoed across the stone moments ago. He was a fearsome being.

"I said stop."

Asher had twitched in their direction but froze again. Amara pressed the gun harder, grinding the barrel against Hannah's skull.

"I will shoot her. Don't even doubt it. And I'll be careful to paralyze her. I can do it, you know how good I am. She can be my juice box for the rest of her short life."

That was a horrifying option that hadn't occurred to Hannah.

Asher dared to take a step.

"Oh, very good. Very nice. Pretending you don't care if I torture and maim another one of your women, that this is all about you. You even gave this one the necklace. Christ, brother, can't you just get a dog or a goldfish or something? They'd last you just as long."

Asher's expression was severe, his eyes hard gray stones. If he felt anything it didn't show. He continued to stare down at his sister without blinking.

Gone was the girlish sweet tone in Amara's voice. "She's mine," she hissed. "You think you can take the power from me, you giant waste of flesh? I will end you now, brother. You'll be the beginning—well, after Gabriel—but now I'll have time to enjoy killing you for good. I'm going to slowly cut you into little tiny pieces one last time, and you'll die knowing I'm going to pump her dry until I'm the last of our kind."

The pressure of the barrel let up slightly, the angle shifting. Hannah looked up at Asher. Finally, he looked at her.

"That's better, brother. Now what you're going to do is—"

Hannah bit down on her own tongue, the pain bringing tears to her eyes, her mouth filling with blood. A tear must have reached Amara's hand where it was clamped over Hannah's mouth, because she stopped and looked down at Hannah.

"Oh no, it's crying. Poor little—"

Hannah bit her. She sank her bloody teeth into Amara's hand, incisors closing down on the fingers against her lips. The hand jerked away, ripping itself from her teeth, and Hannah spat away blood and bits of flesh.

"Kill her!" Hannah screamed at Asher.

The room froze for a second, but before Asher could reach her, Amara launched herself out the window and ran.

———◆◆◆———

They watched the fire begin to take, turning the black empty windows bright orange with flames. Inside, two people who hadn't thought about their death in a very long time were being turned to ashes. For better or worse—worse, definitely worse, Hannah thought, one of them had been her father.

Hannah told Asher what she knew, what had happened, filling in the gaps she could while they watched the fire grow.

"Are you sorry, about Gabe?" she asked quietly.

Asher shook his head. "No, I am not sorry about Gabriel. Even if he had not betrayed me, he has had innumerable lives. He made a farce of death, used it as a tool, and never thought he would truly experience his own end. I only regret he chose to live this last life so poorly." He looked at the flames flowing out the window frames, licking at the roof like red waters flowing upside down. "I *am* sorry about the others, deceived by my sister. They chose the wrong employ, just normal people who made a poor choice. That did not mean they deserved death."

They stepped back from the heat that pushed outward, scorching the ground around them. When the roof began to buckle he turned and she followed him up a long, overgrown drive that curved away from the burning house until it was out of sight, except for the plume of smoke that rose up above the trees.

"How did you find me?"

He stopped abruptly at her question, reaching out a hand behind to steady her when she nearly collided with him, immediately snatching it away.

"I could not. The car pulled away and you were gone."

Asher looked at her for a moment. Then she understood.

He started walking again, still without turning, and as she trailed behind him she turned the thought over in her head. He had ended his life to find her. Asher must have killed himself, taking the chance that once again it would bring him to her, taking the chance that when he did it, it might be for the last time. He couldn't have known that his end—his true, permanent end—was more possible than either of them had believed. The thought made her shudder.

Finally, they reached the top of the drive, a long empty road in front of them. They paused at the edge of the pavement, nothing visible in either direction.

"She will be back, you know. One way or another," Asher said to the empty air.

Hannah did know. There was no way of telling if Amara was finally vulnerable, or if she was as immortal as she'd always been, just way more pissed off. There was so much that was still pure conjecture.

There were a great many questions left unanswered, but at least there was a modicum of safety for the present. Yes, Amara would come for her, but it was possible it would be as a human. She would bide her time, not rushing in blindly and risking what might turn out to be the rest of her relatively short remaining time. And if Amara *wasn't* human, well maybe that was something Hannah could change.

# 33

Driving away from the house in Savannah, Hannah could see in the rearview mirror the sky beginning its nightly show of summer color over the crown of trees. The day was beginning to give way to the humid heat of evening, and she put down the window and let the breeze blow her hair around her face. She'd cut it, snipping away the uneven, burned ends, trimming away the evidence of what had happened before. In the weeks since, the patterns on the sides of her legs had faded to mere shadows, and there was only the slightest limp if she overdid it. The permanent deep divot in her arm was the only visible mark of the painful past.

When Asher turned off the road and parked the car at a trailhead, it was dusk, the sky beginning to darken, showing off a palest blue sky with hazy purple clouds, their underbellies tipped in peach and lavender.

The trail Asher was on was difficult to follow in the ebbing light, and she lost sight of the sky when they passed under the trees. A root grown up into a loop reached for her foot and she stumbled, but his hand steadied her by the elbow, immediately withdrawing. She walked more carefully now, slowing him down, but making sure to keep her footing so he wouldn't have to help her again.

Hannah picked her way over the rough ground until all at once it shifted into soft grass tenuously rooted in sandy soil. In the minutes she'd been beneath the cover of the forest, the sky had darkened more, the pale undersides of the clouds now solid swathes of striking purple, the last streaks of turquoise in the sky setting off their color.

She followed him to the center of this hidden field, uneven in shape and humped like an overturned bowl. He spread out the blanket he was carrying and sat down, motioning for her to sit beside him. Neither spoke for a time, and they sat there silently, side by side, close but not touching, while the sky finished its display, now dove and heather, the tree tops a circle in silhouette around them.

There was a flicker, a small flash, just to the right of her that made Hannah jerk her head. There was another near her knee. All at once, everywhere around them legions of fireflies began their dance, and they were in the midst of a galaxy of stars that orbited them only, blinking into new constellations with every pulse of light.

They landed on her arms, and she could see the outline of Asher's face in the flashes, see the shape of him in the changing light. She laughed, startled by a green glow on her nose that made her eyes cross.

For a long time they sat watching the intricate and unchoreographed ballet, until a pair of fireflies alighted on her knee and she coaxed them onto her finger. Drawing them close to her face, she tried to predict the timing of their lights, but they danced to a tune only they knew.

Holding her hand skyward, she let them drift away, back into orbit.

"Fireflies are becoming extinct, did you know?" His voice sounded out in the dark. "It is because of all the manmade light. It interferes with their courtship rituals. They cannot find each other. Generation by generation they fade in the artificial light until the day comes when they will cast no glow, no longer exist."

She felt him sit up straighter, leaning toward her but not touching, though she could feel the change in temperature from the nearness; it prickled the hairs on her arms.

"I have come here many times, but I will live to see a time when there will only be darkness. This gift of nature will be extinguished, and I will watch it die, when the last light fades."

For the first time since his very first life more than nine hundred years ago Asher needed to fear a permanent death. But he also had the option of human life. Yet he intended to go forward through time. He intended to see the world die, watch the lights blink out one by one.

She understood then; he'd made his choice. Hannah couldn't pretend she blamed him, but she couldn't deny she'd thought things might go differently, that maybe he would choose one last life, one last span of years to count for something different because of its finality. And she had hoped he would choose it with her.

Silent tears threatened to spill down her face, but she refused to let them, because she was stronger than that. It was silly anyway. If truly faced with death, why would he want to die, or if he had to, spend his final time on Earth with her? She wouldn't argue her case because he wasn't wrong. Why risk giving up an eternity to instead wink out of existence? She wouldn't want it for him, even if he did.

If the stars aligned and luck let her survive to old age, the most she could hope for was the chance to grow old and wither and die. Being near her might accidentally bring him down with her. It was a miracle it hadn't already, when he tended her wounds or touched her in the days they spent together.

She understood why he wouldn't come close to her now, since he'd learned the truth. Where they'd been drawing nearer before, there was now a thin but impenetrable wall. He'd put it up. Because she was poison to him.

They didn't speak, over the dark walk back, through the drive down the empty road to the end of the crushed shell driveway. Hannah slipped up to bed with only a nod, closing the door behind her and leaning against it, listening to his footsteps fade away.

Late that night, when the house was silent, dark and still, and the only light came from the moon through a veil of clouds, Hannah slipped into the shapeless shadows in the courtyard. She fingered the pendant for a moment before she left it lying on the edge of the fountain and then she walked out, into the darkness.

# EPILOGUE

**H**annah carefully pulled the frame from the hive. A single wakeful bee wobbled drunkenly around its edge, and she picked it up gently with her thumb and finger and set it back in the hive. Placing the frame in the tub beside her, she reached for another, repeating the process until the tub was full, then lugged it up the hill to the house. She let it slide, heavy with honey, to the floor of the porch with a thud.

Flopping down into the lone chair next to its tiny table, she took a sip from her lukewarm tea and looked past the hives, across a field of clover to where it rolled down and out of sight into Seneca Lake. In the sun, the blue-black water sparkled with diamond flashes, and sailboats tiny as toys skated across the surface like water bugs.

Another bee, a sneaky worker who had hitched a ride up the hill, buzzed out of the tub and landed on her arm. She let this one sit, watching it fidget its minuscule front legs.

"You're allergic to bees, you know."

"Don't tell the bees that." Hannah had drawn the gun before she finished speaking, aiming in the direction the voice had come from. There was a figure standing at the far end of the porch, blurred by the reflection from the tall bank of windows.

"You stay right there." She leveled the gun and scanned the tree line around her, making sure she wasn't being hemmed in on all sides. Her phone had only signaled this one intruder, with nothing else showing up on the perimeter sensor. She didn't see anything to make her question its accuracy.

"Han," the man's voice said, "there's no way you're going to shoot me. Put the gun down."

That voice.

She stood slowly, knees bent, weight shifting forward, hands steady on the gun's grip. The figure took a step forward from the shade into daylight.

It just wasn't possible.

Hannah didn't twitch, bead locked on the slowly moving target.

"Now, Han, that's no way to be."

No one else ever called her Han, because she hated it. Except for him. But it couldn't be him—because he was dead.

The gun started to wobble and she lowered it slowly as he came out of the blinding reflection. "Uncle Joel," she said, her voice choked off to a whisper. It wasn't possible.

"You need to come with me," he said. "I'll explain everything, but we need to go. She's headed this way."

He was dead.

How was he here?

Alive.

Perfect.

Too perfect.

He was one of *them*.

# ACKNOWLEDGEMENT

The End. Typing those words for the first time was only the beginning. It takes a great deal to move from there to publication. Looking for help in taking my work from my head to here was overwhelming. I encountered more than one editor that prefaced their bio with things like "I don't work with newbies," or "find someone at your level." Dicks, right? The most successful authors in the world were all newbies once. Bottomless thanks to Meredith Tennant Beth Dorward for their meticulous editing, because of which this material far better than it would have been. I am a better writer because of it. Thanks also to Natasha MacKenzie for the beautiful cover and for knowing what I wanted before I did and to Catherine Williams for her design prowess.

Finally, thank you to my husband Nathan. When after a night of far too much champagne I blurted out that I had secretly written a book, he encouraged me to go for it. He also brought me Advil and water in the morning.

# NOTE TO THE READER

## What will Joel's return mean for Hannah?

Dear Reader,

Thank you for reading *Echoes*. This book is a work of fiction ... I think.

There are things in this world we haven't discovered, and possibly, people who have been walking amongst us for longer than we can imagine, unaffected by time.

Not so much for the rest of us, for whom time is of the essence. Thank you for spending some of yours to read *Echoes*. I would be grateful if you would spend a little more and kindly leave a review.

See what Joel's return means for Hannah in Reverberation, the action-packed second book in the *Echoes Trilogy*, available on Amazon.

P.S. Sign up for my email list at amcaplan.com for a personal heads-up about future releases.

Turn the page for a sneak peek at Reverberation!

CAN SHE OUTRUN
WHAT CAN'T BE KILLED?

# reverberation

## A.M. CAPLAN

A NOVEL

# CHAPTER ONE

Hannah carefully pulled the frame from the hive. A single wakeful bee wobbled drunkenly around its edge, and she picked it up gently with her thumb and finger and set it back in the hive. Placing the frame in the tub beside her, she reached for another, repeating the process until the tub was full, then lugged it up the hill to the house. She let it slide, heavy with honey, to the floor of the porch with a thud.

Flopping down into the lone chair next to its tiny table, she took a sip from her lukewarm tea and looked past the hives, across a field of clover to where it rolled down and out of sight into Seneca Lake. In the sun, the blue-black water sparkled with diamond flashes, and sailboats tiny as toys skated across the surface like water bugs.

Another bee, a sneaky worker who had hitched a ride up the hill, buzzed out of the tub and landed on her arm. She let this one sit, watching it fidget its minuscule front legs.

"You're allergic to bees, you know."

"Don't tell the bees that." Hannah had drawn the gun before she finished speaking, aiming in the direction the voice had come from. There was a figure standing at the far end of the porch, blurred by the reflection from the tall bank of windows.

"You stay right there." She leveled the gun and scanned the tree line around her, making sure she wasn't being hemmed in on all sides. Her phone had only signaled this one intruder, with nothing else showing up on the perimeter sensor. She didn't see anything to make her question its accuracy.

"Han," the man's voice said, "there's no way you're going to shoot me. Put the gun down." That voice.

She stood slowly, knees bent, weight shifting forward, hands steady on the gun's grip. The figure took a step forward from the shade into daylight.

It just wasn't possible.

Hannah didn't twitch, bead locked on the slowly moving target.

"Now, Han, that's no way to be."

No one else ever called her Han, because she hated it. Except for him. But it couldn't be him—because he was dead.

The gun started to wobble and she lowered it slowly as he came out of the blinding reflection. "Uncle Joel," she said, her voice choked off to a whisper.

It wasn't possible.

"You need to come with me," he said. "I'll explain everything, but we need to go. She's headed this way."

He was dead. How was he here?

Alive.

Perfect.

Too perfect.

He was one of them.

Her gun dropped to the porch with a thud. Boneless with shock, Hannah started to wilt into her chair, but Joel caught her up in a bear hug, hauling her back to her feet. Being crushed by arms that were absolutely real was enough to convince her she wasn't hallucinating. The feeling was so familiar, all flannel and wiry muscles and the smell of coffee and beat-up leather.

There was a time when Hannah would have questioned her sanity, being squeezed breathless by someone who was supposed to be dead. Not anymore. She snaked her arms around him and stood there for a moment. The man who'd raised her, the man she loved and missed and had mourned and accepted as gone forever was here. Alive.

Hannah hugged back him so tightly her shoulders creaked, basking in the strange, unnatural warmth. But only for a moment.

"Joel, you'd better let go," she said. "This is one of those occasions that turns into someone getting a black eye real quick."

When he laughed and she felt the up and down jiggle it made, Hannah smiled against his chest.

"Fine," he said, "but only because I taught you how to throw a punch." He grew serious, pushing her out to arm's length and studying her face. "Really, kid, I'm not sure how much time we have. We need to head out."

Twisting away from him, she sat down. "Not until I get an explanation." Hannah pulled out her phone and turned the screen toward him. "There's no one else here. I knew someone was coming the second you crossed the first line of sensors. There hasn't been anything else since."

Hannah was damn proud of the defenses she had set up. "I've got the entire perimeter on motion detectors from ground to tree tops," she said, "and there are enough guns and ammo in the house to take down a small army. Even if it isn't the normal kind."

Not so normal was what Hannah was expecting. The intruder she'd gone to such great lengths to detect had a lot in common with the man she was staring at. The too-perfect skin had given him away the instant she'd seen him clearly. Knowing what she knew now, Hannah had instantly recognized Joel for what he was.

There were two types of people walking Earth: the kind that died and stayed that way, and the kind that didn't. Hannah had learned that the hard way. What she hadn't known until now was that Joel was part of the second group.

Someone like Joel died, just like anyone else. But when they took their last breath and their life ended, they just vanished, disappearing without a trace. They didn't stay gone long. They quickly found themselves somewhere far away, alive again and perfect—even slightly better than before. The cycle kept repeating and repeating. Forever.

At least it had been forever, Hannah thought, correcting herself. For the first time, there was a way to break the cycle. Her.

"I have a dart gun loaded with my own blood, if the standard arsenal inside doesn't make you feel better," she said. "There are enough loads to turn you into a regular person a couple of times."

Joel didn't look bothered by that; not that he needed to be. The darts weren't meant for him. Hannah had a specific target in mind, and she had a pretty good idea that person was why Joel was here and so insistent on leaving.

"Good girl," Joel said. "I don't have time to explain the details, but Amara is on her way."

Just hearing the name out loud yanked Hannah's stomach up into her throat.

Amara. Last time the two of them had met, she intended to use Hannah as a weapon to kill every other immortal person like herself and Joel. She needed Hannah's blood in order to wipe out the others and make Amara one of a kind. If she'd succeeded, Hannah would probably be strapped to a table somewhere with a tube in her arm, being drained dry one drop at a time. Or dead.

Before that could happen, Hannah had bitten her own tongue bloody and then taken a bite out of Amara's hand. She hoped it had been enough to make Amara a regular human, the kind you could put bullets into that stayed there. She'd also been holding out hope Amara had been hit by a bus, or maybe pushed down an elevator shaft. The fact Joel was looking ready to shove her out the door made Hannah think that wasn't the case.

Amara's heart stopping for good had clearly been too much to ask. Now she was coming back, and whatever her plan for Hannah was, revenge would be a big part of it.

"Is she human?" Hannah asked.

"I don't know," Joel said. "No one knows. Maybe not even her."

She looked up at him, eyes narrowed. "But you do know she's coming here, and you think we should go to a safer location? Where exactly would that be?"

Wasn't Hannah safest where she was? It was secluded, protected, and she was armed to the teeth. Living like a hermit inside her little fortress had been working out so far.

271

Joel looked at her and smiled and her irritation melted away. She had missed him so much and seeing him again was like a miracle. She got up and threw her arms around him, snugging her head against his shoulder like she'd done when she was a child. So much had gone to hell when he died.

Except died wasn't the right word anymore. For a moment, it didn't matter. "I missed you so much," she whispered.

He kissed the top of her head. "I missed you too. You can't even imagine."

"I'm still not going anywhere, at least not until you sit down and give me an explanation."

"We don't have time. This location won't be safe for much longer. I may have gotten here ahead of Amara, but she won't be far behind."

"Inside then." Hannah jerked her head toward the door. "The sooner you start talking, the sooner you might be able to convince me to go," she said. "Might."

---

Ballistic glass was expensive. And really freaking heavy. The sliding glass door stuck in its track, and Hannah had to rock it back and forth, putting her weight behind it until it closed. Reaching behind the long blackout curtains, she pulled the retractable security gate across the glass, securing it to the steel plate bolted through the wall.

Metal grids were already pulled down over the room's two small windows; Hannah checked they were locked and yanked the blinds down over them. The front door was dead bolted—as always—and she dropped a steel bar as wide as her arm across it and pushed it into its slot, where it fell into place with a comforting, solid clunk.

Tapping the screen of the tablet on the kitchen counter, Hannah brought up a visual rendering of the security system with rings of green, yellow, and red arranged in a concentric cylinder like a 3D bull's eye. The black target at the center was the shape of a tiny house.

Joel leaned over her shoulder. "How far out do the sensors go?"

"Motion detectors start four hundred yards out in all directions. There's a ring every hundred yards until you get to the house." Hannah pointed to the two places where the outermost green ring was overlaid with a large dot. "There are overlapping sensors at the obvious points of entry—the lakefront and driveway. They're programmed to disregard anything that's obviously not human. A black bear tripped them a couple times, but otherwise it works."

Satisfied everything was quiet, Hannah pulled up a four-way video feed. Each quarter of the screen showed an image from one of the cameras mounted on a corner of the roof. "These are high resolution and you can see out to the hundred-yard mark, at least where there aren't trees in the way." She changed the view again, pointing to a screen split in two. "There are extra cameras at the same places as the redundant motion detectors."

The top half of the screen showed a gravel driveway with a chain stretched across it, the rusty no trespassing sign hanging from its center swaying dejectedly back and forth. On the bottom half of the screen, inky water lapped against the rocks on the shoreline. The picture was so clear she could make out individual maple leaves, white bellies showing like flags of surrender to the storm hovering somewhere over the lake.

The security hadn't come easy. It had taken her weeks of tree climbing and beating her head against the computer to get everything up and running. It wasn't until then, when she was sure nobody was getting to her doorstop unannounced, that Hannah had finally stopped sleeping in a chair with a gun across her lap. She still spent plenty of nights with her hand under her pillow wrapped around the grip of a handgun, but it was an improvement.

"Good girl," Joel said, nodding in approval at the security camera images.

"Stop good girling me, Joel." Hannah pulled out a barstool. "Sit down and start talking."

He paused, eyebrow raised. She stared pointedly until he sat.

Propping the tablet up against the coffee pot where she could see it, Hannah stood across from him, leaning back against the counter. Joel stared at her for a moment, head tilted to the side, but didn't speak. Fine. If that's how he wanted to do it, she'd ask the questions.

"So who was in the can, Joel? It clearly wasn't you."

That was where it all started, with the little metal urn she'd believed held his ashes. Seeing him alive now, her tight-lipped expression slipped a little. Hannah reined it in, but it wasn't easy. Her happiness at seeing him sitting in front of her was at serious odds with the gravity of the situation and how pissed she was about his neglecting to mention not being dead.

"No clue," Joel said. "Did you know you can buy human cremains online? I feel especially bad now, since whoever they were got cremated twice." The can that had held the remains had been lost—along with everything else she owned—when Amara burned down her last house.

"It's not funny, Joel," Hannah said. "You faked your death, and you left me."

"I had to."

Hannah slammed a hand on the counter. The tablet slid flat with a clunk. "You had to? That never would have flown as an explanation when I was a kid, and it certainly isn't flying now. Try again."

"I really did have to," Joel said. "You've obviously recognized what I am. You know we don't age. Someone was going to notice." He was different than she remembered, and not just because she'd learned to recognize the slight differences that gave his kind away. She studied his face.

"I know. I don't look quite the same, do I?" Joel ruffled the front of his hair. "It was a relief to stop dyeing it. Do you know how hard it is to get a convincing fake sprinkle of salt and pepper?"

She remembered the silver that threaded through the hair at his temples. The thick curls were all dark brown now, and his sharp, thin face didn't look a day older than hers. His eyes at least were the same—crystalline green, the corners crinkled in amusement.

He stroked his chin and laughed. "And you thought you hated the beard? It was so scratchy, but I was stuck with it, since it made me look a little older," he said. "Which still wasn't enough. I'm glad I was able to find that tattoo artist. She was an absolute wizard."

Joel saw her confusion. "Wrinkles. Inked-on crow's feet. They were so good, I swore I was going to be able to feel them. Impressive, since I can't imagine she'd had much practice. How many people walk into a tattoo parlor looking for wrinkles?" His grin fell away. "Even that wouldn't have worked forever. You would have figured it out eventually, that I hadn't really changed in twenty years." Joel reached over and took her hand. "It was time. You were grown up and perfectly capable of taking care of yourself. You didn't need me anymore."

Hannah jerked her hand away. "Easy for you to say. You have no idea what it was like after you left. You could have just told me." Did he think she wouldn't have believed him? It turned out his secret was well within her ability to handle.

She hadn't found out about Joel's world from him, though in a small way it was because of him. So much had changed since the night she glanced away from the road to pick up the container of his ashes from where it rolled under the seat. Hannah had looked up just in time to see the man in the road before she'd ended his life. Or so she'd thought. The man had returned.

And brought a whole lot of trouble with him.

Joel opened his mouth, but she didn't give him a chance to speak.

"You should have told me the truth," she said. "I knew nothing about who I am. My entire life was a lie." A lie, and a dangerous one. Keeping the details secret about what he was—and who she was— hadn't protected her. It made her more vulnerable, ignorant of the danger that was going to come for her. Joel hadn't warned her about her father.

Referring to the man as her father was distasteful, even in her mind. Michael. Hannah hadn't known Michael existed until a year ago. She certainly hadn't known he'd been like Joel, living over and over again.

Unlike Joel, Michael hadn't been interested in seeing Hannah alive; quite the opposite, in fact. She didn't feel any remorse that Michael was dead now—permanently dead—because of her.

"You have no idea how miraculous you are," Joel said. "It's hard to believe you survived at all. Whatever intuition your mother had about him saved your life. If Michael had been in the picture when you were born, you wouldn't have made it to your first birthday."

Pity the intuition hadn't saved my mother's life as well, Hannah thought. And miraculous? There wasn't anything miraculous about Hannah. It was sheer luck Michael hadn't managed to kill her.

"Did you know?" she asked.

"Know what?"

"What I am. Did you know? Is that why you rescued me and raised me?" Hannah picked up the tablet and flicked back and forth between the images on the screen. She didn't want to look at his face while he answered. He'd kept enough else from her; would it be so hard to believe he'd kept the knowledge of what her blood could do to immortals from her as well?

He reached over and put a finger under her chin, forcing her to look him in the face. "I had no idea. None whatsoever, not until I found out Michael was dead for good. No one could've known."

Maybe that was true; Hannah wanted to believe him. And Michael had been fathering children and killing them to see if they came back like he did for hundreds of years. As far as anyone knew, she was the first of his children to survive. Could anyone have known what she was?

Joel shook his head and smiled. "I picked you up and took you because I didn't want to see another child die at his hands. I hid you, because I knew he'd be back to finish you off some day. I intended to erase your identity and place you with a family somewhere so he could never find you."

"So why didn't you?"

"Because after a couple days, I couldn't bring myself to give you away."

Joel smiled at her. "You were a very cute baby."

A ping made them both freeze, the tone reverberating around the bulletproof box of a room. Hannah picked up the tablet.

"We have company."

# About the Author

A.M. Caplan is the author of *Echoes, Reverberation* and *Dead Quiet*, the *Echoes Trilogy*. She resides in scenic Sayre, Pennsylvania, watching the river roll by with her husband and writing about people that only exist in her mind.

You can connect with me on:
    **https://www.amcaplan.com**
    **https://www.facebook.com/annmarie.caplan.7**

Subscribe to my newsletter:
    **https://www.amcaplan.com/page-2**

Made in the USA
Coppell, TX
05 November 2024

39620235R10166